The Right Man

The Right Man

by
Ward R. Jones

Writer's Showcase Press
San Jose · New York · Lincoln · Shanghai

The Right Man

Published by Writer's Showcase, an imprint of iUniverse.com, Inc.

For information address:
iUniverse.com, Inc.
620 North 48th Street
Suite 201
Lincoln, NE 68504-3467
www.iuniverse.com

ISBN:0-595-00032-0

Dedicated to memory of my father,
Ward Tillman Jones, and my mother,
Mary Caffery Jones

Your representative owes you, not his industry only, but his judgement, and he betrays, instead of serving you, if he sacrifices it to your opinions.

From Edmund Burke's message to the voters of Bristol, 1774

The great conservative revival of the 1980's is over. Government is bigger, taxes are higher, family values are weaker, and the Democrats are in power. What will the Right do next?

From David Frum's "Dead Right", 1994

Chapter 1

It had been six months since Doug and Priscilla Crane had moved from Albany to Atlanta. Doug had served as the District Attorney of Albany County for six years before moving to the city. It hadn't been an easy decision for him to leave the place in South Georgia where he had grown up. His father still lived on the small farm by the Flint River and Priscilla's parents owned a cotton plantation only a couple of miles away. Doug loved dove hunting in the fall, the lazy afternoon horseback rides along the river, and most of all, the friendly people of Albany, most of whom he had known since he was a little boy. These were his friends and neighbors who had helped him win his race for District Attorney.

Albany was also the place where Doug had first met a very pretty girl with silky black hair named Priscilla Smithers. She had moved to South Georgia New Orleans. That was twenty years ago.

But it was now 2009 and Doug had come to realize that he was ready for a change, for something more challenging in his life. So when Balding and Bell, the second largest law firm in Atlanta, had offered him a partnership as the head of their new criminal litigation section, Doug had said he was interested. And after thinking it over for several days and talking with Priscilla, he had finally accepted.

They had bought a house in the Virginia Highlands area, close to downtown, with two big bedrooms, two baths, a kitchen with lots of cabinets, a living room with a fireplace, and an oak paneled den. It was a recently remodeled one-story house with high ceilings. The exterior was painted yellow and there were white shutters beside each of the four front windows.

There was room for children, but Doug knew that he didn't have time to be a father, at least not for a while. He not only had a heavy trial docket, he also was responsible for hiring and training a half dozen young lawyers. Priscilla felt differently about having children now and he could understand her anxiety. She would be thirty-six next January. He had hoped that she would take more of an interest in her art gallery and that the issue of a baby would fade from her consciousness. But he could tell from the look in her eye whenever she saw a young mother with a baby that it hadn't. He realized that there was a void in her life that a husband and a career couldn't completely fill.

They had had many lengthy conversations of the subject of parenthood. More than a few had ended with raised voices followed by prolonged periods of cold silence from Priscilla. He had always tried to make up with flowers and kisses and promises that they would have a baby as soon as things settled down at work. But there never seemed to be any abatement of Doug's workaholic schedule.

He was tired when he got home from work. It was a little after 7 p.m. He put down his briefcase and momentarily studied her profile as she sat there on the den sofa. Priscilla had her mother's luminously dark Creole eyes and the same flawless complexion, skin the color of light honey. Priscilla Crane's wavy raven hair was cut just below the back of her long graceful neck.

"Hi. How was your day?" he said brightly.

She never stopped noticing how handsome he was. His eyes were as clear and blue as a cloudless country sky. His soft hair was the color of the sand on the beach at Sea Island. It was parted on the left side of his head and combed back across the top of his ears and just touching the back of his collar. He was a young man of virile intensity, with powerful shoulders and arms. He was also a little bowlegged.

He walked over and kissed her on the cheek.

She smiled and said, "We got some new things in today at the gallery."

"Really," he replied enthusiastically. "Tell me about them." He took his jacket off and draped it over the back of a flame-stitched wing chair.

"They're from a lady who lives in Dothan, Alabama. Really nice. Pine trees and an incredible sky taken while she was lying on her back."

"So when are you gonna have a showing?"

"I think I'll do it in a couple of weeks when she can come to Atlanta. She looks after her mother in Dothan and has to make arrangements." She stood up and walked over to him, then kissed him lightly on the mouth. "So how was yours?" she asked, her hand at his chest holding his tie.

"Good. I hired a new lawyer. He's from Dustan and Bradley. He's been over there about three years, went to law school at Duke, Order of the Coif. And besides all that, he's a good guy."

He walked over to the chair and sat down. " Also, I got a call from Sam Brinkman."

She arched her dark eyebrows and looked up at him, wondering why the owner of all those furniture stores would call Doug. "What did he want?

"He wants me to run for Congress."

"What!" She put her hand over her throat. "What did you tell him?" she stammered.

"I told him I'd think about it."

"Doug, you can't be serious. I mean, you just started at Balding and Bell six months ago."

He held up his hand. "I know, I know, but…I've been doing a lot of thinking lately about the way things are."

"What do you mean *the way things are?*"

"About the way we've let the federal government take over our lives. Every time you pick up the paper there's some new program from Washington doing for us what we ought to be doing for ourselves." He glanced at the clock on her dressing table. "Hey, it's almost seven. I'm gonna duck into the shower before we meet the Jensens for dinner." He was quickly walking away.

"Doug, we need to talk about this, we really do." Her last few words were spoken to herself.

Politics and making money were the two things Sam Brinkman knew best. Since he gave a hundred dollars to a county judge twenty years earlier, which was before he'd divorced the first of his three ex-wives, Sam Brinkman had gotten hooked on politics. He'd learned early on that money was the life-blood that politicians had to have to keep their hearts beating. It was also the one sure-fire way you could make your voice heard and really influence things.

His hefty contributions enabled him to hob knob with politicians from all over Georgia, mostly Republicans, giving the furniture store owner an aura of respectability as well as the access to powerful legislators. He became a member of the National Republican Party's "Million Dollar Club" and was a regular invitee to VIP meetings with the Party's leaders.

He was a big, gregarious, freckle faced man, the size of someone who could have played guard for an NFL team. He had orange-red hair and a big round face, a space between his front teeth and bulging eyes. He looked a little like a circus clown without the costume. He never wore a coat or tie, preferring pressed blue jeans and brightly colored custom made shirts.

He'd made a fortune in the furniture business. Thanks to his ubiquitous television commercials, Sam Brinkman was widely known as the Furniture King of Atlanta. His big round face had always turned a shade closer to red than pink as he'd shouted his sales pitches from one of his fourteen furniture showrooms around the city. And thousands of people had flocked to his stores each year heeding the call of Wild Sam Brinkman to "steal a deal" on a new king sized bed or a new breakfast room table, or a hundred other pieces of low priced furniture.

When he wasn't working for a Republican candidate, Sam spent all his time working at one of his stores. He loved to mix with his customers, tell them jokes, but also listen to what they had to say. He worked ten hours a day and then he'd go home to his mansion and work some more.

The house that Sam had built had a living area of a little over eight thousand square feet. It was fronted by a portico consisting of limestone arches and a sloping copper roof, with mosque like towers on the front corners of the house extending ten feet above the third story. On each side of the double-doors at the entrance were two large ceramic elephants.

His office on the first floor was cherry paneled and the size of a large living room. Through a large expanse of glass at the rear was a pastoral view of the rolling hills of northwestern Georgia, only part of his two hundred acres.

It was late evening and Sam Brinkman was in his home office. He was on the phone with Senator Oliver McSwain, the National Chairman for the Republican Congressional Campaign Committee.

"We've got a young man down here that's the spittin' image of what Robert Redford used to look like. I tell you, Doug Crane is gonna get every damn woman's vote in the Tenth District, I guarantee it."

"What does Dick Bannister say?" said the Senator, referring to the Chairman of the State Republican Party.

"He's as gung ho as I am, Oliver."

"Look, Sam. It's awfully late. We've only got a few months left before the election."

Sam's voice was rising. "Well hell, nobody else was willin' to take on Nat Thompson."

"Might have something to do with the fact that he hasn't lost a race in thirty years," said the senator dryly.

"I think Doug Crane can cause him some problems. I really do," said Sam.

"Well, you tell him we've gotta know now."

"Okay, okay."

"Have you had somebody check his background?"

"Yes, and it's as clean as a baby's bottom after a fresh diaper. I tell you this guy's your All-American boy. Grew up on a farm, star athlete, got a scholarship to Georgia. After that graduated at the top of his class from Duke Law School. He's really a bright young guy."

"Has he ever run for office?"

"He won the DA's race in Albany County three times. Folks I know say he was *very* popular down there. And he's married to a good lookin' young gal who's inherited a lot of oil money."

"Well he's going to have to make a lot of people in the Tenth District crazy about him in a hurry if he's going to have any chance against Thompson."

Sam was rubbing his face. "I know. I'll call you tomorrow."

The Furniture King hung up and looked down at his desk calendar. He picked up a pen and wrote: GET ANSWER FROM DOUG CRANE.

Late that night after their dinner with the Jensens, Doug and Priss were lying in bed. The lights were out but neither of them could go to sleep. They were still thinking about whether he should run for Congress.

She rolled her head in his direction and said, "Didn't your friend Ben O'Neill serve in Congress for a couple of years." She was referring to a law school classmate of Doug's.

"He did." He was looking up at the ceiling.

"Well, what did he say about it?"

"He said it was the most rewarding experience of his life."

She frowned. "I thought I remembered your telling me it almost broke up his marriage."

"He and Doris did have some problems, but that was because she didn't come to Washington with him. They had three children and she didn't want to leave home."

They lay there in the dark without speaking.

Priss finally whispered, "I suppose I could sublease my art gallery space for a couple of years."

He reached over and took her in his arms.

Chapter 2

Doug and Priscilla were sitting at their breakfast room table. There was the smell of coffee in the room and the beeping sound of a garbage truck from outside. He had on tan suit pants with a long sleeved white shirt and cranberry colored tie. She and was wearing a pink satin robe. They were both reading the newspaper.

He put down the paper and looked up at her. "Can you believe this." His eyebrows were raised.

"Believe what?" she said absentmindedly, reaching for her coffee cup.

"A fifty billion dollar class action lawsuit has been filed against McDonald's."

She frowned. "Why?"

He leaned on his forearms and looked down. "Here's what the lead plaintiffs' lawyer says: 'McDonald's intentionally sold to the public dangerous food products, which it knew were laden with life threatening saturated fats, but concealed such information by not properly labeling their food packaging, as a result of which millions of innocent people suffered arterial blockage and heart failure.' So he wants McDonalds to fork over fifty billion, of which he'll probably take home about a third." His face contorted as he spoke the sarcastic words.

"That's the craziest thing I've ever heard of," she said.

"Maybe so, but after the gun manufacturers and the liquor industry paid so many billions to those other plaintiffs' lawyers *and* the federal government, I guess these guys couldn't resist another juicy target."

She laughed at his choice of words.

He walked over to the refrigerator, opened the door and reached in for the orange juice.

She was reading again when he came back and sat down beside her. She looked up at him. "How long has it been since President Hinton left office?"

He was chewing a mouthful of cereal and thinking. He wiped his mouth and said, "I'd guess a little over ten years ago, why?"

"There's an article here that says the Hinton video tapes will be released to the public next week."

He rolled his blue eyes. "Oh, my God."

"What?"

"You don't remember."

"No." She had a blank expression on her face.

"Priss, those were the famous tapes that were recorded in the Oval Office, the ones that damn near cost Hinton his presidency."

She narrowed her dark eyes. "Did they have something to do with him and that intern?"

"Right. He'd forgotten about the surveillance camera. And they were doing it on top of his desk in the Oval Office."

Her eyes opened wide and she held up her hand. "*Now* I remember."

Doug said, "Somehow a *Washington Post* reporter got wind of what was shown on the tapes. And his story exploded on the front page like an atom bomb. But despite the initial shockwaves, Hinton's lawyers managed to keep the tapes under raps, and the President held on and served out his term." Doug shook his head. "Phil Hinton…I hadn't thought about him for a long time, not since he was shot."

She nodded tentatively. "I think I remember that. It was out in California, wasn't it? And wasn't he with some woman at the time?"

"Yeah, it was the woman's husband, that doctor from Australia that caught them in bed."

"Wasn't she a Miss Australia or something," she said, brushing a lock of black hair out of her eyes.

"She was Miss Universe, Priss. Don't you remember? He'd hired her to be his 'special assistant' while he was writing his memoirs."

Her eyes suddenly brightened. "That's right, and it was right after that when the first lady finally said she was going to leave him." Priscilla was stirring her coffee. "I can't believe she put up with all of that stuff for so long."

"She got what she wanted," said Doug. "United States Senator Valerie Hinton." He got up and walked over to the refrigerator again, then turned around.

"I guess it could have been worse."

"What do you mean?"

"She could have been on the Supreme Court if the Senate Judiciary Committee hadn't blocked her nomination." Doug thought about the scandal involving her insider trading involving an initial public offering of a red-hot technology stock.

She looked up at him again. "These people in Washington…Are you absolutely sure you want to do this? Doug."

The sounds of birds could be heard from outside.

His face became pensive and his eyes locked onto hers. "Do you remember when we had that income tax audit last year and I had to drive up to Atlanta with that cardboard box full of my old telephone bills."

She nodded.

"Well, I don't know whether I ever told you the complete story." He paused to take a sip of his coffee. "When I got to Atlanta, I lugged that damn box up six flights of stairs to the IRS office. I remember that for some reason both the elevators were out of order. Anyway, I sat down in the waiting room. There must have been fifty or more people sitting in a space not much bigger than our garage, all on folding metal chairs under bright neon lights. After about an hour, they finally called my name.

"I walked down this long hallway and into this gigantic room." He held his hands far apart. "Priss, it was the size of a large warehouse, divided by all these gray partitions into what must have been more than a hundred little cubicles. The guy who was my examiner looked like one of those airport security guards you used to see staring at conveyor belts. He was sitting there behind a boxy little desk with barely enough room for one chair in front. The only thing on his desk was a stack of sheets of paper. I could see he had a long list of questions on the top sheet."

Doug took a bite of a piece of whole wheat toast and chewed for a few seconds, then resumed his story. "He asked me my name, address, phone number, all that kind of stuff, then moved on to bank account numbers, securities account numbers, and then he started asking about whether we had a maid, how many cars we owned, where we went to church, the clubs we belonged to. He even wanted the names and addresses of our friends, for God's sake.

"After about thirty minutes of this—I think it was when he was asking where we go out to dinner—I'd about had it. I pulled out a copy of the IRS letter and pointed out that the only information requested by the IRS related to the last two years of my telephone calls. But that didn't phase this guy. He didn't even look up, kept right on reading from that damn list."

Priscilla shook her head incredulously.

"But what really got me was what I could hear from the other side of the partition. It was an old man with a raspy sounding voice. Every now and then I'd hear him coughing. He said he owned a little farm about half way between Valdosta and Waycross, and that he'd gotten up at 4 a.m. and driven about two hundred miles to make his nine o'clock appointment with the IRS. I remember it was close to eleven. This poor old guy was trying to explain that he only had two hours to spend in Atlanta because he had to get back home to give his wife her medicine."

Doug's eyes took on a fiery intensity she hadn't seen in a long time. "That old farmer's the reason I want to run for Congress."

She reached out and put her hand on his shoulder. "You really think you can change the tax system?"

"I can damn sure try. Maybe I can make people see how we've allowed ourselves to become a bunch of dependant sheep grazing on the green grass of government handouts until we're sheared every April fifteenth."

She flashed him a dazzling smile. "Congressman Doug Crane does have a nice ring to it."

He jumped up and pumped his fist in the air. "Look out Nat Thompson, here I come!"

Later that morning Doug was at his law office at One Peachtree Plaza. Among his law partners at Balding and Bell was a punctilious man named Paul Davidson. A year before Doug had joined the firm, Paul had served as the campaign manager for a candidate for a seat on the Atlanta City Council. She'd won in a landslide due in large part to Paul Davidson's organizational skills and sharp political instincts.

And Doug was aware of this.

He walked down the hall and saw that Paul's door was open. A life long bachelor, Paul Davidson had a narrow face with a head of close cropped, gray-blond hair. He had a habit of wearing corduroy jackets with leather elbow pads and dark brown Cordovan shoes. He looked more like a college professor than a lawyer.

Doug knocked on the door to get his attention. "Got a second?"

Paul looked up. "Sure. Come on in."

They exchanged pleasantries for a few minutes and then Doug told Paul about his decision to run for Congress. And then he asked Paul to be his campaign manager.

The professorial looking lawyer took off his glasses and began wiping them with a white handkerchief. "You understand, Doug, that I haven't ever done anything…of this scope. I mean, it's going to take a lot more money to do this than it took for that city council race."

"I know. I think I can get some help from my father-in-law."

"I assume you know that single donor contributions are pretty limited, given the restrictions in the new federal campaign finance law."

Doug heaved a sigh. "I guess I'll just have to work my butt off, Paul. But I could sure use your help." He was standing there with his palms held up in the air.

Paul put on his wire-framed glasses and he gazed out the window for what seemed like a long time. Finally, he turned around, his face showing the trace of a smile, and said quietly, "It would be an interesting challenge."

Chapter 3

Nathaniel Thompson was a man who oozed political power from every pore of his short, fat body. He was a man who, when he entered a room, would cause conversations to cease and eyes to look in his direction. That was because Nat Thompson was Chairman of the House Appropriations Committee, and being *The* Chairman, as he was so often referred to, this diminutive politician was one of the most powerful men in Washington. He had the power and he used it, to mold and shape and twist to his satisfaction an annual federal budget that was now approaching four trillion dollars.

Endowed with so many billions by the ubiquitous federal tax collectors, and being a primary decision maker as to the disposition of such mind boggling sums of money, Nat Thompson was accustomed to the obsequious supplications of many people, including his fellow congressmen. He had become a master at trading favors in ways that provided the maximum benefits for the people back home who kept him in office.

As mentioned, Nat Thompson was not a particularly imposing figure. In fact he was a rather ugly man. He was several inches less than six feet tall, but his hands were unusually large. He had a habit of standing on his tiptoes when he gave speeches and wearing white linen suits with navy blue ties. His hair was long and silver and combed straight back. His eyes were sunken in his pale face like small pearls. The combination of his beady eyes, his long, narrow nose, and his very thin lips gave him a reptilian look.

A life long Democrat, he had been born in northeastern Georgia, in the foothills of the Blue Ridge Mountains. He had moved from there to a tobacco farm outside of Macon when he was five years old. Later, he had gotten his first job as a teacher in a one-room school.

He had been the county school superintendent when he first ran for political office. A seat in the state legislature had been vacated and it offered more money. He won by less than a hundred votes. That was the last close election he'd ever had. Six years later he had run for Congress and won again. Since then, the voters of the Tenth Congressional District, which included portions of DeKalb, Cobb, and Fulton Counties in the Atlanta area, had reelected him to fourteen consecutive terms.

He was not a particularly gifted public speaker. He had a high, nasal sounding voice. This he tried to offset by speaking as loud as he could. He also suffered the handicap of not having a smiling wife and doting children that could be displayed to the voters to show what a wonderful family man he was. And surprisingly, for a man that had spent so much of his time winning thousands of people's votes, he had very few close friends. In fact, Ab Connell, the Majority Leader of the Democratic Party, was about the only person that he could really call a close friend.

But Nat Thompson had attributes other than his powerful chairmanship that made him a supremely potent political adversary. He was a tenacious campaigner of seemingly limitless stamina and energy. In the early days he would drive around in his old Mercury Cougar, starting just after daybreak. He'd pick out a neighborhood street and start walking the sidewalks and knocking on doors until he'd shaken hands with everyone within a mile of that Cougar. Then he'd move on to another neighborhood and repeat the process, until he'd rung the doorbell of every single house in the district.

And he listened to people. He found out what they wanted. If somebody was having trouble getting a tax refund or a Social Security check delivered on time, he'd personally contact the IRS or the Social Security

Administration, and most of the time, because of Nat Thompson's efforts, the check would be delivered to his thankful constituent.

Over the years it was this type of personal service and the sense he conveyed that he really cared about people's problems, no matter how petty or complicated they might be, that had cemented his reputation as the friend of the little guy, the one you could always depend on to look out for you when you needed help.

But it wasn't only the little guy that Nat Thompson helped. The wily Georgia Democrat made sure he took very good care of his largest financial contributors. One of his biggest backers was a man named Luke Dorning, a real estate developer who owned fifteen thousand acres of land dotted with scrub oaks and a few head of cattle. The land was located about a hundred miles south of Atlanta.

At that time there was a movement in Congress to trim the Pentagon's budget. Nat Thompson joined in. He managed to push through the House a bill he claimed would save the Pentagon billions of dollars. His plan was to consolidate all the landing fields used by the Air Force in the southeastern part of the United States. Nat proposed a location south of Atlanta that, unbeknownst to others, included almost all of the Dorning property. After the bill was signed into law, the House Appropriations Committee allocated eighty million dollars to buy the land for the new air base. That sum was about twenty times what The Chairman's financial supporter had originally paid for his fifteen thousand acres.

And it wasn't long thereafter that Nat Thompson bought a twenty room, ocean view mansion in West Palm Beach. He used it for entertaining his friends and supporters. Among his most frequent visitors was Luke Dorning.

Norton's was a restaurant in Georgetown and one of the most expensive places to eat in Washington. A New York strip steak cost about thirty dollars and a baked potato or a serving of broccoli another eight. Many of Washington's most powerful politicians were wined and dined by lobbyists, members of the press, and others wanting favors that only a few could deliver.

Nat Thompson was a frequent customer at Norton's. So frequent in fact that there was a small alcove just off the main dining area that was reserved for him. There was even a small brass plaque mounted on the wall directly behind the chair in which he normally sat. The plaque was engraved with the words: "Nat's Nook". And those who knew the important players in Washington didn't have to ask who Nat was.

Nat Thompson was there having lunch with his old friend, Abner Connell, who was the Majority Leader of the House. The burley New Yorker had a wide face and eyebrows that were a tangled mass of black and white hairs, so thick and bushy one had to wonder how he could see. He had an equally unkempt gray moustache that extended from above one corner of his wide mouth to the other.

Known to his friends as Ab, the Majority Leader was a fierce partisan whose worst nightmare was that the Republicans would regain control of Congress. Consequently, he made sure he knew everything there was to know about the status of the congressional races going on around the country, including the ones in Georgia.

"Nat, there's talk around town you may have a new challenger for your seat." The cigar protruding from the corner of Ab Connell's mouth bobbed up and down as he spoke.

Nat slurped a spoonful of his lobster bisque and then wiped his white table napkin across his lipless mouth. "That so," he said curtly. He reached across the table and there was the sound of French bread breaking.

"They say he's a good looking country lawyer who recently moved to Atlanta. Joined one of the big law firms down there. They say he's got a wife who's a real knockout."

Nat was sipping his short crystal glass of Wild Turkey and squinting in the direction of the main dining room.

"I've often wondered why you never got married. I mean, a man like you could've had any number of women. Not that you needed any help on the campaign trail. But nowadays, with all this feminism we've got, it's helps to have some balance. Not that you need any balance, Nat, but—"

"Pass the butta." The words came out slowly.

After pushing it across the tablecloth, the big New Yorker took a long sip of his martini and then continued. "Our majority is only ten, you know. The last election cost us some real war horses for the Party, guys who'd been around almost as long as you. I'm hoping like hell we can hold on." He took the cigar out of his mouth. "Of course, yours is one of the few seats I don't have to worry about. But you can never take anything for granted, can you?"

"If you think I'm worryin' about some piss ant pretty boy who's never run for office and hasn't a clue about the way Washington works, then you're dummerin' I thought. And I don't care how beautiful his wife is." He stabbed a piece of prime rib. "The people of my District are not idiots."

The New Yorker broke into a smile so wide you could see some of his yellow teeth under his bushy moustache. "Hey, this is your buddy, Ab, remember. I know how many Republican country club butts you've kicked over the years. All I'm saying is spend a little more time down there doing what you have to do. Spend a few more bucks on television and hire one of those attack dogs the President uses. You can dump on this kid big time. The Party will come through with whatever financial help you need. You do those things and its a cake walk, the same as always."

Nat raised his eyebrows and his beady eyes locked on Ab's. "You're afraid I might lose, aren't you."

The Majority Leader held up his hand. "Hell no!"

The Chairman's face was beginning to turn red, accentuating the contrast with his white linen suit. He said, "Don't you know my name is on fourteen federal office buildin's in my District alone, and that Nat Thompson is the main reason the state of Georgia now has the third lowest unemployment rate in the country. That if it weren't for Nat

Thompson half the federal programs in this country benefitin' poor folks wouldn't exist!"

"I know, I know, it's just…well, the fact of the matter is you're not as young as you used to be, Nat." The New Yorker saw the eyes of a snake flashing hotly in his direction. He hesitated, flashed a wide grin, then said, "Oh hell, I know you're in perfect health and you don't look anywhere near your age. All I'm saying is don't take this kid for granted, that's all."

The knuckles of Nat Thompson's hand were white as he gripped his knife. "Fuck you, Ab."

The first thing Nat did when he got back to his office in the Longworth House Building was telephone his campaign manager.

Mike Ruby was a wiry, frizzy haired young man who was six inches taller than The Chairman was. He was also the son of a federal judge from Massachusetts who hated Republicans and everything they stood for. Growing up in such a household, the judge's son had absorbed the liberal dogma spoken so frequently that it became his gospel. He was inspired to somehow get into politics so that he could make the world a better place. He was not lacking in brain power, and after graduating with a law degree from Columbia, Mike Ruby found a position on the staff of the junior Senator from Georgia.

That's how he met Nat Thompson. They were introduced after Nat's campaign manager was diagnosed with cancer. The junior Senator from Georgia, also a Democrat, had told Nat about his bright young staff member who was looking for a new challenge. Nat liked the young man's intensity. He also knew that his lack of experience wouldn't be a problem, given the fact that Nat usually trounced his opponents.

And so, although they were about two generations apart and from totally different cultural backgrounds, this odd couple formed a relationship. And it had worked for both of them.

The strategy had always been pretty simple: Let Nat be Nat. The fact was that The Chairman was always running for office. Every time he sent out his monthly newsletter or answered a phone call or paid a visit to a constituent, he solidified his position as the only man who could adequately serve the needs of the people of the Tenth District. Campaigning was a part of his everyday routine and nothing extra was required except for a few extra speeches here and there the timing of which Mike had always arranged.

But this time The Chairman wasn't so sure. He had an uneasy feeling. There was something about the look in Ab Connell's eye and the sound of his voice. So he told himself that he was going to get the message across to Mike that this time they had some real work to do.

"Mike, I want you to find out what you can about Doug Crane." Nat was tapping an ash off the end of his cigar as he spoke to the speakerphone. "Ab Connell told me at lunch today that he's goin' to run against me next fall."

"I've never hear of him."

"I know you haven't, that's not the point," The Chairman said sharply. "But I want you to have somebody take a look into his background an' see if there's anythin' that might cause him a problem. Do you understand what I'm sayin'?"

"Yes sir."

"And Mike, this may not be like it has been in the past. You're goin' to have to be on the ball."

"Yes sir."

Nat sighed, then said. "He's a lawyer with one of the big firms, Baldin' and Bell."

"I'll get right on it."

Nat punched the button on his speakerphone and leaned back in his chair, watching the smoke rising. He still couldn't shake this strange feeling of anxiety. A moment later he reached in his drawer for his silver flask.

Doug had done it. He'd gone on an Atlanta television station and made the official announcement that he was going to run for the United States Congress. There was no turning back now.

Yard signs were being printed with big white lettering on a royal blue background: DOUG CRANE FOR CONGRESS, THE RIGHT MAN FOR THE RIGHT TIME. Space for a campaign headquarters was being leased in a vacant office building on the edge of downtown. Priss was rounding up volunteers. Doug was drafting position papers. Paul was arranging appearances at meeting places around the Tenth District.

There were so many things to do. But Doug told himself he needed to find time to go see his father. So he had driven down to Albany and spent a pleasant spring afternoon with him on his farm.

They were sitting on rocking chairs on the screen porch looking out across the rows of recently harvested cotton plants. There was the sound of cicadas and the smell of camellias.

Doug Crane, Senior, had the same sandy brown hair and clear blue eyes as his son, though his hair was much thinner and grayer and his hairline had receded in a high V shape. He face was deeply lined and had a cowhide looking texture. Like his son's, the nose was finely etched and the jaw was square. He was muscular in the shoulders and arms, unusually so for a man in his late seventies.

Doug's family had owned the cotton plantation since the time his grandfather had bought it at a sheriff's sale during the Depression. His two uncles had no interest in farming. They had wanted to go to college. So his father had agreed to stay home and help his grandfather run the place.

He respected his dad more than anyone else in the world. And that's why he needed to talk with him. "Dad, I hope I'm doing the right thing."

His father took a sip from a glass of iced tea, then said quietly. "I'm proud of you, son."

Doug ran his fingers through his hair and looked over at his father. "Nat Thompson's gonna be awfully tough to beat."

His father was looking out across the cotton field. "Doesn't matter, so long as you're doin' what you think is right." The words were spoken slowly and evenly.

High above them a hawk was circling lazily in the fading light.

The old man's blue eyes looked at him. "Your Mom used to say this was the most beautiful place in the world."

Doug reached over and put his hand on his father's shoulder.

Chapter 4

Sam Brinkman was sweating. The armpits of his custom-made denim shirt were as dark as the circle on the seat of his blue jeans. He'd been helping lift a large sofa into the back of a truck at the loading dock of one of his furniture stores. His employees had never ceased to be amazed that their multimillionaire boss would actually do this kind of backbreaking work.

He had always told them the reason he did it was to remind himself of the way things used to be when he first started out. But that was only part of his motivation. He also wanted to send them the message that if they worked their asses off, they could do what Sam Brinkman had done.

"Damn, that was one heavy son of a bitch, wasn't it boys," he said wiping his big dripping forehead with a folded handkerchief. "Jake, hand me that cell phone, would ya."

A tall black man handed it to him and Sam punched in a number. "Doug Crane, please ma'am."

Sam heard his voice come on the line. "Hello Doug, it's me, Sam." He spoke loudly to make himself heard over the noise on the loading dock.

"Sam, it's good to hear from you. How are things in the furniture business?"

"Busy as hell, I'm glad to say. I got some good news for you. I got you a spot lined up on the Al Wilder Show."

"Great…I think," he laughed, then asked, "How'd you manage that?"

Sam felt a trickle of perspiration moving down his lower back. "We buy about a hundred thousand a year worth of advertising from his station. I played with him in a charity golf tournament they put on out at the Magnolia Country Club last year. Nice little Jewish guy. When you meet him in person, he's nothing like what he sounds like on the radio. You listen to that big deep voice of his and you're thinkin' he's a big, tough lookin' guy. But in person's he's really kind of a nerdy lookin' little guy. Skinny, wears black horned rimmed glasses, and he's got this black shiny hair that looks like a toupee."

"Well, I think Paul will agree it's a great idea. After all, exccpt for Rush Limbaugh, he's got the top rated radio talk show in Atlanta."

"That's why I got you on. You're bound to be quoted in the *Monitor*, and you might get some television coverage, too."

"So when do I make my grand appearance on the Al Wilder Show?"

"Next Tuesday morning. He usually has a little monologue for about fifteen minutes to get started off. Kinda like Limbaugh, you know. And then he'll probably introduce you around nine-fifteen or so and have you take calls for about an hour. They said for you to be at the station by eight o'clock."

Doug could hear the sound of a horn blowing in the background, and then Sam yelling. "Jake, tell that fucker to hold his horses, for Christ's sake. Can't he see we got stuff that has to be moved before he can back that friggin' rig in here!" The big round face scowled in the direction of the offending truck driver.

"Sorry, Doug, we got a little confusion goin' on out here."

"Sounds like you're busy so I'll let you go. I really appreciate for your help in arranging the talk show."

"Okay, we'll all be listenin'. Good luck, Doug."

Doug hung up and walked down the hall to Paul Davidson's office. His campaign director was sitting in his high-backed chair reading something on his desk.

"Hi, Paul, have you got a minute?" said Doug.

Paul took off his wire-rimmed glasses and looked up. "Sure come on in. I was just reading your position paper on Social Security. What's up?"

"Sam Brinkman called and said he'd gotten me on the Al Wilder show."

"Terrific. He's marvelous at waking up our apathetic citizenry."

Doug told him about the time schedule and was about to leave when Paul said, "Oh, by the way, have you seen this." Paul handed him a folded newspaper and pointed to an article, which Doug began to read.

Man stabs 2 Social Security workers over his missing check

DECATUR, Ala. (AP)-An irate man stabbed two Social Security workers in their office Monday during a dispute over his missing check. Harry Malcolm Everett, 32, became angry when told his Social Security check had not arrived because the office thought he was in jail, witnesses told police. "They said they would get it all straightened out," said David Southfield, who was in the office at the time. "He got up and that's when he stabbed the first lady. We all ran out the back door."Police said Everett used a butcher knife to stab Gayle Bowman in the throat, then stabbed office manager William Floyd in the forehand and hand. Everett surrendered in the building lobby and was held on two counts of assault, Decatur police Lt. Harold Bradley said. Bowman underwent surgery and was listed in critical condition. Floyd was released following treatment."

Doug looked up and shook his head. "How in the world could a guy like that think he was entitled to a Social Security check."

"Where's your compassion," Paul said sarcastically. "That poor man was suffering from a mental disorder and he's entitled to be paid for his malady."

"Our federal retirement system is even more screwed up than I thought it was," said Doug, shaking his head.

The campaign manager sat down behind his desk and put his glasses back on. "I thought we might work this Decatur episode into your position paper on Social Security."

"Yeah, that's a good idea," Doug said absentmindedly, his blue eyes were still staring at the newspaper article. He sighed and tossed the paper on Paul's desk. "Unbelievable," he whispered as he walked out the door.

Doug was back in his office sitting in his dark red leather chair. He leaned over and put his hands around his ankles, trying to stretch his lower back. His back had been injured when he was a teenager playing baseball at Albany Academy. He had collided with the catcher at home plate during the state championship game. He'd scored the winning run, but he'd ended up in a hospital in traction for two weeks, and since then his back had never been the same.

He and Priss had been to a cocktail reception the night before that had lasted until almost midnight. A little over a hundred people had showed up. It was a surprisingly good turn out considering the fact that it had rained hard all evening. But it had been a little like preaching to the choir, he realized. His friends and the people they brought along were all conservative Republicans like he was. They lived in Buckhead or other affluent neighborhoods, belonged to the Atlanta Country Club or the Piedmont Driving Club, or some other very exclusive private club. Besides being wealthy and privileged, they were all protestant and white.

But then he asked himself, What about all those other people who live in the Tenth Congressional District who weren't invited to my cocktail reception and who would have probably felt totally out of place if they had accepted an invitation? Most of them have never heard of Doug Crane. Could he relate to them?

He knew that he had to if he would have any chance of beating Nat Thompson. And then he thought about the radio talk show. Some of them were going to be calling in to the Al Wilder Show. He wondered if he would have the right answers. Would he say the things they wanted to hear? An hour taking telephone calls from perfect strangers is a very long time, he thought. Did he need a trial run of some sort to get ready? He closed his eyes and rubbed a hand across his forehead.

Then he suddenly remembered what his Dad had told him, Stand up for what you believe in. And he suddenly felt better.

It was late the next afternoon that Doug received a telephone call from a man named Albert Higgens. The stranger had a smooth, resonant voice. Doug punched a button on his console and saw a face come up on the screen of his computer monitor. Albert Higgens looked like he could have been a movie star. He had distinguished good looks, clear gray eyes and a cleft chin below a patrician nose.

"Sam Brinker gave me your name, Mr. Crane. My company runs a nationwide chain of nursing homes, Higgens Health Care. You may have heard of us." The man's teeth looked like they had been capped.

"Yes, as a matter of fact I have," said Doug.

"Well, the reason for this call is to let you know that you can count on us for some support in your race against Nat Thompson."

"That's certainly nice to hear. I appreciate that."

"Yes, we're willing to place a bet on the right man, even if he is a little bit of an underdog. So long as he realizes how important health care is to a city like Atlanta." The distinguished looking man on the computer screen pushed some gray hair at his temple back behind an ear.

"Well, I'm sure there's going to be a continuing need for nursing homes."

"Glad you agree, Doug." He hesitated, then continued,"Mind if I call you Doug?" The white teeth flashed again.

"Of course not." Doug watched as the man's expression suddenly turned more serious.

"Doug there's some very important legislation pending that will deserve your immediate attention, if..." he grinned and corrected himself. "...make that *when* you're elected to Congress."

"And what exactly is the legislation you're referring to, Mr. Higgens," said Doug.

"There was a front page story in last Sunday's edition of the *Atlanta Monitor.* It was a bunch of crap about how one of our nursing homes in Atlanta had failed to keep alive a couple of women in their eighties. Anybody with a grain of common sense would have known they were about to die from natural causes and that our staff had absolutely nothing to do with what happened to them." His handsome face was sneering. "It's truly amazing what a reporter and a fast talking plaintiff's lawyer can come up with these days that masquerades as being newsworthy."

He reached up to touch his hair again, flashing a gold cuff link. "Anyway, this so-called news report has stirred up a bunch of old codgers down there in Atlanta as well as that old fart Thompson, and he's introduced a bill that would make us subject to all sorts of unnecessary regulations and mandates. Doug, we just can't live with what's in that bill. It would put us out of business down there. Do you understand what I'm saying?" The handsome man's hazel eyes were sternly focused under bushy eyebrows.

Doug looked at the aristocratic face and replied coolly. "I'm afraid I don't have all the information I need to give you an opinion about the Thompson bill. But I'll try to look into it."

"You do that, Doug. And when you do, you call me. As soon as we're all on board the same train, you can count of us for some *significant* financial help with your campaign."

The way he said the word "significant" triggered something inside Doug. And he felt a sudden surge of anger. The guy on the screen was trying to shake him down.

He hung up without saying good bye and watched the man's face stammering words he couldn't hear.

Chapter 5

Al Wilder was winding up his monologue. The talk show host and Doug were seated at opposite ends of a table in the middle of which was an electronic control panel with wires and rows of tiny glass bulbs. Above each man's head was a microphone attached to the end of a boom that was tilted in a downward direction.

The radio host was bony-faced man with sunken cheeks and hair that was as shiny and black as his horned rimmed glasses. He was wearing a fire engine red short sleeved shirt and a thick gold link bracelet. The first two buttons of his shirt were unbuttoned and partly visible was a thin gold chain with a disc bearing the Star of David.

He was leaning on his elbow with his hand cupped under his chin as he talked. "…and that brings us to our guest for today, Mr. Doug Crane, who recently has announced his intention to run for Congress. The race is in the Tenth Congressional District. The challenger has the unenviable task of trying to unseat a legend in Georgia politics, the venerable Nathaniel J. Thompson, the current Chairman of the powerful House Appropriations Committee. As most of you know, Congressman Thompson has served for fourteen consecutive terms and has never lost an election."

He looked up at Doug and said, "So, how about it Doug. Don't you feel a little like Emory kicking off against the Georgia Bulldogs?"

Doug laughed and looked up at the microphone.

"Well Al, I hope I'm not *that* much of an underdog. The reason I've decided to run for Congress is that I got tired of sitting on the sidelines and watching us punt the ball down the field. Over the past sixty or seventy years, we've allowed ourselves to become so dependent on the federal government that we've forgotten how to do things for ourselves. If you look back, say to the late nineteen nineties, the annual federal budget was a little less than two trillion dollars. Today we're more than double that. The interest we owe on the national debt now consumes about half of every dollar we earn. Our taxes have gotten so burdensome that we work almost all year just to pay them. And one of the main forces in Washington promoting this drift toward government dependency is Nat Thompson. And if—"

The toupee suddenly bobbed up, "Hang on there a minute, Doug. Let's give our callers a chance to get in on this." He pushed a button on his speakerphone. "Harry, you're on the Al Wilder Show."

"Thanks for takin' my call," said a man's voice that could barely be heard over the sound of a barking dog. "Hush, damn it. Hello Al,uh…" more loud barking. "I'd like to ask Mr. Crane what he plans to do about the tax increase bein' talked about for deer huntin' licenses."

Al frowned and looked over at Doug. "I think the caller's question was, Do we need a tax increase for hunting licenses? "

Doug turned in his swivel chair.

"Harry, your deer hunting license fee is not subject to federal law. You need to write a letter to your state representative in the legislature. But I can tell you that as a general rule, I'm strongly opposed to any tax increases. And for your information, that includes a state lottery."

"Let's take another call." Al stabbed the button on his speakerphone. "Charlene, you're on the Al Wilder show."

A woman's voice came on. "Yes, Mr. Crane, what's your position on abortion?"

Doug blinked then said, "Charlene, it's my opinion that the abortion issue is one that should be left up to the people of Georgia. Just as I was saying to our first caller, we ought to make our views known to our state representatives and get them to do what we think is the right thing on the abortion issue."

The caller then said, "Okay, but what's *your* position about killing the unborn?"

"Charlene, I don't mean to sound like I'm dodging your question, but what I just said *is* my position on abortion. I don't think the federal government ought to be telling you the conditions under which you can or can not have an abortion. If you read the Tenth Amendment, they don't have the constitutional authority to do that.

"Now, if you were ask me what I would do if I was in the state legislature, I'd tell you I'd want to keep the parental notification requirement we've got now and perhaps even add a few other restrictions. But my main point is that the federal government needs to leave us alone and let the people of Georgia work out solutions for these kind of personal problems. We're never going to—"

Al was raising his hand. "Hang on, Doug we got a bunch of callers waiting." Little red lights on the control panel were flashing like Christmas lights. "Maureen, you're on the Al Wilder show."

A stridently high-pitched female voice came over the speakerphone. "I heard that right wing religious nut you just had on ranting about killing the unborn. Mr. Crane, are you suggesting that we deny a woman's right to choose?"

Al chimed in. "How about it, Doug, you taking sides?"

Doug took a deep breath. "What I'm suggesting is that our state legislature should be free to impose reasonable conditions on abortion without any interference from Washington."

Al Wilder punched up the next call. "Bob, you're on the line."

"Mr. Crane it sounds to me like you're just passing off a lot of stuff to our state legislature. Don't you have any strong feelings on the issues?"

Doug sat up straight. "I certainly do Bob, and I'm glad you asked that question. The first thing I'm going to do when I get to Washington is introduce a bill for an across the board tax cut. The second thing I'm going to do is introduce a bill to abolish the Internal Revenue Code and replace it with a flat tax."

"A *what* tax," said Bob.

"That's a tax that was first considered by Congress about fifteen years ago. It didn't get very far because the tax lawyers, accountants, corporate lobbyists, and people like Nat Thompson all joined together to kill it. As a result, our tax laws have gotten more and more complicated. The fifteen thousand-page tax code we now have is the most incomprehensible monster on earth, but complexity is exactly what the Washington establishment wants. They thrive on passing those arcane exemptions for the special interests, because that's the way they get the money to fund their campaigns. But what about the rest of us who don't have the clout to carve out all those juicy little tax breaks? We get nothing but more mindboggling rules and a greater share of the tax burden.

"But once I get to Washington, we're going to change all that. We're going to get rid of the Internal Revenue Code once and for all. And we're going to have a flat tax system that let's us file our returns on a post card that can be completed in less than ten minutes."

Al Wilder held up his hand again. "Bill, you're on the Al Lewis show."

"Doug, I'm twenty-two years old and last month I started working for Coca Cola as an assistant distribution manager. When I got my first paycheck I couldn't believe how much money was being taken out. I mean, after they deduct for income taxes, Social Security, and Medicare, there's not much left."

Doug felt as though he finally had someone he could really relate to. "Bill, what you've discovered is exactly what I think is—"

Al Wilder butted in, "Hold it Doug, we've got to break for a quick commercial." The talk show host was slipping a CD into a slot on his electronic control panel.

He took off his earphones and turned to Doug. "Got a bunch of fire breathing women today. Happens every time you mention the A word." He shook his shiny black head. "And how about that guy with that damn dog. Unfortunately, we get a lot of bubbas like him calling in all the time."

Doug nodded. He was starting to develop a migraine headache.

A man was pointing at Al.

"We're back on folks. Bill, are you still with us? Bill..." Al was frowning, and Doug was eager to talk about the Coca Cola assistant manager's tax burden. Al repeated, "Bill?" More silence at the other end of the line. "Okay, let's go to Paul. Paul, you're on the Al Wilder Show."

"Mr. Crane, I'm sixty-five years old. I bought my house thirty five years ago. My mother is going to be ninety-eight next month. Six months ago we converted our garage into an apartment and she—"

Al broke in. "What's the question, caller?

"Well, after we converted our garage to an apartment, we had a small fire. She wasn't hurt or anything, thank the Lord, but—"

Al stabbed the button on the speakerphone. "Jane, you're on the Al Wilder show."

"What experience does Mr. Crane have that would compare to the lifetime of service rendered by Nat Thompson to the people of the Tenth District?"

Doug said, "Jane, I'm glad you asked that question. Let me tell you a little bit about my background. After graduating from law school, I worked as a county prosecutor down in Albany County and then served as District Attorney there for six years. My wife and I moved to Atlanta about seven months ago and I'm now a partner with the law firm of Balding and Bell.

"Although I'm a lot younger than my opponent and I haven't had the experience he's had in Washington, during my thirty-six years I've read a lot and thought a lot about the issues confronting this country. I've also listened to people and talked with people, and during that time I think I've developed an understanding of what needs to be done to make this a better country."

"Marvin, you're on the Al Wilder show."

The man's words were loud, harsh, and passionate. "Why do some Euro-Americans kill people of color? Why do they profit by redlining and discrimination? Why are we sent to prison for longer terms than white people? Why do they dump their drugs in places we live? Why do they—"

"Hold on Marvin, let's give Doug a chance to answer."

"Well, you've asked me a lot of questions, but let me start by saying that I believe our civil rights laws should be enforced. If a case is proven that someone has been discriminated against, then they should be given the remedy the law provides. But I'm not in favor of Affirmative Action. I don't think we ought to give any racial group special preferences. Everybody should have to make it on his or her own merit. That's what Arthur Ashe believed. That's the way he lived his life and that's why his statute is standing on Monument Avenue in Richmond, Virginia next to other honorable and great men like Robert E. Lee and Stonewall Jackson." Doug reached down and took a sip of water.

"As to the issue of capital punishment, which I think one of your questions alluded to, I'm a strong believer in the death penalty. As a former county prosecutor, I've seen how effective it can be in reducing murders and rapes."

Al was circling his index finger in the air. "Let's take another call."

A woman came on the line. "Yes, Mr. Crane I was so impressed by what you had to say about our tax system. I couldn't agree with you more and I want to—"

"Can you believe that folks, we're all out of time." Al Wilder pushed a button and the little red lights stopped blinking.

"I want to thank you, Doug Crane, for being here this morning." He was reaching across the table to shake hands. "And I want to wish you good luck in your upcoming race." Al leaned back and said, "When we return from this commercial break, I'll tell you about next week's guest, Atlanta Police Chief Dan Ball, who's going to be talking about the new teen curfew law recently passed by City Council. Don't touch that dial, we'll be right back."

A lady wearing a headset came over and disconnected Doug's earphone. The boom swung overhead as he stood up. He thought about how good it felt to stretch his legs.

He walked around a glass partition to a door opening to a hallway. As he came out, he saw Priss walking toward him.

She was smiling as she hugged him.

"How'd I do?" he asked.

"You were great." She kissed him on the cheek leaving a small red mark.

He put his arm around her and they started walking down the street. "This is gonna be harder than I thought it was," he said.

She gave him a playful jab. "Hey, you've just started, Congressman. You've gotta learn to take a little heat."

"There was definitely some heat in there."

He looked over and noticed her smile had suddenly disappeared. She was staring straight ahead. A young mother was laughing and pushing a baby carriage in their direction.

Chapter 6

Nat Thompson was out of breath. The elevator on the first floor of the Longworth House Building was out of order and he'd had to walk up three flights of stairs. He could feel the pain in his chest.

As he was walking into his office he reached in his suit pocket and felt his bottle of pills. He swallowed two and sat down in the big black leather chair behind his old desk made of north Georgia pine. The wall behind him was covered with framed photographs taken over the last thirty years. They showed the smiling Congressman separately framed in a variety of political poses exchanging handshakes with many people, including Georgia tourists, CEOs of Coca Cola, IBM, and Boeing, five Air Force generals, and three presidents, including the current one, Paul O'Banion.

The election was less than six months away. The Chairman hadn't been able to shake his feeling of anxiety about this race since his meeting with Ab Connell. And while the polls showed he was still far ahead of his young challenger, by a margin of almost thirty- percent, they also showed that there had been some narrowing in the last couple of weeks.

Nat wondered whether he needed to make any changes in his television commercials.

He sat there at his desk with his big hands behind his head, his beady eyes gazing into space. He was thinking about his meeting with the campaign ad guru that Mike Ruby had found. Nat knew that Derek Jacobson was going to be expensive as soon as he'd seen his double-breasted tailor-made suit, the kind designed by Italians and worn by young investment bankers after they made partner. His hair had been long and fluffy and parted in the middle, and his cheeks had been smooth and pink as a baby's. He'd looked like he'd never shaved before.

After thirty minutes with this kid, Nat was convinced that he was absolutely the biggest bullshitter he'd ever heard, and The Chairman had heard a lot bullshit in Washington. The baby- faced consultant had presented a thirty minute video with samples of his work, including detailed graphs and charts showing how his commercials had been so devastatingly effective in turning voters away from the victims of his attack ads.

Nat disliked this egotistical and obnoxious kid, but he couldn't argue with the results.

So he'd agreed to pay his ten thousand-dollar a month retainer. And the high priced consultant had gone to work for Nat.

During the last few months, Derek Jacobson had written some terrific negative ads blasting Doug Crane. One of The Chairman's favorites involved an outdoor scene with three actors. It started with a shot of a sweet looking elderly couple standing by their mailbox. In the background you could see a flowerbed of begonias in front of their neat little red brick house.

Nat played the action back in his mind. He could see the whistling mailman opening their white picket fence.

"Mornin' folks," says the friendly letter carrier, tipping his hat. The camera pans over to the old folk's faces. They're both frowning. "Gee, Mr. and Mrs. Green," says the mailman, "you all look awfully worried. Is somethin' wrong?"

There's a close up of the husband's wrinkled face. He's standing there, his eyes glistening with tears. And then finally, he says. "Oscar, they say that this right wing lawyer, Doug Crane, wants to pass a bill in Congress to take away our Social Security checks, the ones you bring us every month along with those friendly newsletters we get from Nat Thompson."

The mailman takes off his hat and scratches his gray head. "Why, that would be awful, Mr. Green. I know how much you folks depend on that money, just like I will next year when I retire."

Their camera closes in on the old woman. She's putting the palms of her hands together under her chin, and she says, "We better all pray to the Lord that Nat Thompson is reelected."

The old man's solemn face reappears and he says earnestly, "Yes Dorothy, and we all need to go vote for him, too."

They're all nodding their heads as the camera fades to black, and then words appear on the screen in big, bold letters against a white background: "OUR FUTURE SECURITY IS AT STAKE. KEEP NAT THOMPSON. HE CARES ABOUT US."

Nat blinked and rubbed his long, narrow nose as he remembered another one of his favorites attack ads.

It had showed a photograph of Doug Crane's head superimposed upon the plump shoulders of a screaming baby in a diaper. The caption had read: "CAN WE REALLY AFFORD TO TAKE THE TIME TO POTTY TRAIN DOUG CRANE?"

At Derek's suggestion, Mike had spent several days organizing the videotapes of Nat's public appearances in Atlanta during the last ten years. After a little editing here and there, Derek had used portions of some of them in his commercials, like the sixty-second clip showing him at a ribbon cutting ceremony in Atlanta. Nat had been there as the honoree for the opening of the fourteen million-dollar Nathaniel Thompson Veteran's Hospital. Cheering faces had surrounded the proud Congressman as the red ribbon had fluttered to the ground.

Nat smiled and said to himself, A novice like Doug Crane can't come close to matching that kind of wonderful display of public service. Who cares if Doug Crane looks better than I do, he told himself, I'll still win. I always have.

He remembered how many times his political enemies on the right had tried to pin labels on him: Ultra liberal. The King of Pork. Washington Fat Cat. But none of that garbage had stuck. Nat Thompson knew who he really was: The peoples' lobbyist.

And he didn't mind being called a lobbyist. That's what they hired me for, he reminded himself, and that's why they've kept reelecting me all these years—to go to Washington and get as much from the federal government as I can and bring it back home. Because if I don't, somebody else up there will sure as hell get it for their voters.

And he'd delivered. He felt a profound sense of pride thinking about all the libraries, post offices, government agencies like the new IRS building, and so many other monuments to his hard work for his people. How could they not reelect him given this unparalleled record of service?

He rubbed his sunken eyes. He was tired. The last few weeks of endless hearings before his Appropriations Committee had taken a toll. As the deadline had approached for submitting the annual budget, the horse trading among his committee members had intensified into a feeding frenzy. It was as if a pack of Piranha were attacking a drowning cow.

His mind went back to their last meeting. It had been after 11 o'clock at night. The room had smelled of tobacco smoke and there had been little piles of crumpled yellow paper scattered all over the long mahogany table. Nat had been sitting there in his big chair at the end, holding his cigar and glaring at the weary faces.

"I'll say it one last time, gentlemen," thundered The Chairman, "we either set aside an additional two billion for the North Georgia Interregional Airport or a lot of you fellas are going to be goin' home empty handed."

A bespectacled man from Louisiana had looked up and said, "But Nat, you've already got ten billion in here for all that other stuff in Georgia—the libraries, the bridges, the post offices. For God's sake, we just can't add anymore."

The Chairman had given the man a long cold stare that would have stopped an attacking Grizzly bear. When Nat had finally spoken the only sound in the room had been the ticking of the grandfather clock.

"Lionel, do you want that armory in Shreveport or not. Didn't I hear you tell us earlier all that shit about how your Army Reservists needed a new place to keep their guns and ammunition, along with the five jeeps they drive down to Gulfport every summer." He moved his beady snake-like eyes around the table.

"Well gentlemen, I ask you, is it our fault that Lionel's weekend warriors decided to convert a United States Armory into a basketball gymnasium." He slammed his hand down on the table. "No it's not! And I'll tell you what, Lionel. Your folks back home can kiss a new building good bye unless we fund my airport. Am I understood!"

In the end they had all been allowed to join the feast, but the choicest cuts were reserved for The Chairman.

Just down the hallway from the floor of the House of Representatives was a marble bathroom. The Democratic Majority Leader was there, sitting in a stall. The only sound he could hear came from a television mounted high in the corner of the bathroom. It was a simulcast of someone speaking out on the House floor. A member had introduced a resolution to recognize the one hundred and fiftieth anniversary of Dry Prong, Ohio.

The Majority Leader's mind shifted back to the upcoming elections. Ab Connell was worried and his stomach was tied in knots. The Democratic margin of ten seats in the House had shrunk to five. Three of the oldest Democrats in the House had suddenly decided to take their six figure pensions and retire. Then, a week later, one of the House's most popular liberals had been diagnosed with an inoperable brain tumor. And, if that wasn't bad enough, two days ago, a pro choice New Jersey Democrat had been forced to resign when it was revealed that she was having an affair with a Washington D. C. policeman.

Why can't this happen to the Republicans? Ab asked himself.

He knew that the Party could still keep control of the House, but at least ninety percent of the Democrat incumbents would have to win. He knew that was cutting it awfully close.

He started thinking about Nat Thompson's race in Georgia. He'd seen some of the television ads that were running down there. The contrast in their physical appearances had become too painful to watch. Doug Crane looked like a movie star and Nat looked like the old man that he was.

He wanted to tell Nat to stick with the ads like the one of the old couple and the mailman and forget about replaying all those ribbon-cutting ceremonies. But how do I tell him he looks bad on TV without pissing him off, he wondered. He remembered what happened during their lunch at Norton's, when Nat had been so mad. But, hell…there was so much at stake.

"God, don't let it happen," he whispered to himself.

There was the sound of someone opening the bathroom door.

The Majority Leader felt a painful tightness in his gut. It lingered for a long time as he sat there straining. On the television screen the Congressman from Ohio was still blathering on about his resolution. The Majority Leader closed his eyes and tried to tighten his stomach muscles. He suddenly felt a blessed release and heard the sound of a volcanic fart echoing off the marble walls.

A voice from outside the stall said, "*Jesus.*"

Ab sat there for a few minutes, waiting for the man to leave. When he heard the door close, he walked out of the stall. While he was washing his hands, he looked up at the television set. The lonely Congressman from Ohio was still singing the praises of Dry Prong, Ohio.

Chapter 7

Doug was working out at the Q Club of Atlanta. It was only a couple of blocks down Peachtree Street from his law office. The carpeted room, which was surrounded by mirrors, had a long row of Stair Masters and stationary bicycles on one side and a long row of chrome-plated weight machines on the other.

The noontime crowd was an assortment of young professionals, men and women who worked downtown. Most of them were pumping, peddling, or straining, and watching the row of televisions suspended from the ceiling.

When he'd first joined the fitness center Doug had established a well-defined workout routine: thirty minutes on the Stair Master, another thirty minutes on the weight machines. And until he started running for Congress, he'd adhered to this workout routine religiously since the first day he'd joined eight months earlier. But during the last couple of months, with all of the luncheon meetings and speeches, he'd been lucky to squeeze in a half an hour.

It had also been hard for him to get used to all the attention. Today was no exception.

He could see the heads turning to look at him when he walked in. A young woman wearing a yellow leotard and holding a lightweight barbell in one hand looked over at him and smiled.

Doug walked up behind a Stair Master to wait his turn. A pot-bellied man wearing a sweatband on his forehead was furiously pumping up and down. He glanced back at Doug and suddenly the machine stopped. He climbed off and bent over panting. Then he raised up with a big smile on his dripping face.

"Hey! Doug Crane, how're you doin'! The man held out a sweaty palm.

"Pleased to meet you," said Doug, shaking is hand.

"Bob McAndrews. I'm with Shade Rite."

Doug was punching in the maximum speed on the computerized control panel. His feet started pumping.

"We distribute lamp shades. Third largest distributor in the southeast. I'm District Manager."

"Really," said Doug, moving up and down.

The lampshade manager was taking off his sweatband. "We do about sixty percent residential, and—"

There was a young woman's voice. "Excuse me."

Doug felt a light tugging sensation at the back of his T-shirt and he turned around.

It was the young woman in the yellow tights. Doug said to himself, She looks like an Atlanta Falcon's cheerleader.

"When you get through," she cooed, "can I get your autograph?"

"Sure."

The lamp shade manager's eye got as big as silver dollars as he watched her walk away. The yellow leotard had only a narrow strip at the crevice of her buttocks that broadened as the material arched high above her thighs. There was little left to Bob McAndrew's imagination.

"Man, that's a nice piece of work, huh?"

She walked back over to the floor mat and started stretching again.

The lamp shade manager gestured in her direction with a big smile. "That's one of the main reasons I come here."

Doug was pumping up and down and beginning to sweat.

The pot-bellied man said, "Business has been great lately. We sold over five thousand shades last month."

He kept talking about his company, his friends, and the Atlanta Braves for the next thirty minutes. Doug climbed down from the Stair

Master and wiped his face with a towel, then walked over to the bench press machine, trailed by his loquacious admirer.

There was a beeping sound. Bob McAndrews reached in the pocket of his gym shorts and pulled out a cell phone.

"Yeah…no…that's not what was on the invoice." He frowned as he sat down on the vinyl seat of the machine next to Doug's. "No it wasn't Joe. Okay, okay, I'll be there in about twenty minutes."

"Sorry, but one of our order's gotten screwed up, and I'm gonna have to get back to the office."

Doug was on the bench, lying flat on his back, his muscular arms straining to hold the weight above him. Through his clenched teeth he said something that sounded like, "I hope you get it straightened out."

"I'm gonna go by your headquarters and pick up some yard signs."

Doug managed a half smile and kept on lifting.

After the lamp shade manager left, Doug worked on a few other machines and then decided he'd had enough. He glanced in the mirror. The perspiration had rolled down his pectoral muscles, creating two dark curves on the front of his T-shirt in the shape of UU.

He was walking down the hallway toward the locker room when the girl in the yellow leotard came up to him.

She smiled at him coyly. A narrow shoulder strap was hanging loosely off her tanned shoulder. She extended her arm. "I'm Sally Wainwright."

He shook her hand and felt something in his palm.

"What's this?" he said frowning. He looked at the piece of paper and saw a phone number.

She was standing there smiling at him. Doug knew the message her Caribbean Sea eyes were sending: You can do whatever you want with me. He felt a sudden shortness of breath and weakness in his knees.

"Didn't you say, I mean…I thought you said you wanted my autograph," he stammered. As soon as the words left his mouth, he realized how stupid they sounded. With a look like that and a body that could put her in the running for Miss Nude America, Sally Wainwright was obviously interested in a lot more than an autograph.

He took a deep breath and said, "If you'll excuse me, I'm afraid I'm on a pretty tight schedule."

His heart was pounding by the time he got to his locker. He took a long cold shower.

Later, as he was getting dressed, he started laughing.

At about the same time that her husband was working out at the fitness center, Priscilla Crane was working at the recently opened campaign headquarters. It was a couple of miles away from the Omni Complex on the edge of an industrial area. Across the street was a rail yard owned by Southern Pacific. The office they'd rented was on the first floor of a three-story stucco building. It looked like it had been built before the Braves had moved to town. There were a few white spots on the grimy facade where the plaster had fallen off. A big blue and white sign, CRANE FOR CONGRESS, was taped to a corner of a large plate glass window that extended across the front.

Priscilla had been spending eight hours a day there. She'd hired a temporary office manager to look after her art gallery. Before she started, Paul had spent a lot of time with her laying out an organizational plan for the campaign. With his usual careful attention to detail, he had spelled out everything she needed to do from the time she made the coffee in the morning until the time she turned out the lights at night.

She had also benefited from having done a lot of charity work. Since she and Doug had moved to Atlanta, she had served on three separate organizing committees to raise money for medical research. Although most forms of cancer had already been cured, she had taken a special interest in raising money for research into heart disease. Her father's best friend, Jim Ferriday, had died of a heart attack when he was only 58 years old.

But while he charity work had given her experience in fund raising, she wasn't now just part of a committee, she was *the* person in charge.

And the pressures and pace of managing a congressional campaign office were much more frenetic and intense than anything Priscilla had ever experienced.

Four long folding tables had been set up on each side of the room that was lit by a bank of fluorescent ceiling lights. The beige walls were bare except for the blue andwhite campaign posters. Telephone books and sheets of paper with long lists of names were stacked on each of the tables.

Priscilla moved around the room like a mother hen tending her chicks. The volunteers were eight women and two men. The women were all matronly looking and middle aged to elderly, except for a well-dressed doctor's wife and Marjorie Rodriquez who was eight months pregnant. The men were elderly and retired, one bald and the other white haired.

Paul had worked up a list of names he'd gotten from the county records of registered voters. It listed the people in the Tenth District most likely to vote Republican. Priscilla had carefully reviewed Paul's script with each of her volunteers.

This is how it read:

> "Hello, my name is_______, and I'm calling from the Crane for Congress Campaign Headquarters. Doug Crane supports smaller government, lower taxes, and more personal freedom and responsibility. We hope you'll support him and vote for him on November third." Wait for response. If negative, say "Have a nice day," and hang up. If positive, ask for a contribution of $25 or more. If they say they will contribute, tell them to make their checks payable to the "Crane for Congress Campaign." Remember, *don't badger people*. Be polite to everyone, no matter how they respond to your call. Don't try to answer a question if you are not sure of the answer. Ask Mrs. Crane for help.

Someone had brought a radio. It was tuned to an "easy listening" station, the type that played a lot of Frank Sinatra and Tony Bennett recordings. Now, a red haired lady was waving at Priscilla from across the room. "Mrs. Crane, I've got a man on the line here who says he wants to make a contribution, but he wants to send cash. He says he doesn't have a bank account. What should I tell him?"

"Tell him we appreciate it, but we can only accept checks."

"Mrs. Crane!" Marjorie Rodriguez was yelling and waving. Her large stomach couldn't be concealed by her frilly cotton maternity dress.

Priscilla came running over. "Yes, Marjorie, what is it?"

"I just got a call from my babysitter. She's gonna have to leave to catch the bus early. I'm gonna have to go home. Is that okay?"

"Sure, I can handle your phone. Where's your list?"

The pregnant woman reached down and picked up a sheet of paper that was soggy and brown. "Sorry, but I spilled my coffee."

"You better get going," said Priscilla. Her head was starting to hurt.

It was seven o'clock and Priscilla had just gotten back to the apartment. She was in the kitchen putting a paper carton of *egg fu yung* in the microwave when she heard steps on the parquet flooring.

Doug came in the kitchen and kissed her on the mouth. He stood there looking in her eyes with his arms around her thin waist.

She recognized the look in his eye. "Hey, we've got to have supper first," she said, smiling and tucking a loose strand of dangling black hair behind an ear. She walked over to the microwave again.

"So, how goes the life of an aspiring United States Congressman?"

"Okay, but it seems like a lifetime until next November." He took off his tie.

"Anything new from your polling guru?"

"He says we're down by less than fifteen percent."

"That's great!"

"I also found out that Thompson's rejected our latest request for a debate. Let's see, that's either the third or fourth letter we've written, I'm beginning to lose track. And every time they tell us to get lost."

"Well, I hope you're making an issue of his refusal to debate." She was scooping rice out of a paper carton.

"We are. You'll see my sterling interview in the *Atlanta Monitor* tomorrow. Full of outrage about what a disservice it is to the people of the Tenth District that the old fart still refuses to debate the issues."

"Of course, you know why he won't do it," she said.

Doug was unscrewing the cork from a bottle of California Chardonnay.

She answered her own question. "He knows damn well that he looks like somebody's great grandfather and you look like some Greek God."

He laughed. "Think we can work that line into a new campaign ad?"

He poured her a glass of wine.

"Thanks." She gave him a warm smile.

"So how'd it go with you, Mrs. Future Congresswife?"

"The usual. Chaos and confusion. Majorie spilled her coffee all over the phone list. I think she's gonna give birth in the campaign headquarters any day now, I really do. I mean, can you see it?" She waved her arm through the air. "Front-page news in the Monitor: Candidate's *loyal campaign worker has baby while dialing for votes.*"

He laughed until tears filled his blue eyes. "Hey, we can use it!" he said, holding his side.

They both had tears in their eyes now, laughing until their sides hurt.

There was the sound of a siren from somewhere outside.

Doug put his glass of wine down on the kitchen counter and walked over to the refrigerator again. "Take out again, right?"

"Right. What time do you start in the morning?" she asked.

"Five."

She walked over to him and put her arms around his neck. His eyes were like the sky of a beautiful clear day, she thought. She kissed him softly on the mouth for a long time.

"The take out can wait," he said with a sparkle in his blue eyes. Her dark brown eyes were saying yes.

Chapter 8

It was a warm afternoon at the Smithers' cotton plantation in south Georgia. The Smithers' twenty-five hundred acres of fertile Georgia farmland was located on the banks of the Flint River about two miles southeast of the much smaller farm where Doug grew up.

On the horizon below a cloudless sky, at the end of long rows of green, evenly spaced cotton plants, could be seen two hatless men riding on horses. Their heads were tilted downward as though they were pondering something one or the other had said, and they moved slowly along a dusty path beside the river bank of the avocado green Flint River.

A crow cried out from off in the distance. The muffled clip clop sound of hooves striking red clay was mixed with the sound of the men's voices.

The handsome white haired man, who rode with the ease of a cowboy, was Doug's father-in-law, Boyd Smithers. He had on a pair of faded blue jeans and a button down shirt with sleeves rolled half way up his forearms. He and his wife, Susan, Priscilla's mother, had lived here for the past twenty years, ever since they had left New Orleans.

Doug could see some of his wife's features in his father-in-law's face. He had the same evenly spaced, luminous eyes, although his wife's were darker, more like ebony to his chocolate. The nose was straight, but not too long, every bit as aristocratic as Priscilla's. And he had the physique of a man much younger than one in his seventies.

A slight breeze tousled Doug's sandy hair. There was terra cotta colored dust on one shoulder of his white knit shirt, the sleeves of which stretched tightly across his large biceps. The leather reins hung loosely in his strong hands, while his clean-cut face reflected an air of serious deliberation.

"I think the key issue is going to be Social Security, Boyd, I really do. Thompson can relate to the older people in a way I haven't been able to. Not yet anyway." He sighed and said, "The sun of a gun is a real master at playing to the fears of old people. Even the slightest reform of the system is always painted as an evil plot by Republicans to cast old folks out on the street. The AARP is behind him one hundred percent." Doug was referring to the powerful American Association for Retired People.

"I dropped my membership in that damn organization years ago," said Boyd with a scowl on his tanned face. He shifted in his saddle and then gazed out across the cotton field. "I remember how it was when Tal Shore was president. That son of a bitch won the presidency by getting just about every single vote of those forty million AARP members. He had promised that if he was elected, he'd pass a law to give everybody over sixty-five a fifty thousand-dollar tax exemption. And after the election he kept his promise. But he also jacked up social security taxes on everybody else." He looked over at Doug. "What's it now, thirty percent?"

"Thirty-two point five, to be exact."

Boyd shook his head then looked in the direction of an old windmill. The rusty tin blades were turning slowly in the breeze.

"When I turned fifty-five, the AARP mailed me this red, white, and blue card. I cut it in half and sent it back to them with a letter telling them to take my name off their damn mailing list."

An idea suddenly lit up Doug's face. He turned half way in his saddle and leaned over and tapped his father-law on the shoulder. "How would you like to go on television?"

"What?" Boyd said with a look of bewilderment.

"I said how would you like to go on television, and do a campaign ad for me."

"Oh, I don't know. I mean, I've never done anything like that before," he said, shaking his head.

"Hey, you'd be great. You would. You're articulate, handsome, and best of all I think people will see that you're…*sincere* about the things you believe in."

"Well, that's nice of you to say, son, but I think maybe you're letting your family prejudice get a little ahead of your reason. I'm not so sure other people are going to share your kindly viewpoint of Boyd Smithers."

"You're being too modest, Boyd, really. You'd be perfect. I know Priscilla would back me up on this."

Boyd was stroking the side of his horse's neck. You could tell he was thinking about it. Finally, he smiled. "Well, if you really need me, I will. But I've gotta warn you. I'm a rank amateur at that kind of stuff. All I've ever been good for was lookin' for oil with my old partner Jim Ferriday. And the only reason I made a lot of money doing that was Jim's hard work and a thing called luck."

His father-in-law's self-effacing comments drew a sarcastic reply, "Yeah, right."

Boyd glanced down at his watch. "Let's go back and see what the girls are doin'."

The clip clop sound got louder and faster and the dust billowed higher as the two men headed back to the Smithers' plantation home. They didn't need to shade their eyes as they looked into the orange sliver of sun peaking over the horizon of green cotton plants.

Priss recognized Sam Brinkman's husky voice as soon as she heard it. They'd gotten to know each other on a first name basis during the last few months of Doug's campaign. It was late afternoon and she was at the downtown headquarters when she got his call.

Sam's voice was brimming with excitement. "I tell you, this could be a *really* big break for Doug."

He told her that he had gotten a call from one of his salesmen who worked in a store in Cobb County, northwest of Atlanta. The salesman said a young man had come in with his family, a wife and two little children, and that they had been looking for a breakfast room table. The young husband had told the salesman that he was a computer technician who operated some of the robotic construction equipment at the Lockheed plant. Sam pointed out that the Lockeed Aircraft Company had over fifteen hundred workers now that Lockheed had been named the successful bidder on a major government contract to build a state of the art bomber for the United States Air Force.

"It's one of the largest employers in Cobb County, but most of the folks working out there live in DeKalb and vote in the Tenth District."

"But Sam, Nat Thompson's been Lockheed's patron saint for who knows how many years," she said. "How's Doug going make any inroads with them?"

"I know. It sounded crazy at first to me, too. But let me finish my story. Everybody who works for me knows what a strong supporter I am of Doug's. That's the reason my salesman called. He said he and this Lockheed guy started talkin' about politics. The young computer guy was sayin' how unhappy he was about the fact that a big chunk of his union dues was being used to help pay for Nat Thompson's campaign. He said that wasn't fair since he was planning to vote for Doug."

"He actually said that?" She couldn't hide her skepticism.

"Damn right he did. He said he liked what Doug's been sayin' about family values and lower taxes."

"That's great Sam, but what makes you think there're more people like him out at the Lockheed plant?"

"He told my salesman, Priss! He said there's a whole bunch of people who were fed up with what the union's been doin', sucking all this money out of their paychecks and pumping it into Thompson's campaign. These aren't the same blue collar, dirty fingernail guys that used to work in industrial plants twenty or thirty years ago, Priss. These people are well educated, highly trained scientific and technical types, and they will vote Republican if the right guy comes along."

"I didn't realize." Her eyes were wide open as his words sank in.

"We gotta move on this Priss."

"What do you have in mind?"

"There's a seafood restaurant called Danny's that's about a mile from the plant gate. The young man I've been talking about is named Bill Farrington and he's real gung ho about helping Doug. He said a lot of the Lockheed people head over to Danny's on Friday afternoons. They've got a patio area out back with picnic tables scattered around a concrete space big enough to handle a couple of hundred people. It would be a great place for Doug to meet them."

She was already thinking about contacting the printers about the announcements.

"What's his schedule?" asked Sam.

"Hang on." She reached over and picked up a sheet.

"Let's see…a week from Friday we could squeeze it in. He's got an appearance that afternoon before a group of Rotarians downtown at 3:30. If he gets out of there by 4:30 we could make it to Danny's around 5:30 or 6, depending on traffic."

"If you can get the announcements printed by Monday, we can have 'em posted at the restaurant that afternoon. Might also have somebody hand some out as the Lockheed people are leaving the plant gate. I could take care of that."

"Great." She hesitated for a second, then said, "And one more thing, Sam."

"What?"

"You're a genius."

An hour after Sam Brinkman's call, all of the telephone callers at the Crane headquarters had gone home and Priscilla was about to lock up when she heard the door open. There, standing in the doorway, was an attractive lady dressed in a beautifully tailored blue suit. Her black hair was streaked with gray, but her face was still beautiful. Susan Smithers looked a lot like her daughter.

"Mom! I didn't expect you."

Her mother walked over, kissed her lightly on the cheek, and said, "Dad and I had some shopping to do in Atlanta so we thought we'd come up for the weekend."

"I hope you'll stay with us," said Priscilla.

"Oh, no dear, thank you. We'll be at the Ritz Carlton. The last thing Doug needs right now is to have some unexpected visitors."

They both sat down on the folding chairs and Priscilla's mother reached into her purse. "I've got something for you."

Priscilla watched as her mother took out a white, letter size envelope and handed it to her.

"These are from some of my old Garden District friends."

Priscilla reached in the envelope and pulled out some checks.

"We were in New Orleans last week to see the Van Gogh Exhibit. They all wanted to help Doug."

Priscilla leaned over and kissed her on the cheek.

There was a moment of silence as they exchanged a warm look.

Priscilla was beaming as she fanned the checks out like a hand of cards. "Thank you *so* much. This will really mean a lot to us."

"You're quite welcome, dear."

She told her mother about her conversation with Sam Brinkman.

"That sounds like a wonderful opportunity," her mother said as she reached up and took off one of her diamond earrings. "The morning paper had a story saying Doug's gaining ground on Thompson."

Priscilla's eyes glowed. "People are starting to listen to what he's saying, Mom. We're all really excited about his chances."

"Well, if there's anything else you can think of your father and I can do to help, let us know."

"Tell Dad we really appreciate his doing the commercial." Priscilla remembered that her father's commercial was scheduled for taping the day before Doug's meeting with the Lockheed workers.

"I actually think your father's looking forward to it." She smiled radiantly. "He's always been a little bit of a ham, you know."

They hugged and mother and daughter walked toward the door.

"Thanks again, Mom. You and Dad have been wonderful."

Susan Smithers was walking out the door when she suddenly stopped and turned around.

"Oh, I forgot to give you this."

"What is it?"

"It's for good luck. Your father gave it to me on our twenty-first wedding anniversary."

Priscilla looked down in her mother's palm and saw a small silver cross. She looked at it more closely and read the engraved words: "Love Conquers All."

Chapter 9

A world away from the events taking place in Georgia and in Washington, D. C., a crisis of epoch proportions was taking place in the Middle East. Iran, a country that for years had been a ticking time bomb of religious zealotry and political fanaticism, finally exploded. More than fifty intermediate ballistic missiles were fired from Iranian soil at Persian Gulf oil fields. The plumes of towering black smoke from the raging fires could be seen as far away as India.

With the destruction of their major oil fields and the consequential loss of their oil revenue, one by one the capitals of Saudi Arabia, Kuwait, Bahrain, and the other Persian Gulf states began to collapse like Bedouin tents blown down by an Arabian sandstorm. A horde of rampaging Islamic fundamentalists began pillaging and plundering the cities and towns. Their clerical leaders, each of whom was a puppet of the Iranian government in Tehran, finally restored order by threatening to chop off the hands of anyone caught looting. And soon after the revolutionary governments had taken over the oil fields, Abdul Jassim Gazarrani, Iran's Prime Minister, issued a declaration that henceforth no oil would be sold to the blood-sucking infidels of the West.

In response to this crisis, the Democratic President of the United States, Paul O'Banion, called an emergency meeting of his top military and national security advisers. The President heard the pleas of his generals and admirals who wanted to mount an immediate counterattack. They presented a plan to launch a thousand cruise missiles programmed to hit each of Iran's major oil fields, its principal military bases, and it radar sites. This was to be followed by high altitude saturation bombing of Tehran. And then a fifty thousand Marine landing force would storm ashore at the Strait of Hormuz and move inland to take control of the capitol.

After hearing this detailed plan of attack, President O'Banion told his assembled advisers: "I can not approve of such bellicose actions without the approval of each of the Western European heads of state and the President of Russia."

So following his meeting with his advisers, the President called the Prime Minister of Great Britain, the presidents of France, Germany, and Italy, the Queens of Belgium and the Netherlands, the King of Spain, and the Russian president. With the exception of King Carlos of Spain, they all told President O'Banion that the United States had to have the approval of the United Nations before any type of military action could even be considered. The President agreed.

The Secretary General of the United Nations was a distinguished Sudanese gentleman named Henri Mubowi. A career diplomat with a post doctorate degree in Political Science from Harvard, Secretary Mubowi was a debonair African who spoke five languages and was *Time* Magazine's most recent Man of the Year.

President O'Banion invited the UN Secretary General to come to the White House to discuss the Iranian crises. Mubowi arrived in his black Rolls Royce and was greeted by the smiling President. They went inside as the White House Police held back the sea of onlookers.

Two hours later the two men emerged into the sunlight and stepped out into the Rose Garden. People were pressing against each other and the crowd took up every square foot of space on the manicured lawn. They were all standing on their tiptoes and straining to hear the President's words as he began to speak.

"It gives me great pleasure to announce to you that Secretary General Mubowi has graciously consented to use his good offices to mediate the grave international crises brought about by the reckless actions of the Iranian government. The Secretary General has agreed to fly to Tehran tomorrow morning where he will meet with Prime

Minister Gazarrani. The United Nations will make known to the Prime Minister their dismay and deep concern about what has happened in the Persian Gulf."

Paul O'Banion turned and looked at the gray haired African, then said, "We wish you God's speed in your mission to restore normal commerce in the Persian Gulf so that oil shipments to the United States and the other members of the United Nations may be resumed as soon as possible."

There was loud applause from around the Rose Garden.

The President nodded in the direction of the African diplomat, who then walked over to the podium.

"Thank you, Mr. President O'Banion." There were so many flash bulbs going off it seemed as though he were standing in front of strobe lights. "I will do my best to convince the Iranian government that it is in its own best interests to make peace with the western world." His words were spoken with a trace of a British accent. He reached into his hip pocket and pulled out a white handkerchief and wiped his forehead.

"The people of Iran are a peace loving people, as are those of the United States. We must reach out to them and show them that we want to build bridges of friendship and respect. This I hope to do, not only during my visit to Tehran, but in all places around the globe where there is inequality and oppression, human misery and suffering." He bowed his gray head and said. "Thank you very much."

The President had walked over and put his arm around the diminutive Sudanese as the flash bulbs started flashing and reporters began shouting questions. The two men just stood there, smiling.

The next morning the Secretary General took off for Tehran and the world held its breath. And then, just as his Boeing 877 was entering Iranian air space, a heat-seeking missile was launched from somewhere down below. It made a direct hit on the big airliner, which exploded into a fireball and then vanished from the sky, leaving behind only a wispy trail of gray smoke.

The next day President O'Banion made a nationwide address to the American people. His big Irish face was red with rage.

"Yesterday, the world lost one of the most decent and honorable men I have ever known. Secretary General Mubowi was a man of peace on a mission for peace. An evil, cowardly, despicable tyrant whose infamy will be remembered for generations ordered the murder of this noble civil servant and twenty-five innocent civilians who accompanied him on this journey for peace."

His right fist was clinched as he glared into the camera. "My fellow Americans, this dastardly action will not go unpunished, you have my sacred promise."

But in the weeks that followed, nothing happened. No cruise missiles were launched, no bombs were dropped, and no Marines were landed.

The price of gasoline shot up to ten dollars a gallon. It was a lot like the Arab oil embargo of the early nineteen seventies, except that this time it was even worse. Now, no matter how long they waited in line, millions of people were unable to buy a drop of gasoline.

And the oil crisis, of course, became a very hot political issue.

Nat Thompson was feeling the heat. He was covered with an avalanche of e-mailings and faxes from the people back home. They wanted answers to their questions: How could we let something like this happen? When is it going to end? What are you going to do about it?

He knew he had to develop some kind of coherent strategy to deal with the problem. So he decided to ask his friend, the Majority Leader, to join him for lunch.

They decided to meet at the House of Representatives cafeteria. There weren't any cabs or limos to give them a ride over to Norton's.

The crowded capitol building dining hall was a beehive of legislators, secretaries, pages, and clerks, all milling around the brightly-lit room holding their trays, and trying to find a place to sit down. Nat Thompson and Abner O'Connell had finally found one. They put their trays down at a small round table next to the cashier. A black woman counting change behind the counter was laughing out loud at something someone had said to her.

"This is really shitty," observed Ab, listlessly stirring his glass of iced tea. "How much longer do you think we're going to have to put up with this crap?"

"Hell if I know. I don't think O'Banion does either." Nat moved his fingers along the crease of his white suit pants.

"Well, I wouldn't want to be in the President's shoes right now."

"Me neither," said Nat. "Pass the ketchup, would ya."

"It's gonna be real tight, Nat. I guess you know that." His fingers were tugging at one end of his gray mustache.

"You keep reminding me, so how could I forget." The Majority Leader's eyes were suddenly trained on the massive chest of a young woman with long blonde hair. She was standing there holding her tray only a few feet away. "My God, would you look at that," he whispered.

"Ab, listen, I need your help."

"What…oh yeah…what?" The Majority Leader was obviously still shaken by what he had seen.

"It's this fuckin' oil crisis, for Christ's sake, what else would it be!" The veins of his short neck were standing out like cords. Nat ran a hand through his silver hair and frowned. "Listen, this Crane kid is crucifyin' me on this. I've seen the papers back home. All those editorials blastin' the administration for not having the balls to do somethin' to Iran. And I'll tell you this, in case you don't know it. It's all Democrats, not just O'Banion, who're bein' roasted by the media." He paused to sip his cup of coffee, then looked up. "I need somethin', a position paper, a new ad. *Somethin'* to distract the public's attention. But whatever it is, I need it now!"

Ab held up a hairy hand. "Okay, okay, I know there's a problem and we're working on it.

His eyebrows were contorted into bushy knots. A few seconds later his face lit up. "Shit, this should be easy." He leaned over and said, "Listen, all you've got to do is go down there to Atlanta and hold a press conference. You say something like 'At a critical time like this, it's vital for our country to maintain the strongest possible national defense.' You with me?"

Nat was spreading butter on a piece of French bread.

"Then you could say, 'and I would remind you that Nat Thompson has been the best friend our national defense industry ever had'. Sounds pretty good, huh?"

"In case you forgot, I'd remind you that the O'Banion administration has cut defense spendin' by more than twenty percent durin' each of the last four fiscal years. That's why we're such toothless tigers when it comes to dealin' with people like this maniac Gazarrani."

"I know that and you know that, but I'll bet those hayseeds down there—excuse me, constituents—down there in your district don't. I'll bet most of them never read the *Wall Street Journal* and haven't got a clue about what's been going on at the Pentagon."

"Maybe not, but this Crane kid is educatin' them. People are listenin' to his bullshit about how Paul O'Banion and the Democrats in Congress have crapped on the American people." The Chairman glanced down at a gold cuff link, then said. "You and those DNC guys have got to come up with somethin'. If you don't, those of us takin' all this flak are goin' down. And if we do, next January you're gonna have your ass sittin' on aisle Z, right there with all those freshmen members who can't do dick."

Ab heaved a sigh and said, "So what do you want me to do, Nat?"

He pondered the question in silence for a long time, then said. "You should pay a little visit to the President. He needs to know what's going on down there."

Nat was stirring his coffee and gazing into space. A moment later, his slit lips showed the trace of a grin. "O'Banion might be able to pull some strings and create a nice little scandal involving Mr. Perfect."

The Majority Leader sat their expressionless.

Nat's beady eyes fixed on Ab's. "You tell him I need some help with this guy."

"Ab, come on in."

The President stood up from behind his desk as his secretary let the Majority Leader into the Oval Office. Paul O'Banion's desk was the same one that had been used years before by John F. Kennedy. The Kennedy Museum in Boston, a city that happened to be the current president's hometown, had loaned it to the White House.

Paul O'Banion was a bear of a man, well over six feet, with milky blue eyes an jowls and cheeks that were translucent, revealing a web of tiny blood vessels. The big Irishman idolized the Kennedy family. His devotion was partly due to the fact that he shared the same sort of heritage, being a Catholic and the grandson of a poor Irish emigrant who had used the money he'd made from bootlegged whiskey sales to build a chain of video rental stores.

"Thank you Mr. President," said the Majority Leader, who sat down in a chair in front to JFK's desk.

"Well, how do things look for November?" asked the President, as they finished shaking hands.

"Frankly, Mr. President, it's looking a little shaky right now." Ab Connell took a pen out of his chest pocket and began nervously tapping it on his knee.

"How shaky?" O'Banion's big face showed deep crevices across his forehead.

"The way things stand right now, it's too close to call."

"Shit." The President rubbed his fingers across his closed eyelids.

Ab shifted in his chair, and said, "I had lunch with Nat Thompson yesterday."

"What's that crusty old bastard up to?"

"He's worried about his race, Mr. President. He's up against a young guy named Doug Crane who's been getting a lot more attention than we hoped he would."

The President turned and started gazing out the window.

"Nat thinks that unless things change, he could lose."

Paul O'Banion swung around.

"What! You've got to be kidding. Nat Thompson's the Chairman of the House Appropriation's Committee for God's sake. Don't those fools down there in his district realize what he can do for them!" He leaned forward on his big forearms revealing gold cuff links engraved with the presidential seal and said, "Are you telling me they might be stupid enough to actually dump someone with that much power for some young guy who's not going to be able to do squat for them."

"There's more to it than that, Mr. President."

The President heaved an audible sigh.

Ab was still tapping his knee with his pen. "It's this oil embargo. Most of the folks down there, like in a lot of other places around the country, can't afford to drive anymore, and even those that can…" The President held up his hand.

"I know, I know, I've heard it all a thousand times so you don't have to remind me."

"Mr. President, we all know how skillful your people here in the White House are at uncovering the political…vulnerabilities of some of these Republican radicals. Nat thought you might be able to use some of your resources to help him uncover something in Crane's personal history that would be useful in turning things around for him."

The President was gazing out of the window again. He said nothing for several seconds and then finally turned around and looked at Ab Connell. He had a little smile on his ruddy face.

"I'll see what I can do."

Chapter 10

The *Atlanta Times* had only a small fraction of the readership of the mighty *Atlanta Monitor.* The smaller news distributor was the latest entry among the large number of on-line news providers. At the end of the first decade of the new millennium, the electronic medium had taken a dominant role in disseminating the news. The home delivery of newspapers was rapidly becoming as antiquated as the Model T.

In order to compete in this New World of sound bite journalism, the *Atlanta Times*, like many other news services, had adopted the policy of featuring the most sensational news stories that could be uncovered by its roving band of investigative reporters. The most experienced and successful of such reporters was a man named Ron Weingarten. He had worked for the *Times* for ten years and during his career he had provided many of the fledgling news service's most sensational stories. In fact, some said it was Ron Weingarten who kept the *Times* in business. He had become something of a celebrity.

The portly, chain-smoking reporter cared little about his personal appearance. His long dirt-brown hair was always unkempt and his clothes were at least a size too big and usually wrinkled. His voice was shrill and his manner of speaking was rapid fire. He had widely spaced eyes, with angular brows that gave him an owlish look.

A native New Yorker, his father had headed a garbage worker's union in Brooklyn. And Ron Weingarten wasn't one who was attracted to the ideas of political conservatives such as Doug Crane. And so, when he received a late night telephone call from the President's Chief of Staff suggesting that there might be an investigation into the

Republican challenger's background, the *Atlanta Times* reporter was more than willing to start digging.

A few days later Ron Weingarten went to Doug Crane's hometown and interviewed people he thought of as the *local yokels* of a hick town. The only thing he was able to turn up was a comment by Crane's third grade history teacher. She remembered that when he was ten years old, he had thrown a baseball during practice that had shattered a library window.

It seemed as though everybody in Albany worshiped Doug Crane. Weingarten thought how nauseating it was to hear all the adulation and praise heaped on the country club pretty boy by these dimwitted farmers and shopkeepers. He had left town feeling completely frustrated.

He had then tried to dig up some dirt from some of Crane's old college fraternity brothers whose addresses he'd been able to track down. But nothing of value turned up. Nor had he been able to find anything damaging from two of Crane's former classmates at Duke Law School. The sad fact was that Doug Crane was Mr. Perfect in every respect.

But Ron Weingarten hadn't given up hope. He was still racking his brain trying to think of a way to find something when a thought suddenly struck him: Priscilla Crane. The beautiful wife in her fancy clothes, always with that sickeningly bright smile, waving to the mindless crowds of rich supporters. There just might be something in her past.

He decided to find out.

Ron Weingarten had gone to New Orleans in search of Jason Carrington. And it hadn't taken him long to find him. They were sitting on bar stools beside each other having a drink at the Old Absinth House. The New Orleans bar on Bourbon Street was crowded with people who had dropped in after work for Happy Hour. There was the sound of laughter and glass tinkling and the smell of popcorn.

Jason Carrington was a stockbroker. His ponytail and earring, which he wore when he'd dated Priscilla Smithers, had been replaced by neatly trimmed short hair parted down the left side. He had on a cord suit with a maroon and black-striped tie, both of which he'd bought at Joseph A. Bank.

Ron Weingarten's approach to prospective sources like Jason Carrington wasn't very subtle. He told them up front that he was in the business of buying and selling information. He'd told Jason that he would pay him five thousand dollars for any information he had about Priscilla Crane. But only if the information was newsworthy enough to merit publication in the *Times*. The bottom line was that it had to be sufficiently sensationally titillating to get the readers' attention.

"So Jason, you were Priscilla Crane's boyfriend in…when was it?"

"It was probably sometime in 1993."

"How old were you?" The reporter was looking down at the little black recorder sitting next to his drink.

"About 15."

"And Priscilla?" The reporter brushed away some of his dark tangled hair from his forehead.

"She was a year younger than I was."

"And what kind of relationship did you have with her?"

"We dated. I'm not sure what you mean by 'relationship'?"

"Did you ever screw her?" Weingarten asked the question in a casual tone while stirring his drink.

The boy's eyes widened. "No." He was swinging his hips on the barstool seat. "Oh, I may have got my hands down her pants a few times, but that was about it."

"Did she ever perform oral sex on you?" the reporter asked without changing the expression on his face.

"No! Hey, we were only kids, you know."

"What about the other boys? Did you ever hear any stories that she might have had any sexual relations with anybody?" The words came out in rapid fire, like a prosecutor examining someone on the witness stand.

Jason shook his head and lifted his glass of scotch.

"What about drugs?"

"Well, I smoked a little pot a few times."

"While you were dating her?"

"Right."

"And did she?"

"Yeah, I think she may have, once or twice." The stockbroker put a finger under his button down collar.

"What other drugs did you use?"

"Oh, I think that's about all we did." Jason looked out an open doorway into the street for a second, then turned back to the reporter. "Except for the speed."

"You took speed?"

"No she did."

"How do you know that?" His voice was suddenly more intense. "Did you see her taking pills?"

"No, but she told me about it."

"What did she say?" The reporter's voice was louder than it had been.

"She told me she took some little red pills that made her feel really high and that it was speed."

Ron Weingarten was looking down at the little black recorder again. This time he was smiling.

Wire services from around the country picked up the headline shown on the *Atlanta Times'* web site: CONGRESSIONAL CANDIDATE'S WIFE WAS DRUG ABUSER, REVEALS EX-BOYFRIEND. Within minutes after Ron Weingarten's story was released the phones started ringing at the Crane for Congress Headquarters.

At that moment Priscilla was on the phone discussing the wording of the announcements for Doug's meeting with the Lockheed employees at Danny's Restaurant. She heard her name being called from the other side of the room. "Mrs. Crane, there's some reporter on the line who wants to speak with you. He says it's urgent."

She held up a hand and said, "Can I call you right back?"

Priscilla walked across the room and smiled at the young volunteer. "Thanks, Leslie," she said reaching for the phone. "This is Priscilla Crane."

She heard a man's voice she didn't recognize. "Mrs. Crane, I'm with the *Monitor*. Do you have any comment about the *Atlanta Times* story?"

"What story?"

There was a moment of silence. "You haven't heard about it? The *Times* reported that, according to a former boyfriend of yours, you abused drugs."

"They what?" she gasped. "What boyfriend? What in the world are you talking about?"

"His name is Jason Carrington."

She yelled, "Jason Carrington! I haven't seen him in over twenty years!"

"So are you denying the story, Mrs. Crane?"

"Well, of course I am. I was never a drug abuser."

"He says you smoked pot and took amphetamines."

"Listen, I'm not going to make any further comment about this…this garbage." She slammed down the phone, trembling with rage.

The young volunteer was looking up at her. "Are you all right, Mrs. Crane?"

Priscilla was standing there in a daze.

"Mrs. Crane?"

Chapter 11

Doug was as tired as he'd ever been in his life. His legs were sore and his feet had blisters. For the last ten hours he had been walking from house to house in neighborhoods in the Tenth District. He grimaced as he thought about the short-haired terrier that had bitten him on the ankle. It hadn't required a rabies shot, thank God, but it still hurt like hell.

He wondered how many of the two or three hundred people he'd shaken hands with today would actually vote for him. For the most part, he'd gotten a friendly reception and they'd listened attentively to what he had to say, but it was still hard to tell what most of them really thought about him.

The neighborhoods he'd visited reflected the broad range of Atlanta's social and economic lifestyles. Some neighborhoods had houses that looked like something you'd see in *Southern Living*, big houses with columns and looping driveways and beautifully manicured lawns with dogwoods and banks of blooming azaleas. But as majestic as some of the homes were in these wealthy parts of the district, they also seemed somewhat sterile and lifeless, he thought. The only people he'd seen outside were the yardmen and gardeners who were cutting the grass and trimming the shrubbery, and the UPS deliverymen who were dropping off packages.

A few miles away were some one-story brick houses, each with small lots and many bordered by Hurricane fences. He remembered the kids who were tossing a ball out in the street. They hadn't recognized him. They were talking about their favorite baseball players.

Closer to downtown were the row houses lined up next to each other like a string of Army barracks. The sidewalk out front had weeds growing up through the cracks in the cement. He remembered a group of sullen black boys. One of them was carrying a blaring boom box. They ignored him when he said hello.

Doug had been surprised to find that, even in the poorest neighborhood, many of the people he'd talked with really cared about what was going on in the country. And at almost every house he'd visited whoever was home was willing to listen to what he had to say. But it was still hard to know if they really agreed with him of if they were just being polite.

He'd tried to speak from his heart about the things he felt so strongly about. He'd told them that he believed Washington should let people be more responsible for their own lives. That they should be allowed to keep more of their own money and plan their own futures. Most of the people had been surprised when he told them that the average wage earner in the Tenth District had to work almost six months just to earn enough money to pay his federal income taxes.

He was on driving home on I-73 near Memorial Park thinking about these things when he heard his car phone beeping. He picked it up and heard Priss' sobbing voice.

"Doug…something terrible's happened."

"What is it Priss?"

As he listened to her telling him about the *Atlanta Times* story, he felt as though someone was sticking a knife in his back. He could understand the personal attacks on himself. That was the price you paid for running for office. But to savage his wife with this type of malicious sensationalism was something beyond contempt.

He tried to console her. "It'll be all right darling, I promise. Whatever you did happened so long ago. People won't care." He told her he loved her and promised to be home soon. She was still sniffling when she hung up.

He was driving by the Georgia Tech campus and he began reflecting on what he knew about her childhood in New Orleans. When they had first met at Albany Academy, Priss had mentioned that she'd done some crazy things when she lived in New Orleans. He hadn't really cared about what she'd done in the past. All he'd cared about was that she was a very pretty black haired girl with big black eyes and that she was unlike anyone he had ever met before.

He realized it was going to have to be her decision about what, if anything, was going to be said to the media about the *Times* story. If it meant protecting her from further abuse, he was willing to drop out of the race. But no matter what happened with the election, he was going to fight like hell to restore Priss' reputation.

The pain of the blisters and the dog bite hadn't hurt half as much as the sound of her crying. He was almost home now and he couldn't wait to hold her in his arms.

"We ought to sue the bastards!" Sam Brinkman was pounding his fist into his hand as he stood glaring out the window of Doug's law office. Doug was sitting behind his desk and Paul was on the couch by the coffee table.

"Let's put those sum bitches out of business," said the Furniture King.

Paul was wiping the lenses of his glasses. He looked over at Sam and said, "There's a recent case that would make it tough for us to do that."

Doug looked up. "Are you talking about Harrington versus the *National Investigator*?"

"Right."

"What are you guys talking about?" said Sam, frowning.

"Tell him Paul."

"About two years ago, a supermarket tabloid called the *National Investigator* published a story about the wife of a man named Don Harrington. Harrington was a Republican running for Governor of Wyoming. The tabloid claimed his wife had abused alcohol when she was a teenager and also suggested that she still had a drinking problem. The Harringtons sued claiming they'd been libeled and they asked the court for a million dollars in damages.

"At the lower court the only testimony about a drinking problem came from a former high school classmate. She told the jury that she remembered Connie Walters—that was Mrs. Harrington's maiden name—drinking beer at a party twenty-five years earlier and that she later threw up in the back seat of her car on the way home. There was no evidence that Mrs. Harrington had ever had a drinking problem since then."

"Hell, that sounds a lot like this thing with Priss!" said Sam.

"Indeed it does," said Paul. "Anyway, after the lower court found in favor of the

Harringtons, the *National Investigator* got a reversal in the appellate court and then the Harrington's lawyer was able to get the Supreme Court to review the appellate court's finding."

"So, they ruled for the wife didn't they?" said Sam.

"I'm afraid not." Paul picked up a law book from the coffee table and flipped to a page he had marked. "Here's what Chief Justice Winslow had to say: 'The First Amendment of our Constitution clearly enunciates the sanctity of the right of free speech. This right is always paramount, no matter that there be some degree of exaggeration or distortion on the part of those making the comments. This is especially so when the allegedly harmful words are directed at the relatives of public officials, since the public officials themselves are rightly held to a higher standard of permissive criticism.'"

"That's' bullshit, " said Sam. "That lady was slandered or libeled or whatever you call it the same way Priss was."

Doug reached down and rubbed his ankle, and then said, "What's so ironic about this so-called high standard of permissiveness for allowing criticism of politicians is that most of the ones in Washington could do anything short of murdering somebody and still get reelected."

"Well, I'll tell you one thing. My furniture company's spent its last dollar advertising in that good for nothin' *Atlanta Times*, by God."

Sam looked forlornly off in space again. A few seconds later he turned to Doug and said, "You think Thompson's behind this?"

"I don't know."

"Well, what if I go pay a little visit to this sumbitch Weingarten. Maybe use a little friendly persuasion and see if he's interested in making a retraction."

"Sam, wait a second. I think there's a better way to handle this."

Sam slumped down in the chair in front of Doug's desk. "Like what?"

"Well, I talked to Priss last night. She told me the truth about what happened with Jason Carrington. She said that when she was fifteen she and Jason smoked some pot. He was also fooling around with cocaine. He tried to get her to snort some, but she wouldn't do it. She did take some amphetamines. But only a couple of times."

"She also told me that one of the main reasons her family moved to Albany was to get her away from Jason Carrington. Thank God they did."

"So what are we going to do?" asked Sam.

"Priss wants me to call a news conference and she wants to be there to answer questions."

Sam's eyes widened. "My friend, you've got yourself one hell of a wife."

"I know."

The conference room at the at the Westin Peachtree Hotel was filled to capacity. It was humming with animated conversations. Every newspaper and television station in Atlanta had a crew of cameramen and reporters and they were all crowded in the carpeted space between the podium and the front row of metal chairs. There were about fifty rows of the folding chairs with about thirty people seated in each row. They were all sitting there under a long row of crystal chandeliers and you could hear the buzz of animated conversations about what Doug Crane's wife might have to say.

Their faces started to turn as the handsome Republican candidate and his beautiful wife walked into the rear of the large room and began moving briskly down the aisle toward the podium. Wearing a charcoal pin striped suit and dark blue tie, he was smiling and nodding and waving his hand, but there was a look of concern in his eyes. She was also smiling as she held his hand, but instead of waving she moved her head slightly from side to side. She was dressed in a light gray suit with a black velvet collar. Her raven eyes and hair were glistening as she moved by them. Priscilla Crane looked as though she could have been walking down the runway of a style show at the Atlanta Country Club.

They arrived at the podium and Doug stepped forward. "Ladies and gentlemen, I want to thank you all very much for coming here this morning. The last couple of days have been a very trying experience, especially for my wife. Because of my candidacy for the United States House of Representatives, I've become a target of some who are opposed to the things I believe in. I do want to make it clear that I don't have any information that Nat Thompson was in any way responsible for the report that appeared in the *Atlanta Times*. So far as I know, the motivation behind this attempted character assassination rests solely with Mr. Ron Weingarten.

"Mr. Weingarten's standards as a journalist have obviously reached a new low. He has always had a reputation for seeking out the sensational, rather than the newsworthy. He's always been the type of reporter who looks for that salacious tidbit of gossip, while ignoring any thoughtful consideration of important issues. And as demonstrated by his report on my wife, he will distort something perfectly innocent into something vulgar and tawdry, whenever doing so can help him sell a story."

"Priscilla and I find it hard to believe that anyone would seriously consider her childhood indiscretions of more than twenty years ago worthy of all the attention Mr. Weingarten's report has generated. But the fact is the *Atlanta Times* story has cast a dark cloud over my wife's reputation, and that's why I called this press conference."

He reached behind the podium and picked up a glass of water, took a sip, and then continued. "Had I married a woman of lesser character, she wouldn't be standing here by my side as she is today. But she is a woman of character, ladies and gentlemen. She is in fact the finest and most honorable…" He could feel a lump forming in his throat and he reached the glass of water again. "Excuse me…she is the most honorable…" His voice was cracking.

Priscilla moved quickly over to the podium and put her arm around his waist. "Would anyone like to ask me a question?" She was smiling and looking at the audience.

A cacophony of shouting voices erupted.

She held up her hand. "One at a time please. Just hold up your hands." She pointed at a man in the front row.

"How many times did you smoke pot with Jason Carrington?"

"Well, let me think. It could have been two or three. I'm not absolutely sure. It was a very long time ago."

Another hand shot up and a tall lady with her hair tied in a bun stood up. "Mrs. Crane, what about the amphetamines?"

"What about them?" responded Priscilla coolly.

"Well, how many times did you take them and how often did you take them?"

"I think I took two pills one time. I remember they were little red pills and I also remember that they made me very sick. That's why I never took them again."

The tall lady fired another salvo. "But what about other drugs, you know, cocaine, heroin, those types of drugs?"

"Absolutely not. I never experimented with anything like that."

A gray haired man with no coat and suspenders was next. "Are you planning to take any legal action against the *Atlanta Times?*"

She looked at Doug, who stepped forward.

"We're not planning to take any legal action at this time. But I should add that we would hope that you, the members of the press, would apply your own standards of journalistic comment and criticism to the sordid tabloidism practiced by parasites like Ron Weingarten. The public deserves better, and they also deserve to be informed about what's happening to our culture."

"Mrs. Crane, do you still think all this publicity about your private life is worth it? Do you have any regrets that your husband decided to run for office?" The loud voice came from bearded man holding a pencil and pad.

"Absolutely not. I fully support what my husband is doing, and will continue to work as hard as I can so that he can help bring about the changes he's talked about."

Doug felt her squeezing his hand and saw the warm look in her eyes when she glanced at him. He whispered something only they could hear and then raised his hand. "That's all we have for now. Thank you all for coming."

Doug and Priscilla walked down the aisle holding hands. The people in the room were all clapping and rising to their feet.

The next day there was a two column editorial in the *Atlanta Monitor* under the heading: RON WEINGARTEN'S NEW WORLD OF SENSATIONAL JOURNALISM: WHAT HAVE WE COME TO?

Chapter 12

The Chairman of the House Appropriations Committee had been sitting alone in his office at the Longworth House Building. He had been watching the president's speech on his digital 28-inch television set. Nat punched a button on his remote control and the Paul O'Banion's somber face faded into black.

The Chairman put his big hands behind his head and leaned back in his black leather reclining chair. A trace of a smile was forming at the corners of his slit lips.

The President had given a wonderful performance, he thought. He had assumed an air of righteous indignation at the greed demonstrated by the big oil companies that had brazenly raised their gasoline prices in response to the oil crisis. Never mind that anyone with even a rudimentary knowledge of economics realized that whenever any commodity, including oil, was in short supply, prices always rose.

Nat believed that Paul O'Banion was one of the slickest actors to ever hold the presidency. Oh, there might be some that would argue that the real master, the champion con man of all time, was Phil Hinton. And he probably was. He could charm the pants off his worst political enemy, or the panties off the girl with the biggest tits, whichever target happened to be in his sights. But, based on tonight's performance, Paul O'Banion had to rank a close second.

He heard a beeping sound and punched his speakerphone.

"Did you see it!"

He recognized Ab Connell's booming voice.

"Of course I saw it. You told me to watch, remember."

"Well, wasn't that one hell of a performance. I mean accusing the big oil companies being 'capitalist predators' and then putting emergency price controls on gasoline prices so people can still buy gas at a buck a gallon! That was a master stroke."

"Yeah, that was pretty good, alright," said the Chairman dryly.

"Look, this is gonna be big, and I mean really big. You gotta jump on it."

"What do you have in mind? "

"Call your own press conference. Say you're backing the President one hundred percent in his efforts to protect the consumer from corporate greed. Force Crane to take a stand on the issue. You can nail his butt to the wall on this."

The Chairman was watching the ash of his thick cigar fall into a crystal ashtray. "Okay, I'll talk it over with Mike and see what we can do."

"You do that and let me know if you need any help," said Ab.

"Okay." Nat hung up and looked down at the pile of papers on his desk. Letters from his constituents.

They always want something, he thought. And I always deliver. That should be enough. But he knew it wasn't…this time, anyway. Not with this God damned buttoned down pretty boy running around spouting his so-called conservative principles about smaller government and lower taxes. He was making people think Washington was some kind of evil empire. Why? They had never felt that way before. That liked what Nat Thompson could get for them. They like it when helped get their Social Security checked sweetened and delivered on time, when their grandkids got Thompson grants so they could go to college, when their children got a job at one of the fifteen federal agency buildings in Atlanta because of telephone calls by Nat Thompson, and when he did the thousands of other things he'd done for them for so many years.

He had thought that the Weingarten story about Doug Crane's wife would halt his slide in the polls. It sounded very promising at first, all the talk about Priscilla Crane being a drug abuser. Unfortunately, the story didn't' have "legs," he thought, using the vernacular of the press. That son of a bitch Crane and his prissy Priss had somehow managed to turn the press around. And now that poor Jew reporter from the *Atlanta Times* was desperately trying to save his job.

Christ. He breathed an audible sigh and ran a finger down his long thin nose. He decided to see what Mike thought about Ab's idea of holding a press conference.

He punched a button on the console on his credenza. "Mike could you come in here."

A few seconds later the skinny, dark haired campaign manager walked into the Chairman's spacious office holding a stack of papers.

Nat said, "Ab Connell thinks I need to get down to Atlanta and hold a press conference showing my support for O'Banion puttin' a lid on gas prices."

Mike Ruby sat down on the couch. "The President really came across as a champion of the people tonight, just like you said he would. He ought to get a nice bounce in the polls from this."

"You got some ideas on how we can cash in?"

"Well, one way we could play it would be for you to point out that Crane's father-in-law made a killing in the oil business, just like the big oil companies did before the President stepped in to protect the consumer."

The Chairman's beady eyes brightened and his slit lips curved into a smile.

The crowd at Danny's Seafood Restaurant had not been what Doug had hoped for. The bad weather had been part of the reason for the small turn out. It had been stormy all day, with lightening, gusting winds, and periodic heavy rainfall. When it had started raining the wind was blowing and the striped tent that Priscilla had rented wasn't big enough to keep some of the people from getting wet.

The little Dixieland band had tried in vain to brighten the gloom. The four smiling musicians, all of whom had looked like they were way past retirement age, had been dressed in bright red jackets and flat-topped straw hats. One had played the harmonica, two had strummed banjos, and the other had plunked away on a big bass violin. But the band and the keg of beer hadn't been able to enliven the gathering, mainly because the weather was too lousy and there weren't enough people.

Doug and Priscilla were pulling out of Danny's parking lot.

"Well, that wasn't so great, was it," she said dejectedly. She slipped off her wet shoes.

"I really thought we'd get a better turnout." Strands of his sandy brown hair were matted to his forehead.

"Do you think it was just the weather?"

"Oh, I'm sure that was part of the reason."

She shrugged her shoulders. "Well, we had plenty of handouts about your appearance distributed at the plant as well as that big sign at Danny's."

"I think it's mainly the fact that people like what O'Banion's done to keep gas prices low. They see a Democrat President taking a bold action to protect them even though all he's really done is make the problem worse. There's going to be even less gasoline available now than there would have been without the price controls."

"People are so easily manipulated."

He sighed. "The shifting sands of politics, Priss. I guess, we're just going to have to get used to it."

She took off a small silver earring and rubbed her ear lobe, then looked over at him again.

"How can all those highly trained, intelligent people who work for Lockheed not care about all the things you stand for. Don't they want their taxes lowered so they can spend more of their own money on their families? Don't they want more control over our their schools so that they, instead of Washington, can decide what's best for their children?"

Her reference to children hung in the air for a few seconds with neither of them saying anything. Then, in a quieter tone, she said, "You realize, of course, that if you do win, it's going to be even more difficult for us to start a family."

"Priss, please. Let's don't get into that now."

They rode in silence as the Atlanta skyline loomed in the distance.

A few days following Doug Crane's appearance at Danny's Seafood Restaurant, a telephone call was received at Nat Thompson's Atlanta office.

The Chairman's receptionist answered, "Congressman Nat Thompson's office, may I help you?"

"I want to speak to the congressman." The man's voice was deep and raspy, like a three pack a day smoker's."

"I'm sorry, but he's in Washington, sir. Do you want the number of his office there?"

"You tell him Virgil Wilson's got some important information on somebody *real* close to this Crane guy he's runnin' against."

"Would you care to tell me what that information is so I can pass it on to him? Congressman Thompson has a very busy schedule right now."

"I ain't sayin', but you tell him I called."

"All right Mr. Wilson. Let me have your number." She jotted it down and hung up. She called the Washington office and heard her friend Karen's voice.

"Congressman Thompson's office."

"Karen, it's me, Sally. I just got a call from a man down here who says he's got some important information about somebody who's supposed to be very close to Doug Crane. He says he wants to talk to the Chairman. Do you think it's worth his time?"

"I don't know. He's on the Hill right now. I'll give him the message when he gets back."

"Okay, thanks."

When Nat Thompson returned to his office late that afternoon, he decided he would listen to what Virgil Wilson had to say.

Chapter 13

The news of Sam Brinkman's indictment sent shock waves through the city of Atlanta. The man whose big clown face was known to thousands had been arrested for cheating on his income taxes.

The federal Grand Jury had reviewed the evidence presented by the United States Attorney and after five hours of deliberations had rendered its decision. People were streaming out onto the steps of the Jimmy Carter Federal Court Building. They gathered around a small bald-headed man wearing an impeccably tailored double-breasted suit, silk tie, and gold stickpin collar.

United States Attorney Ben Wattenberg held up a hand, attempting to calm the mass of humanity swirling around. They were barking questions at him faster than he could answer them. He was only five feet four inches tall and the top of his bald head was only visible by those who were standing next to him. But everyone in the crowd could hear his resonantly plumy voice.

"Today the United States Government has obtained an eleven count indictment from a federal Grand Jury against Samuel F. Brinkman. The charges are based upon evidence that Brinkman unlawfully concealed more than a million dollars of income from his furniture business, a retail enterprise known as Sam's World of Furniture. The unpaid taxes owed by Mr. Brinkman to the United States Treasury are in excess of four hundred thousand dollars."

"At trial the Government intends to prove that Mr. Brinkman also conspired with others to conceal evidence relating to his crime, and that he willfully obstructed an investigation being conducted by the Internal

Revenue Service." The U. S. Attorney took off his tortoise shell reading glasses and put them in his breast pocket.

A tall reporter standing some distance away yelled, "When do you plan to take him into custody?"

"My understanding is that Mr. Brinkman is being taken into custody as we speak." His words were spoken with the precision of a sharp knife.

A hand shot up from a young woman several feet away. "What about those who say that these charges were trumped up because Sam Brinkman is a close friend and supporter of Doug Crane?"

"That is absolute rubbish," the little man said defiantly as he glared in the direction of the unseen reporter's voice. "The facts presented at trial will speak for themselves, and we intend to get a conviction on each and every count."

The U. S. Attorney reached down and picked up his briefcase as some of his dark suited federal lawyers began pushing the crowd back. "I'm afraid those are all the questions I can take at this time. Thank you very much."

The mass of bodies began to part as the federal prosecutor and his entourage of legal assistants made their way down the long concrete stairway. The reporters kept shouting more questions. As Ben Wattenberg climbed into the back seat of the black Lincoln Town Car, he waved a dismissive hand. It wasn't until the car was half way down the block that the reporters stopped shouting.

Doug had never seen his friend Sam look so bad. His clothes were wrinkled, his orange hair was sticking out in all directions, and he had dark circles under his bloodshot eyes. He looked like he hadn't slept in a week. Sam had explained that he'd spent the last twelve hours in jail waiting for his lawyer to get a judge to hear his request for bail. The judge had finally agreed, but he'd also required a five-hundred thou-sand-dollar bond.

Sam's lawyer was Charles Danberry. The silver haired lawyer was in his late sixties and had one of the sharpest legal minds of any criminal defense attorney in the South. He had silky smooth baritone voice that could mesmerize a jury. He had only lost two jury trials in the last ten years.

At this moment, Charles Danberry was sitting in an upholstered chair next to his disheveled client. They were in Doug's law office on the thirty-fifth floor, one of the six floors in One Peachtree Plaza that was occupied by Balding and Bell. It was early evening and most of the firm's 287 employees had left for the day. Doug's secretary, Jane Winfrey, was among the few that were still there.

Doug looked at Sam and said, "Can I have Jane bring you something to drink?"

Sam shook his head without speaking.

Charles Danberrry looked the young lawyer straight in the eyes. "This is a setup, Doug."

Doug was sitting with his forearms crossed on top of his desk. He looked over at Sam and said, "What's this all about, Sam?"

The Furniture King still had a dazed look on his big face.

"Tell Doug what you told me, Sam," said Danberry.

"I still can't believe it. This all seems like a bad dream." Sam rubbed a hand across his eyes. "Virgil Wilson." He looked up at the corner of the ceiling and was silent for a few seconds. "He worked on the showroom floor at our store on I-75 near Memorial Park. He sold living room furniture. That's the high end of our business where our salesmen can make the best commissions. " He ran a hand through his tangled orange hair.

"Virgil sold a lot of stuff for us. He was a member of our Golden Housing Club. You had to sell a half million a year to qualify, and he did, three years in a row." He sighed."I guess it wasn't enough."

Doug's secretary opened the door. "I'm sorry to bother you, Mr. Crane, but there's a man from the Atlanta Monitor outside and he says he needs to speak with you as soon as possible."

"Tell him he'll have to wait."

She nodded and closed the door.

Charles Danberry said, "Tell Doug what Virgil Wilson did with the invoices."

Sam pushed his loose shirt tail inside his leather belt. "We couldn't figure it out at first. I guess I wasn't payin' close enough attention. Virgil had figured out how to fix up fake invoices. He was chargin' customers who came in the store to look around, but who didn't actually buy anything."

"How'd he manage to do that?" said Doug, frowning.

"Somehow he got all the information from these people he needed to fill out our purchase slips—names, addresses, credit card numbers, the works. Don't ask me why the customers would do it, but they did. Virgil had always come across as a real friendly guy and I guess he just bull- shitted with them until they told him everything he needed."

"Anyway, after he made up these phony invoices, he'd have one of our delivery guys haul the furniture off."

"But didn't people raise hell about not wanting to take delivery of furniture they hadn't bought?" said Doug.

"Oh, he didn't take it to their houses. He'd put down a different address on the shipping forms."

"So where did it end up?"

"He'd set up a little operation with a used car dealer named Al Blunt. They'd rented an old warehouse on the East Side of town and were selling it as furniture being dumped in a factory closeout. So here was old Virgil makin' it both ways—fat sales commissions from me and fifty percent of the money he and Al Blunt made."

"What finally tipped you off?"

"Luckily we caught on pretty early. He only got two or three shipments out the store before a customer called one our store managers. He said he was upset that Virgil had been pressin' him for so much personal information. So we did some checkin' and found out that Virgil had fixed up a phony invoice for this guy."

"Did you call the police?" asked Doug.

Sam shook his head.

"Why in the world not?"

He hung his head and said, "Oh hell, I know now that I damn sure should have." He spread his arms apart. "But at the time I didn't want it to get out that we had a crooked salesman working for us. And I guess I was thinkin' that since we were the only ones that had suffered a loss, nobody else was gonna care about prosecuting him." He rubbed his hands together. "And to be perfectly honest, we didn't want the bad publicity. Our reputation means everything to us. If something like that got in the papers, it would've killed us."

Charles Danberry turned toward Doug. "Virgil Wilson's going to be the government's main witness. Had this guy been convicted or even charged for what he did to Sam, I doubt Ben Wattenberg would've given him five minutes when he came in with these trumped up charges. So you're right. In hindsight Sam should have turned him in. But Sam knows a hell of a lot more about running a business and about public relations than either you or I do Doug, so we can't really fault him, can we?"

Doug looked at his friend's weary face. "No, I suppose not," he said quietly. "But there's still one thing I don't understand? Why would this Virgil Wilson, a man that who you saved from criminal prosecution by ignoring his stealing, go running off to the U. S. Attorney's office with a bunch of lies about you cheating on your income taxes?"

"That's the question I keep asking myself. But I just can't find the answer."

Danberry put his hand on Sam's shoulder. "I'm going to look at everything Wattenberg's got in his file. We're entitled to that under the law and we'll get to the bottom this, Sam. I promise you that." The lawyer's gray eyes shone with intensity.

Doug stood up and walked around his desk. He put a hand on Sam's other shoulder and said, "You can count on me, too."

Tears welled up in Sam's bulging eyes. "I never doubted it."

Virgil Wilson was staring at the little white ball on the whirling roulette wheel as it rolled around and around. It started to slow down and finally landed in little red square.

"Red twenty one!"

A blonde woman wearing the starched white shirt, bow tie, and black satin vest, was raking in his tall stack of chips across the green felt. "Would you like to go again, sir?" she asked, looking over at the gray haired, pot-bellied man with a scar on his left cheek. He had on a double-breasted blue blazer with gold buttons and a big diamond ring on the little finger of his left hand.

"Yeah." Virgil glared down at the numbers shown on the game board, wiped his hand across his forehead and took another long drink of bourbon. He pushed a tall stack of chips onto a rectangle surrounding the words, "ONE THROUGH NINE."

It was his last stack of chips. He wondered how he could have lost all those others. He stared sullenly at the spinning wheel that had turned become so treacherous during the last hour, praying that this time his luck would change.

The ball started slowing down again and it fell into a black square.

"Black thirty-two!"

"Shit." Virgil glared at the woman standing next to him who was squealing with delight.

The croupier glanced at him again. "Sorry, sir."

His voice was hot with anger. "Listen you, don't give me anymore of that 'sorry sir' crap. Just give me some fuckin' numbers!"

The blonde woman looked over at someone standing nearby and a moment later the gray haired man felt a tug on his shoulder. He turned around and saw a burley black man dressed in a tuxedo.

"Excuse me, sir, but I think you may want to call it a night."

"Who the hell are you?"

"Security sir. I will be happy to escort you to your room."

"Fuck you."

The security man grabbed his arm.

"Hey!" The gray haired man felt a sharp pain in his shoulder. His arm was being twisted behind his back and he was being pushed out of the room toward the hallway.

His legs felt like they were being lifted off the floor, and before he knew what was happening he was up the elevator and back in his penthouse suite. Virgil had been dumped on his king-size bed and now he was lying there watching the chandelier above him spinning out of control.

The next morning when he woke up, his head felt like a knife had gone through it. His mouth felt like it was filled with cotton balls. He still had on all his clothes. He'd paid cash for them at a fancy shop in the Mirage.

The sickening memory of last night's disaster at the roulette wheel made him feel like vomiting. He wondered how much money he had left. He knew it couldn't be much.

Virgil staggered over to the dresser drawer and pulled it open. He could see that his gold money clip held only a few bills. He pulled them out and counted them.

"Oh my God," he whispered to himself. Virgil sank to his knees and started crying.

Chapter 14

Nat Thompson was sitting in a lounge chair beside a rectangular shaped swimming pool. He had flown down to his place at West Palm Beach for the weekend to get a couple of days of rest and relaxation.

There was the smell of roses coming from a flowerbed bordered with monkey grass that surrounded the patio of polished gray stones. Water cascaded over the edge of a rock garden at the shallow end of the large pool. On the side closest to Nat's lounge chair was a semi-circular plaster terrace, the top of which was covered with a dark blue tile that was fronted by five submerged barrel-shaped bar stools. On the other side of the pool, behind the flowerbed, was a tall hedge of photinia beyond which was the beach. The entire area on that side was shaded by a row of tall palm trees.

It was late afternoon and the swaying palms cast angular shadows that moved rhythmically across the turquoise water of Nat Thompson's swimming pool. He was alone, except for his staff of three house servants. He looked up as one of them appeared with another crystal glass of ice and Wild Turkey.

"Bring me some more cashews, wouldya?"

He took a sip of the whiskey and then reached over and picked up the newspaper. He lay there on the lounge chair dressed in white slacks, velvet slippers, and a bright yellow open necked short sleeved shirt. He was reading the *New York Times* and enjoying the late afternoon Gulf breeze and the sound of the waves. He felt a surge of pride as he read a flattering story about his work to establish stricter regulations for nursing homes. He made a mental note to take the author of such a perceptive piece to lunch the next time he was in New York.

He flipped over to the editorial section and started scanning the opinions. His face suddenly showed a look of disgust as he glanced at the editorial written by the conservative columnist, William Saffire. It was a long-winded piece criticizing what he claimed was the public's growing dependency on 'big government.' Thank God that most of the American people didn't share that reactionary viewpoint, thought Nat. The truth was they were more interested in getting what they could get from the federal government than in doing things for themselves.

Nat and most of his Democrat brethren, including the President, had understood this for a long time. It was probably the main reason why Paul O'Banion had been able to maintain his high public approval ratings, despite all the scandals involving his administration. But Nat also understood that there were other factors at play in his own race and that he couldn't rely on the national polls. It had become clear that there was trouble brewing in his home district. For the first time in Nat's long career in Congress, a Republican opponent had been able to energize the conservative cause and create a crack in what had been an invincible political machine. No doubt Doug Crane's youth and charisma played a large part in his success. But Nat had faced other young men over the years, most of whom also had good looks and pleasing personalities, and he had always prevailed on election day by wide margins. But this young man was different. He had a way of communicating his ideas the others didn't have. He had a fire and a passion that made his simplistic right wing solutions sound very convincing. And Doug Crane was beginning to convince a growing number of people that it was time for a change.

Nat knew he had to do something to regain his footing. And then he'd gotten the telephone call from somebody named Virgil Wilson.

The Chairman had listened when the stranger told him he had important information that could help bring down Doug Crane. But Nat had known it was foolish to discuss anything that sensitive over the telephone. So he had suggested they meet at his office in Atlanta and he had his secretary schedule an appointment.

But a few days latter, the instant Virgil Wilson had walked into his office, Nat had known the man couldn't be trusted. The man had looked like a crook. His milky gray eyes had been sunken below bushy brows and they had darted from one side to the other like a hawk's. The scar on his left cheek had looked like it could have been the result of a knife fight. He had been wearing a shiny, royal blue suit, neatly pressed gray trousers, and tasseled alligator loafers. The combination of the scarred face and flashy clothes had made Virgil Wilson look like he was a member of the Cosa Nostra.

Nat remembered how their conversation had played out.

"What is it you wanted to see me about, Mr. Wilson?"

"I used to work for Sam Brinkman." The voice was raspy.

Nat held up a hand and glanced at his manicured fingernails, then replied coolly, "I know the name."

"Most folks in Atlanta do. He's made a pile of money in the furniture business."

Nat sat there in his big leather chair without commenting until the stranger said, "I know he's working for your opponent, this guy Doug Crane. Throwing his weight around raising money and telling folks you're not doing such a great job up there in Congress. 'Course folks like me know you're doin' real good for us and want to keep you up there," he said with a sly grin.

Nat pulled open a drawer and pulled out a cigar. He lit it and blew a circle of smoke in Virgil Wilson's direction.

"Anyway, while I was workin' for Sam Brinkman I discovered some things." He stared at The Chairman who was gazing at the end of his cigar. "Some *very* interesting things."

"No need to be coy, Mr. Wilson."

"I made copies of everythin' before Brinkman ordered me to destroy 'em. I got a big box of 'em at home."

"Copies of what?"

"Sales invoices. Covered home furniture worth over a million bucks."

Nat leaned forward. "Are you tellin' me that Sam Brinkman wanted you to destroy sales records so he that could avoid havin' to pay taxes."

"That's what I'm sayin'."

Nat looked at the man and thought, He's probably lying, but what if he does have a box full of invoices, and what if they look valid? His mind started considering the possibilities. His beady eyes glowed with a white-hot intensity as his snake tongue slithered over to his cigar.

"I'm not one who would normally be involved in something like this, Mr. Wilson, but I'm always willin' to help one of my constituents." He paused and then said, "If you'd like my opinion about the authenticity of your documentation, I would be willin' to take a look at what you have."

"Oh, they're authentic, all right."

Nat looked at him coldly, the slit lips straight across, then spoke in a tone as low as his nasal voice would allow. "What is it you want from me? Mr. Wilson."

There was a moment of dead silence. Virgil Wilson reached down and ran his fingers along the crease of his slacks, then replied, "A million dollars."

Nat studied the end of his cigar for several seconds, and said somberly, "Good day Mr. Wilson."

"Wait a minute. I might be able to take a little less than that, if you can get me the money real quick."

Nat looked down and started reading something that was on his desk, as though he had lost interest in their discussion. A few minutes later Virgil Wilson had agreed to take a hundred thousand dollars.

And now that Sam Brinkman had been indicted, The Chairman thought that the hundred thousand had been money well spent. He knew the indictment could do some real damage to Doug Crane. The Republican challenger would suffer not only because of his close association with a known tax cheat, but also because of the loss of his main fundraiser. It could be the turning point in the election Nat had been searching for.

As Nat lay there on his lounge chair, his mind drifted to the man who would soon be trying the case, United States Attorney Ben Wattenberg. The little Jew was a streetfighter type of a trial lawyer. He not only had the tenacity of a bulldog, but he also had one of the best legal minds in Atlanta.

The Chairman had known him since his was a little boy. His father had been a file clerk in the Fulton County Court House and had always been a big supporter of the Democratic Party. The year before he had died, he had been selected as an alternate to the state Democratic convention. His mother had worked in the Julian Bond Public Library. When she had been a little girl she had participated in the famous civil rights march with Martin Luther King, Jr. when they all walked from Selma to Montgomery.

Nat remembered a comment that Ben Wattenberg had made to him once when they were sharing a drink at the Mayflower bar. He had said that Sam Brinkman was from an even poorer family than Ben's was, but that Brinkman had made his money by sucking up to rich bankers and fat cat politicians. Nat also remembered that when Ben Wattenberg was fifteen years old a bank had foreclosed on his father's house and the boy and his mother had been forced to move in with Ben's grandmother.

The cell phone on the glass top table next to his lounge chair started beeping.

The Chairman put down his drink and answered. "Hello."

"Nat, this is Ab. How's the weather down there?"

"Sunny, the way it always is in Florida." Nat spoke in a lazy drawl.

"Right, well, it's not too sunny around here, and I'm not just talking about the weather."

"O'Banion feelin' some heat about those gas rationin' coupons?"

"Well, he didn't really have much choice. He had to do something else."

Nat said, "He shoulda figured that gas supplies were gonna dry up even more after he put a ceiling on prices."

Ab said, "It's a really shitty situation for us, especially this close to the election."

"Maybe he ought to just nationalize those fuckers."

"He's thinking about it." There was a momentary pause and then the Majority Leader changed the subject. "Listen, Nat, I was talking again with O'Banion about your race. I told him what a good job you did down there at your press conference. You really put it to Crane and his father-in-law. But we all know you're gonna to have to keep hammering away and it may be time for you to do something even more dramatic."

"What do you mean by more *dramatic*?" said Nat without hiding the sour sound of his skepticism.

"We think it's time you accepted Crane's challenge for a debate."

"You do, do you? Maybe you all are figurin' Doug Crane's an easy mark, somebody who'll choke in front of the TV cameras and people will see he's not fit to serve. Maybe you and Oliver should come down to Atlanta and debate him yourselves. You can say you're actin' as my agent, if you want to. But I know one thing, I won't be there."

"Wait a minute, I think you're putting yourself down to much. Hey, you're an attractive man, an influential man who's spent a lifetime serving the people of your district. Don't you think when people look up there on that stage and see the two of you standing there, they're gonna figure out pretty quick which one's the man with the experience, the man who knows the way Washington works and can get things done. Hell, you're the Chairman of the fucking House Appropriation's Committee."

"Yeah, and I'm also almost seventy-five years old and this guy looks like he could do push ups in his sleep, not to mention the blond hair and blue eyes that'll probably cost me ninety percent of the female votes in my district."

"I think you're underrating yourself, Nat. You're a sharp dresser, I mean with those white suits, and—"

"Would you cut the bullshit. I'm not debatin' Crane and that's final."

There was another long silence at the other end of the line. "I think you're making a mistake, Nat, I really do."

Nat moved a hand through his long silver hair. "How much more money did Oliver say I was going to be gettin'. My campaign money is runnin' pretty low, you know."

"Well, we'll do what we can. But you've gotta understand that yours isn't the only tight race going on around the country. We've got almost twenty districts where the polls are showing the outcome is too close to call."

"If you want to see the chairmanship of the Appropriations Committee turned over to a Republican, just say so." His anger was boiling over now.

"Now hold on. Who said anything about not wanting you to stay in power? Did I say that? Oliver and I aren't going to short change you, you know that."

"Just send me the money." Nat rubbed the back of his short neck.

"We'll do what we can."

"You do that." The Chairman abruptly pushed the off button on his cell phone. He closed his eyes and leaned back on the lounge chair.

They want me to debate him. Why? It would be suicide, he thought.

He'd never had to face anybody like this kid. Crane had kept bouncing back, no matter what. All the negative campaign advertising that had sucked his campaign funds dry, and the story in the *Atlanta Times* about his wife being a drug abuser. And none of it had worked.

Sam Brinkman indictment might still be enough to turn the tide. If it weren't, then maybe I'll have to accept Crane's call for a debate, Nat thought. But only if there was no other alternative. He prayed that it wouldn't come to that.

Virgil Wilson was back in Atlanta. He was sitting in his Mercedes convertible in a line of cars waiting for some gasoline. A barefooted man in front of him was sitting on top of his trunk, reading the newspaper. Virgil had been in line for almost an hour.

As he was sitting there in his luxury automobile, Virgil had been pondering his predicament. He desperately needed more money now that he'd blown almost all the 100,000 the congressman had given him. His mind was turning over the possibilities as he looked around at the walnut and beige leather interior. He had loved the smell of a new car, especially a Mercedes. It really was beautiful, he thought, and less than a hundred miles on the odometer. He wondered how much he could get for it.

And then something clicked in his memory. Al Blunt. He was the used car dealer who helped him sell the stolen furniture. He might be interested in the Mercedes, thought Virgil, and he might also be interested in doing some other business.

He lit a cigarette and then pushed a button and his leather seat purred into a reclining position. As he watched a plume of blue-gray smoke snaking over the top of his passenger side window, his scarred face began to brighten.

Chapter 15

For many large metropolitan areas around the country the gas crisis brought on by the Iranian oil embargo had had a devastating effect. And in the first few weeks following Iran's attack on the Persian Gulf, there was a great deal of fear about gasoline shortages in Atlanta. And the President's emergency order invoking a mandatory system of gas rationing made that fear a reality. There were long lines at gas stations in Atlanta for a couple of months that followed the order. But the citizens of the South's largest city hadn't suffered as much as might have been expected. To understand why, one had to go back to the late 1990's, and consider what Atlanta had been like then.

As the twentieth century had been drawing to a close, Atlanta was a city of gigantic proportions. Indeed, it had grown so much that by 1999, in order to get from the north end of the city limits to the south end, it was necessary to drive a hundred and ten miles. There was so much urban sprawl that the average commuter had to travel almost thirty-five miles to get to work.

Civic leaders had known they had to do something to deal with the mobility crisis. A rapid transit system had been operating for several years. But there still had been so much driving going on, a stunning 100 million miles a day, that on most days a blanket of dirty looking haze had shrouded the vast stretches of concrete weaving all over the huge metropolitan area.

But then things had started to change. The federal government had started withholding subsidies for highway construction projects. This was because Atlanta had been chronically in violation of the Clean Air

Act with over 200 tons of nitrous oxides having been pumped into the air every day. And companies like Hewlett-Packard had started canceling their plans to build office buildings because they knew it was going to take too long for their employees to get to the new buildings.

There were other victims of the mobility crisis besides the office employees, like the tenants in the giant Perimeter Mall located north of the city. The tenants there had started canceling their leases because there hadn't been enough customers coming into their stores. People had just gotten tired of fighting all the traffic.

The founder of CNTen, Fred Burner, had agonized that congestion was turning his hometown into a "hellhole." And then the litigation had started. Lawsuits had been filed by the Georgia Conservancy, the Sierra Club, and Georgians for Transportation Alternatives. They had all been seeking to halt highway projects that had an astounding combined value of almost a billion dollars. And the environmentalists had won.

So it was that with all these things going on the city limits of Atlanta had finally stopped expanding. And it wasn't long thereafter that the size of the city had actually begun to shrink. This trend of suburban contraction continued, and by the time of the congressional elections in 2010 the distance of the city limits from north to south was a mere sixty miles.

The rapid transit system had been expanded throughout the Atlanta city limits so that there was a lot less driving than there had been. Atlanta had even managed to come into compliance with the Clean Air Act.

The result of these developments was that once the initial hysteria of the Iranian attack had melted away, the people of this still great Southern city realized that the gas shortages they were experiencing were more of an inconvenience than a crisis.

And because it wasn't a major problem for most people in the Tenth District, Doug Crane had not been able to take advantage of the issue the way many Republican candidates in other parts of the country had. Doug realized he was going to have to win his race on other issues. And that's what he was trying to do. But he was about to run out of money.

Doug tossed his tie onto the satin comforter at the foot of their four poster bed. He was exhausted. It had been another long, foot-hurting, doorbell-pushing, handshaking day. And after ten hours of it, he was glad to be back home.

Priscilla was in the bedroom when he walked in. She was taking off her blouse and putting it on a coat hanger. She smiled at him. "Hi honey." He returned the smile and kissed her on the cheek and walked over and sat down in a chair on the opposite side of the room. He took off a sock and rubbed his foot, then looked up at her and said. "I got a call from a *Monitor* reporter today. It was on my recorder when I got back to the office."

"What about?"

"My letter to the editor about Thompson's refusal to consider any reforms to the Social Security system and the fact that it's going to start running a deficit in the next couple of years if we don't do something."

She was unzipping her skirt. "What did he say?"

"He said they were going to run it in the Sunday edition, but because of space limitations they were going to have to abbreviate it."

"Well, at least you'll get some of your ideas across."

He shrugged his shoulders and then took off his other sock and started rubbing his foot.

She walked over and picked up his shoes, then looked down at the red blisters on his feet. "Ugh, you need to put something on those places."

"I will, " he said wearily.

She put the shoes in his closet then said. "Have you talked to Sam lately?"

"As a matter of fact, I dropped by to see him on the way home."

"How is he holding up?"

"He's really hurting. I've never seen him so…quiet. It's like he still doesn't know what hit him."

She walked over to the her a chest of drawers, and said, "I hate to tell you this but our telephone callers are hearing a lot of people say they won't contribute to your campaign because of what's happened to Sam."

He looked down at the floor and ran his hand through his sandy hair, then whispered, "Hell."

She was folding back the bed sheets. "Maybe you should avoid seeing him for a while, Doug."

He clenched his fist. "No, I'm not going to abandon a friend who's in trouble."

"But Doug."

"Priss, if we stand by Sam, we're going to show people we think he's an innocent man. And he *is*. I know he is, Priss."

"I hope you're right."

"Hey, why don't we get him to take us to the Vultures game on Sunday." Doug was referring to the professional football team located in Atlanta. Sam's furniture company had leased a luxury box.

"Okay, but what are we going to do about our contributions?"

"I met with Dick Sampson today," he said, referring to a friend who was a loan officer with one of Atlanta's largest banks. "He said the bank would lend me the current value of our stocks if I bring him the certificates."

"Doug, you know my father will help us if you ask him," she said pleadingly.

"He's already done enough. I'm not going to ask him for anything more."

"But Doug, all our stocks, what if—"

He held up a hand. "I know," he replied weakly, then walked slowly toward the bathroom.

She finished putting on her gown and climbed into bed. The only sound was the sound of running water from the bathroom. She reached over to her bedside table and turned on the radio. It was tuned to a classical music station and she heard the sound of a Beethoven sonata.

She lay there with her book, starting to relax when the music ended. A commercial came on: "On November third the voters will have a choice. They can vote for a man who is seasoned with wisdom and experience gained from thirty years of service or—"

She reached over and turned off the radio.

The new Fulton County football stadium was designed to seat sixty-five thousand fans. There was a reason why it seated a lot fewer fans than the old stadium. Only twenty thousand seats were available to the general public and they were all end zone seats. A general admissions ticket for one of these seats cost 100 dollars. The rest of the seats were in the luxury VIP lounges, large plate glass fronted living rooms with kitchens and bathrooms. They were each expensively decorated to suit the tastes of the corporations who leased them at rates ranging from two hundred to five hundred thousand dollars a year. These luxury suites were located on each side of the stadium, stacked one on top of another to a height of twenty-five floors, and stretched from the corner of one end zone to the other. Sam's World of Furniture had leased a VIP lounge on the third level right on the fifty-yard line.

The Atlanta Vultures were about to start their season. The previous January, at the Super Bowl game in London, the Vultures had lost in overtime to the Los Angeles Conquistadors. Sam was optimistic the Vultures could make it to Tokyo for this year's Super Bowl. He was looking through his binoculars as the players ran out onto the field and started bumping their chests against each other and doing head butts.

Doug and Priscilla were sitting on a cranberry colored velvet sofa by the mahogany coffee table. They were nibbling on some of the crackers and caviar that was on a silver platter. Sam came back over from the large plate glass window and sat down in a big leather Lazy Boy.

"Mat Simpson's not playing," said Sam dejectedly, referring to the Vulture's star quarterback.

"Why not?" said Doug.

"He's still in arbitration over his salary. We're gonna either have to give him the ten million a year or forget about him."

A waiter in a white jacket was pouring Priscilla a glass of wine.

Sam looked over at Doug. "I read your letter to the editor in the *Monitor* about the need to fix the Social Security system. You were dead right to call Thompson a coward for failin' to offer any kinda solution that would take some of the burden off our young folks."

"I guess I should be grateful they ran it, but they left out about a third of what I had submitted. I had some specific proposals about how we can phase in private savings accounts to replace low yielding government managed accounts. But at least I got the point across that the people, and not the government, should have the right to manage their own retirement funds."

"You damn sure did." Sam looked over at a waiter and waved his arm. "Bring these folks some of those beef tenders."

A moment later the waiter reappeared with another large silver tray upon which was a large loaf of fresh bread bearing succulent squares of beef tenderloin attached to the bread by toothpicks.

Suddenly there was an eruption of wild cheering coming from each end of the stadium. A player wearing the red and black Vultures uniform was streaking down the sideline trailed by players wearing orange and blue.

Sam ran over to the plate glass and looked down onto the field. "Go...Go...Go...Alright!" he yelled, raising a clenched fist high in the air.

Doug smiled, thinking this was the first time he'd seen Sam this excited and happy since his indictment.

The Furniture King came back over and sat down and they talked about football for a while, and then Doug said, "What's the latest from Charles Danberry?"

"Well, we got our motion approved. You know the one that's supposed to give us all this information the District Attorney has showin' exactly how I'm supposed to have done all this cheatin' on my income taxes." He offered a wry smile.

Priscilla leaned over and patted the big man on the back. "You've got the best criminal defense lawyer you could possibly have."

"I know." Sam got up and walked over to the plate glass window again. He was looking down at the football field, but you could tell by the distant look in his bulging eyes that his mind was somewhere else. He finally said softly, "Virgil Wilson got some kind of pay off for doin' what he did. We just gotta find out how…and why."

Doug walked over to Sam and put a hand on the big man's shoulder. "We will, Sam. We will."

Chapter 16

Boyd Smithers was sitting alone in the mahogany-paneled study of his remodeled plantation home in South Georgia. The sun had been down for over an hour. The only sound in the room was the humming of the ice machine in the bar.

Doug Crane's father-in-law had an air of gentility and grace. His cream colored Sea Island cotton shirt had button down collars and his initials, BRS, monogrammed in small maroon lettering on his shirt pocket. The faded blue jeans, a belt with fabric showing tiny oil derricks, and his shiny Bass weajuns were something a younger man might wear. He was a picture of robust health with clear blue eyes, a bronze tan on ruggedly handsome facial features, and a trim waistline. His wavy and still thick snow-white hair was long enough to comb back at his temples and was parted on the left side of his head.

The telephone on his credenza rang and he reached over and picked up the receiver.

"Hello, Dad, it's me."

He recognized his daughter's voice. The sound of the people talking in the background made him realize that she was calling him from Doug's campaign headquarters. "Hi, sweetheart, it's good to hear your voice," he said warmly.

"Did you go horseback riding today?"

"You know, I haven't been out in the past few days. Been having a little back pain so I thought I'd give it a rest for a while."

"That sounds like a good idea," she said encouragingly. "How's Mom?"

"She's fine. Would you like to talk with her?"

There was a pause and then Priscilla said. "In a minute. Dad, the reason I called is…hang on a second would you." He heard a woman's voice asking for a list of names. A minute later Priss came back on.

"Sorry about that. The reason I called is because we're getting pretty low on our operating funds and I was hoping you might help us again."

"Of course, I will," he said in a strong voice. " I'll mail you a check first thing in the morning." He had a second thought. "Or do you need it wired?"

"No, the regular mail would be fine. We're not quite that desperate yet." She gave a little laugh, and then she said, "You've already given us the maximum amount you can give under current federal law, so Mom will have to sign the check."

"I wish it could be more than that."

She said quietly, "I'd appreciate it if you wouldn't mention this to Doug."

"Whatever you say, sweetheart. I only wish we could do more to help."

"Dad, you've done so much already. Your television commercial was wonderful."

"Thanks sweetheart. Now, let me let you talk to your mother." He pushed an intercom button. "Susan, Priss is on the line."

He leaned back in his chair. Priss' request had reminded him of his discussion with Doug about the new campaign finance law. Doug had explained that under the new rules Boyd couldn't contribute more than five thousand dollars a year to any candidate for a federal office. While this was a much higher limit than there was back in the 1990's, it came with some strings attached. Doug had pointed out that because of Boyd's income tax bracket, there would be a twenty-five percent surtax on his contribution. So it was going to cost him 1,250 dollars to give his son-in-law the five thousand dollars. Doug said the surtax money was being put in a government trust fund for redistribution to people below the poverty level. They would each get two hundred dollars. But only if they registered to vote. Robin Hood strikes again, thought Boyd with a rueful smile. The Democrats were masters at rigging the system to turn out their voters.

Boyd wondered what the Founding Fathers would have thought about this idea of punishing wealthy people whom had the gall to support the political candidates of their choice. In those days, the wealthy people were the only people qualified to lead the new Republic. They wrote a Constitution that contained the revolutionary idea of letting the people control their government. But they planned a Republic, a nation led by responsible leaders, not a pure democracy led by populist demagogues like Paul O'Banion.

He could feel his heart pounding. He knew Susan would warn him about his blood pressure if she knew what he was thinking.

He stood up and stretched his back. It was starting to hurt again. He wished he was twenty years younger, back in New Orleans with his partner, Jim Ferriday.

He thought about all the dry holes he and Jim had drilled before they finally struck oil at Bayou Chauvin. All the worry and anguish and sweat about so many things—whether they could raise the money to drill a well, whether they could get the drilling permits, hoping it wouldn't be raining too hard so they could build the board road to get the drilling rig onto the location in time to save their leases. And whether, when they hit the really big one like they finally did at Bayou Chauvin and the son of a bitch blew out, whether they could bring it under control.

During their long career together, he and Jim had faced all these challenges and they'd won. They had made more money than they'd ever imagined they would.

And now, after all that, those bastards in Washington pass a law that says if I want to support my son-in- law for Congress I have to pay a big tax because I've made too much money.

He walked over to a cabinet mounted on the wall on the opposite side of the the room. Below it was a marble-topped sink and next to the sink was the ice machine.

He fixed himself a Chivas and water and went back to his desk and sat down.

He thought about the current oil crisis. How terribly short-sighted it had been for us to allow our own oil industry to die, he thought. At the time the Iranian missiles started raining down on the Persian Gulf oil fields there were fewer than two hundred rigs drilling in the entire United States. He remembered that back in the early 1980's there had been more than four thousand rigs searching for oil and gas all over the country. He knew there was no way to renew that kind of massive exploration effort. There just weren't enough trained engineers and geologists. Almost all of them had been laid off years ago.

He took a long sip of the amber liquid and started thinking about another new law that Doug had told him about. It was even more damaging, Boyd thought, than that damn campaign finance law.

Doug had told him that a couple of years ago a Democrat sponsored bill was introduced in Congress to redefine the family. The definition of a "family," Doug had said, was important because it set the conditions for qualifying for a whole slew of federal entitlements. The conservatives in Congress had fought like hell to keep it from passing, but they had failed and Paul O'Banion had signed it into law.

Boyd remembered how angry it had made him to hear Doug read the bill's new definition of a family. He could still remember every word:

"A family for purposes of receiving any monetary benefits payable by the United States Treasury pursuant to any federal law, rule, or regulation shall be defined as two or more persons, one of whom is at least 18 years old, who have cohabited with each other for a period of not less than six weeks."

Boyd could feel his blood pressure rising again as he thought about the fact that the federal government was now promoting the idea of kids shacking up. The world had gone mad.

He knew Doug would try to stop that kind of insanity if he was elected to Congress.

Why couldn't we have more good people like my son-in-law in Congress? he wondered.

What's happened to our values?

Boyd stood up painfully and tried to stretch his aching back. He whispered to himself, "God, I hope he wins."

Virgil Wilson was reading the want ads. He'd sold his new Mercedes to Al Blunt for fifty thousand dollars in cash. Al had said he was willing to try another scam with him if Virgil could come up with an idea. That's why Virgil was scanning the want ads. He was looking for something he and the used car dealer could use to make some money.

He turned a page and saw something that caught his eye:

> Wanted experienced salesman.
> Attractive commissions selling the world's most famous
> motorcycles.
> Cycle City Imports

He'd driven by the place a hundred times. It was located near the Perimeter Mall on the north side of town. He remembered that Cycle City Imports had the largest showroom and the largest inventory of any motorcycle dealer in the South. They did millions of dollars of business each month.

He folded the newspaper and reached for the phone.

Chapter 17

Nat Thompson felt the tightness in his chest and took another deep breath. He wished he were still down in West Palm Beach. It was a miserable day in Washington, gray skies and an incessant rain. Adding to the gloom was the sudden resignation of the President's Secretary of Commerce. It had been all over the papers that Earl Butterworth had been caught trying to extort money from a Fortune 500 company. It had also been revealed that a major drain on Secretary Butterworth's financial resources had been the expensive tastes of his Parisian mistress.

Nat was in his Georgetown house, dressed in a lightweight wool bathrobe, drinking coffee and reading the *Washington Post*. The house was much larger than he really needed—a three-story wood frame structure, painted white with green shutters beside each of the six front windows. Two round white columns stood on each side of the front door. The copper mailbox had turned a blueish green. The front yard was small but large enough for three elm trees. There was a heavy wrought iron fence painted black running parallel to the sidewalk.

As Nat was reading the newspaper in his breakfast room, he could hear the rain on the roof. At that moment a heavyset man appeared at his front gate. He was hunched over and, despite the umbrella he was carrying, his gray bushy eyebrows and mustache were dripping wet.

Nat heard the doorbell and went to the door.

"God, what a day!" Ab was leaning over shaking his umbrella just outside the doorway.

"Couldn't find a cab huh?" The Chairman's slit lips curved into a little smile.

"My feet are soaked. I stepped in a fuckin' water puddle."

Nat pointed to the floor mat. "Wipe them off before you come in hea'."

They walked into the breakfast room and sat down.

"You want some coffee?" asked Nat.

"Yeah." Ab took off his jacket, the shoulders of which were spotted with raindrops, and draped it over the back of his chair.

Nat handed him a steaming cup.

"Thanks."

"I've been readin' about Earl Butterworth," said Nat.

Ab heaved an audible sigh. "I saw it on the news last night. Christ, that's all we need, another scandal."

"The media is gonna be all over this."

"And so will the Republicans." Ab morosely gazed down into his coffee cup. "Does it say how they caught him?"

"Telexon was biddin' on a communications license from the FTC and Butterworth told their Senior Vice President, a guy named Tom Andrews, that unless he was taken care of financially Telexon's bid was going down the toilet. Andrews refused to be accommodatin', and instead, went straight to the FBI. After hearing his story, the FBI put a wire on him and told him to go back and have another visit with the Secretary. Andrews did and that dumb ass Butterworth threatened him again. And then the FBI turned to tape over to the Justice Department."

"Why the hell didn't the Attorney General cover it up?"

The Chairman was spreading jam on a piece of toast. "Somebody musta' leaked it before she could get it locked up."

"Hell." The Majority Leader frowned and took a sip of his coffee, then looked over at the refrigerator. "You got any doughnuts?"

"No."

Ab slumped down in his chair and gazed out the window watching the rain dripping from the eves of the roof. He sat there in silence for several seconds with a distant look in his eyes and then said, "You know Nat, about three years ago I was in Paris. I'd gone over there to attend the unveiling of a statue of Lafayette. Supposedly we were there to show the Frogs how much the American people still appreciated all the help Lafayette gave George Washington during the Revolution, and all that shit. I've never liked any Frenchman I ever met but it was nice getting away from Washington for a while."

"Anyway, the Speaker—he was also on the trip—and I decided to go out to dinner after this statue ceremony ended. He'd heard about a restaurant not too far away that was supposed to have great French food. It was just a few blocks off the main drag…you know, where that big arch is…"

"The Champs-Elyssees," interjected Nat dryly.

"Right. So the Speaker and I come into this little restaurant. It only has about ten tables, all dimly lit with candles, and I look around and guess who I see over in the corner."

"I'll take a wild stab and say the Secretary of Commerce."

Ab frowned at Nat and continued, "So we walk over and there's Butterworth with this drop dead gorgeous babe. I say 'Hello, Mr. Secretary, what a surprise to see you here,' and he's got this expression on his face like he's about to shit in his pants. Both the Speaker and I look over at her sitting there sipping her glass of wine, cool as a Cheshire cat, a little smile on her face, like she's kind of enjoying watching ole' Butterworth caught with his ass in a crack." Ab took another sip of coffee, his bushy eyebrows rising. "I'm looking at her thinking this babe could be a Las Vegas show girl, I mean, the big hair, the long eye lashes, and boobs about to bust out of her tight fitting low cut top. Jesus, with a body like that, she could've killed that poor bastard."

Nat said, "I hope he enjoyed what she had to offer, because, where's he's going, he won't be dipping into those pleasures anytime soon."

The Chairman stood up and walked over to the coffee percolator on the kitchen counter.

Ab looked over at him. "I guess you saw O'Banion's response to the Republican leader's demand that the President take some action against Iran."

Nat nodded.

"I liked the part where he said it's part of our human nature to want to strike back when we feel victimized and that we sometimes listen to 'the lesser angels of our human nature'." He frowned and looked at Nat. "Wasn't it Lincoln who said that? Or was it Roosevelt?"

"I don't remember," said Nat.

"Well, he had to say something. He couldn't just let the Republicans keep beating him up about the gas shortage, but the truth is it's getting pretty damn tiresome for a lot of people.

"The press is gonna keep given him shit about it, you can count on that."

The Majority Leader was looking at Nat's empty plate. "You got any bagels?"

"No."

Ab loosened his tie. "I don't know if I'm going to the Hill today. The weather's so crappy. I told the Majority Whip to make some calls about the President's SUV legislation."

"Ab, with a gallon of gas costin' damn near five bucks, nobody in their right mind gonna be buyin' Sports Utility Vehicles. Why in the world does the President still think we need all those rules and regulations?"

"My friend, you need to read the newspapers more carefully. If you did, you'd know there's a twenty-five billion-dollar class action lawsuit against all the big car companies who manufacture SUVs, or as O'Banion likes to call them, those 'killer cars'. And Nat, who do you think's gonna be in line for a nice big chunk of the plaintiffs' lawyers' thirty percent contingency fee when the case is settled."

Nat smiled. "You guys've really got it down to an art."

"Your damn right we do. We've had to compete with those fuckin' country clubbers who can raise more money than God."

There was the sound of a garbage truck out on the street.

The Majority Leader put down his coffee cup and said, "I see your lead's back up to ten points."

"It helps to have Sam Brinkman in a box. Crane hasn't been able to buy much television time lately."

"We're gonna really need you to come through for us, Nat. The latest CNTen poll shows us hanging on to our majority, but only by a fingernail. Three or four races going either way could be the difference."

Nat walked over to the window and looked outside. The rain was starting to let up. "I've spent every one of the last three weekends in Atlanta. After we go into recess next Friday, I'll be down there until the election." His shoulders slumped as he put his big hands in the pockets of his robe still looking out the window. He finally turned around, a hand running through his tangled silver hair. "I'll be glad when this son of a bitch is over." His pale face suddenly looked very old.

"That'll do zero to sixty in less than six seconds." They were standing on the showroom floor of Cycle City Motors and Virgil Wilson was pointing at a chrome coated monster chopper, a picture of raw power resting majestically on its kickstand. A boy wearing a baseball cap and braces on his teeth stroked the leather seat as though he we petting a gentle lion. A man in a white short sleeve shirt with a plastic penholder in his breast pocket was standing next to the boy.

"This is killer, Dad!" said the boy.

"Billy, I'm afraid that Harley might be little too much for you to handle, son."

Virgil frowned and then looked around.

"Well, over here we've got the new Yamaha K 40," said Virgil pointing again. They moved across the showroom floor to a smaller motorcycle, one with black mountain-bike wheels, no spokes, and not much chrome. It also didn't have the Harley's windshield over the handlebars.

"We just got this one in last week," said Virgil. "It's got a real nifty new turbo charger that gives it enough horsepower to do eighty on a straight away."

"Awesome!" said Billy.

"That looks more like what we're interested in," said the father hesitantly, "but I need to do a little checking with my insurance agent and see..."

"I'll tell you what let's do," said Virgil, "I know you all are gonna need some time to think about this." He had a little grin on his scar face. "It's a pretty big decision, spending five thousand dollars on a motor-cycle, though a Yamaha like this one's gonna keep its resale value for *at least* ten years, so long as Billy takes care of it."

"I will, I promise! Dad."

Virgil was looking at the boy's father and smiling. "Why don't we step over there into my office and fill out a preapplication form."

"A preapplication form?" said the man frowning.

"It's a form we use, Mr. Milton, to speed up the process, you know, expedite the paperwork so we can get the bike to Billy here as soon as possible. We get everything down, and then when you tell us your ready, you just drive in and pick it up. Or if you'd prefer, we can have it delivered."

The father rubbed his chin, with a look of uncertainty.

"Awe Dad, come on!"

A few minutes later, Billy's father was filling out the preapplication form.

Just as it appeared that the Republicans might be gaining some polit-ical leverage from the revelation about Earl Butterworth's extortion attempt, the Republicans suddenly found themselves on the defense. Ironically, the reversal occurred the day after Nat and Ab were sitting at the Chairman's breakfast room table bemoaning the news about Earl Butterworth, when the *Washington Post* dropped another bombshell. And this time it landed directly on the Republicans.

The ranking Republican minority member on Nat's House Appropriations Committee was a handsome middle aged Midwesterner named Dave Curatin. The *Post* reported that over a period of ten years, Curatin had paid more than six hundred thousand dollars to his campaign coordinator. The Republican congressman had also employed her as a salaried staff member. The woman in question was a 36 year old blue eyed blond who had also worked as a part time fashion model.

Abner Connell had jumped on the story like a tiger pouncing on a wounded Cape buffalo. He took to the House floor and demanded an immediate and full investigation by the House Ethics Committee.

Following that performance The Majority Leader held an impromptu press conference at his office in the Longworth House Office Building. He affected an air of righteous indignation as he spoke the words he had memorized.

"If the reports about Mr. Curatin's payments to Cynthia Lucas are proven to be true, and I hope that they will not be," he said with a straight face, " I think it will then be incumbent upon him to tender his resignation immediately and set an example that such improper conduct will not be tolerated in an institution in which all of us who are privileged to serve hold so dear."

Dan Curatin had desperately resisted the increasing number of calls for his resignation, but his standing in the polls plummeted and his prospects for reelection became very bleak.

And so as the end of summer approached, the importance of a victory by Doug Crane in his race against Nat Thompson became even more critical to the Republican chances of regaining control of Congress.

Chapter 18

They had been adversaries for years. The feisty little Napoleonic prosecutor and the silver haired, silver-tongued criminal defense attorney had battled in court many times before. But despite their long history of tenacious courtroom combat, there had also been elements of civility and mutual respect in their relationship. They were like two championship boxers, each trying to maintain their balance and land a few blows, but not without observing and admiring the other man's skillfully directed jabs and counterpunches.

It was 10 o'clock on a Friday morning and they were in the U. S. Attorney's office. Ben Wattenberg's domain was a large, tastefully decorated corner space on the top floor of a twenty- five-story federal office building. Engraved across the top in the granite façade above the entrance were the words: NATHANIEL J. THOMPSON UNITED STATES JUSTICE DEPARTMENT, SOUTHEASTERN REGION. There were heavy drawn curtains in a burgundy color hanging beside windows that extended across two sides of the room. An Oriental rug covered most of the polished wood floor. The uneven surface of Ben Wattenberg's early American antique desk was covered with a glass top and was stacked so high with piles of papers that from time to time the little man's bald head would disappear from view.

Charles Danberry had requested the meeting to discuss the charges levied against his client, Sam Brinkman. The courtly looking Southern gentleman was seated in one of the two Hepplewhite chairs facing the U. S. Attorney's cluttered desk. His sonorous baritone voice was emphatic as he waved his right arm in the air.

"Ben, you know damn well that there's not a jury in the State of Georgia that's going to believe a word Virgil Wilson says. He was caught red handed steeling furniture from one of Sam Brinkman's stores."

The U. S. Attorney took off his glasses with the tortoise shell frames and wiped the lenses with his white handkerchief, then said coolly. "I might point out to you, Charlie, that there's no criminal record of any such charge against Virgil Wilson. What you're alluding to is nothing more than hearsay. And don't tell me you plan to put your client on the stand, because a jury will never believe *him.*"

"Come on, Virgil Wilson's a known liar. I can bring you affidavits from—"

Ben Wattenberg held up his hand. "Save your breath, Charlie, I'm telling you we're going to trial on this one."

The defense attorney gave him a disconsolate look. He held out his hands and said quietly, "Why? What is it that makes the government so determined to persecute Sam Brinkman?"

There was silence from behind the stack of papers. The only sound was from a helicopter flying nearby. Neither man said a word for several seconds.

Charles Danberry's eyes began to narrow, a reflection of the anger building inside him. His intense gaze was focused like a laser beam on the darting black eyes of the little man behind the cluttered desk who was nervously rubbing his glasses again. "It's the election, isn't it," said Danberry.

"I don't know what you're talking about. In case you've forgotten, we got an indictment handed to us by a duly constituted federal grand jury."

"Don't give me that crap. We both know you could indict the Virgin Mary the way the rules are written." He paused and then said, "The truth is somebody from Washington told you to shut Sam Brinkman down because he was raising too much money for Doug Crane." He gave the prosecutor another cold look. "Was it Nat Thompson?"

The little man stood up and wiped a hand across his shiny head, then glanced down at his watch. "I'm afraid that's about all the time I've got for you today, Charlie."

There was a loud snapping sound as the defense lawyer shut his briefcase. He said defiantly. "I'm going to file a motion to get all there is to know about Virgil Wilson."

"File whatever you want. We've got nothing to hide about him."

"Good day, Ben. It's been a real pleasure."

They parted company without shaking hands.

Doug Crane had parked in front of a long four-story office building. It was shaped like a box used for packaging a dozen long stemmed red roses. Across the front of the long gray metallic structure were two long bands of darkly tinted glass. It was a sterile looking, if modern workplace, not unlike several others along I-75 that Doug Crane had visited during the last few weeks.

It was also the administrative headquarters of the Tandry Corporation, the largest manufacturer and distributor of bathroom fixtures in the southeastern United States. Based upon a distillation of Tenth District voting records—research Doug had paid for—it had been demonstrated that the Tandry employees like many other white collar workers in the district went to the polls more often than the average person and that they tended to vote Republican.

Doug glanced at his watch and saw that it was almost 5 o'clock. He knew that was when the hourly employees left for home.

He climbed out of his car and opened his trunk. He reached inside a cardboard box and pulled out a stack of Doug Crane for Congress brochures and put them in the hip pocket of his tweed jacket.

He closed the trunk and looked up at the sky. Gray clouds were moving fast from a northwesterly direction. He felt the quickening breeze and whispered a silent prayer that the rain would hold off.

It was the fourth consecutive day that Doug had done this. After six weeks of walking neighborhoods and pushing doorbells, he'd decided it was time to start hitting the office buildings, especially in those areas where his research told him he would do well. It would all be so much easier, he knew, if he could afford to buy more television time. That would enable him to reach so many more people without having to spend so many hours pounding the pavement. But the sad reality was he didn't have the money. A minute of prime time television advertising cost more than 10,000 dollars and it had become a lot more difficult to raise that kind of money in the wake of the negative publicity surrounding Sam's indictment. So he had told himself that he was just going to have to work harder.

The Tandry people were starting to come out now and Doug had positioned himself at the end of the concrete walkway leading from the building to the parking lot.

As the people got closer he tried to push his wind blown hair back in place. At the same time he tried to affect a smile that would conceal his anxiety. Strange as it might seem after all these weeks, he still got butterflies in his stomach whenever he had to introduce himself to perfect strangers.

A short pot bellied man with a crew cut was walking toward him. He was loosening his tie with one hand and looking in the direction of the parking lot.

"How are you, I'm Doug Crane. I'm running for Congress and I'd appreciate your vote on November third." Doug held out a brochure, still smiling broadly.

The man nodded without speaking or even changing his expression. He took the brochure without breaking stride and went straight for his car.

Behind him appeared two young women, talking and laughing. One of them had streaked platinum hair, the other a ponytail. The one with the ponytail looked up at him and said, "You're Doug Crane," her plain face was brightening.

"Pleased to meet you," said Doug, holding out his hand.

"I'm Mary Anne Jankowsky and this is my friend, Trudy VanDyke."

"I hope you'll vote for me on November third." He handed them each one of his brochures.

"Sure we will," said Trudy, giving him a warm look. "It must be hard having to meet strangers like us." She looked at her friend and laughed.

"No. I've really enjoyed it. I've learned a lot about what the people think."

"Well, we think you're great," said Mary Anne.

"Can I get your autograph?" said Trudy.

He reached in his pocket for a pen. The flow of people heading to the parking lot was increasing by the minute.

Trudy moved closer to him holding out a business card for him to sign.

"There you go," said Doug.

"Here's another one you can keep." She was writing something on the back.

He was shifting nervously from one foot to the other. He took Trudy's card and stuck it in his pocket without looking at it. More people were walking by. In desperation, he reached for their hands and started shaking them. "Thank you so much for your support. It was really nice to meet you." The young women's faces were flushed with excitement as they walked away. Trudy looked over her shoulder and smiled at him.

There was the rumble of thunder in the distance. Doug looked up and then heard someone yelling at him.

"Hey Doug! Hope you win!" A man with a huge nose and close set eyes bounded up to him and slapped him on the back.

"Thank you, sir. I appreciate your support."

"I'm with you all the way. That old guy Thompson needs to be let out to pasture." Doug could smell onions on his breath. "You know, there's one thing that really bugs me about what's going on in Washington."

The walkway was crowded with people heading for their cars.

"What's that?" said Doug smiling helplessly at the others passing by.

"Formica."

"Sir?"

"There's something funny going on with the price of Formica. I think there may be some kind of conspiracy among the home building contractors here in Atlanta. A few months ago, my wife Susie and I decided to remodel our kitchen and…uh oh."

Raindrops the size of jellybeans started pelting down as though a giant dam in the sky had suddenly burst. People started racing for their cars. Doug stood there in the driving rain, holding his soggy brochures, his only consolation being the sight of the Formica conspiracy theorist dashing toward the parking lot.

Doug walked into the bedroom and saw Priss in bed. His clothes were soaking wet.

"What in the world happened to you?" Priscilla's dark eyes were opened wide at the sight of him.

"We had a rain out up at that Tandry office. Game called in the bottom of the first," he said dejectedly.

"Oh, that's too bad," she said. She glanced down at the floor and saw little blobs of water. "Honey, you're dripping all over our wood floors. Go get a towel."

He shrugged and went into the bathroom.

After he wiped the floor he went back in the bathroom and took off his wet clothes. She was reading when he reappeared. He was wearing a robe and rubbing his hair with a towel.

She said, "Can I fix you something to eat?"

"No thanks, I stopped on the way home and handed out a few brochures. There's a McDonald's on the freeway just south of Smyrna. Figured I might as well have a burger while I was there."

"As wet as you were, they must have thought you were the candidate from the lost city of Atlantis."

Doug laughed and went back into the bathroom. He took off his robe, turned on the hot water and waited until the shower stall was filled with steam. He got in and leaned against the wall, feeling the hot water hitting his back muscles. He wondered whether he should go back to the Tandry office. He said to himself, I sure as hell didn't accomplish much this afternoon.

When he came back into the bedroom, she was still reading.

He climbed in bed and looked up at the ceiling. "If we could just get back on television it would make so much difference."

"Uh huh," she was still reading.

"Hell, I'd be happy if we could buy a few radio spots."

She put down her book. "We got pledges for about six hundred dollars today."

"Whoopee," he said sarcastically.

"What happened to the hundred thousand dollars the bank loaned us?"

He rubbed his face. "It went to pay bills."

"I never realized things cost so much," she said.

"Well, they do. Paul showed me all the gory details."

She reached over and turned out the light. "So what are you going to do tomorrow?"

"I guess I'll go back out to the Tandry office."

There was the sound of distant thunder from outside.

"Have you ever stopped to think about what this is doing to our financial security? I mean, it's not that I don't think you're going to win, I do, but we're still going to have all this debt to pay off."

He rolled over on his side away from her and said sarcastically, "I'm sure glad you pointed that out. That's the kind of support I really need right now."

Her tone became even colder. "You know Doug, sometimes you can be so...self-centered. It's like nothing else but your winning this race against Nat Thompson matters, regardless of the negative consequences to our family life."

His eyes were closed, but she knew that he was still awake.

A flash of lightening lit up the bedroom as they both lay there in silence.

Chapter 19

The shafts of fluorescent light coming from the towering lampposts attracted a swirling army of knats. At this late hour the only sounds were from the used car lot's line of pennants snapping in the wind, the intermittent wailing of air brakes being applied, and the groaning of gears being shifted as the lonely long distance haulers of freight drove along the ten-lane freeway.

Those solitary truckers were among the few still driving at 3 a. m. on this black and windy night. They drove past an exit sign on the north side of I-20 where the tall lampposts illuminated a gravel used car lot. It covered about an acre of ground at the rear of which was a dilapidated trailer, the type a duck hunter might haul to his hunting lease.

There were two small windows in the front of the trailer and the lights were on. At that moment, had someone inside been looking toward the freeway, he might have seen something barely visible, an indistinct form in the shadows at the end of a long row of cars and pickup trucks. This darkened form was in fact a car, but it was the only one on the row that didn't have a big dollar sign and numbers scrawled across its windshield.

Inside the only car in the lot that wasn't marked for sale was a private investigator. He was sitting behind the steering wheel and he'd been there for over an hour, watching and waiting.

He glanced at his watch again.

And then he saw the headlights of a truck. It was only a little larger than one of those brown package delivery vans. Its beams lit up long stretches of white gravel as it turned into the used car lot. There was a muffled crunching sound as it rolled slowly past the rows of cars and pickups along a corridor leading to the trailer. It kept going until the brakes squealed and it came to a halt.

The private investigator saw a rectangle of light at the doorway of the trailer. A man was walking toward the truck. The driver side door swung open and someone got out. He could hear the faint sound of the two men talking. A moment later he saw that the man who'd been driving the truck was opening the rear door. There was the grating sound of metal against metal as it was raised. The private investigator held up his camera and pushed a button and a zoom lens protruded into position.

The men were now lowering a ramp onto the ground. Then one of them climbed up inside the storage area and disappeared from view. Seconds later he reappeared, his hands gripping handle bars that flashed in the light as he guided it down the ramp. Once it was on the ground, the other man took the motorcycle and rolled it in the direction of the trailer. When he got a few feet away, the man stopped and put his foot on the kickstand and it tilted slightly. The big Harley was now hidden in the shadows.

The private investigator watched twelve other motorcycles roll down the ramp before the men were finally finished. Then the man inside the truck jumped down and wiped a handkerchief across his head. He said something to the other man that the investigator couldn't make out, and then he reached in his pocket for a pack of cigarettes. He turned toward the freeway to block the wind and held the lighter up to his face. Now the private investigator could see the scar on the man's left cheek.

As the gavel came down on the 111th session of the United States Congress, many of its members, including Nat Thompson, took great pride in what had been accomplished by the Democrat majority.

The unemployment rate was less than four percent, the lowest it had been in history. This was partly because, either directly or indirectly, more than a hundred million people were now working for the federal government. Around the country federally funded construction projects were springing up like clover—day care centers, drive through post office-voter registration centers, long term health care and retirement villages, alcohol and tobacco withdrawal centers, tax and Social Security information offices, and even federal burial service centers.

As the end of 2010 approached, nearly a third of all American workers belonged to labor unions. President O'Banion had nationalized a number of run down low tech industries: rusting steel and copper foundries, aging shipyards, antiquated textile and sugar mills, and hundreds of other large failing business which threatened to lay off large numbers of traditional Democratic voters.

President O'Banion's Secretary of Labor was an Hispanic graduate of the University of Wisconsin named Armando Torres. He was a strong advocate of egalitarian wage practices. He had lobbied Congress to pass a law forcing companies to pay their employees the same wages as the most profitable company with which they competed. He had even asked the president to issue an executive order requiring that a start up computer service company pay the same wages to their employees as IBM paid theirs. In response to the U. S. Chamber of Commerce's contention that this would put the start up companies out of business, the Labor Secretary had fired back, "I will not tolerate discrimination in the workplace."

By 2010 American physicians were subject to strict federal rules and regulations limiting not only their fees, but also the cost of prescribed medicines and treatments. It only cost fifteen dollars to see your doctor for a physical, and only a hundred dollars for a heart transplant, but there were only about half the number of doctors that there had been twenty years earlier. Unless the patient was suffering from some life threatening condition, it took several weeks to see a doctor.

But the federal government did provide a lot of free health care: drugs, physical therapy, home health care, including professional nurses, and even psychological counseling. Of course, none of these benefits were available to the "rich," who now had to travel to either Bermuda or the Cayman Islands if they wanted to see their own doctor.

There, colonies of refugee physicians worked in hospitals where they could charge fees free of government control.

Back in the US, the flimsy conditions attached to receiving government entitlements became even flimsier. It had even gotten to the point where some benefits were dependent on *not holding* a job. So more and more people were content to just stay home and do nothing but surf the web or play golf at a federally funded course.

Because of all this government spending, the federal deficit was now so large that almost half of all the money paid in taxes was used to pay interest on government bonds. This even though the 111th Congress had raised payroll taxes for the third time in less than three years. After the latest tax increase, more than sixty percent of an average American's paycheck was being withheld for taxes.

America was starting to look a lot like Sweden. But most people didn't seem to care. They were happy the way things were. That is until something totally unexpected happened that shocked the American people unlike anything since the bombing of Pearl Harbor.

Sam Brinkman had flown out to Honolulu to watch his beloved Vultures play an early season game with the Hawaiian Islanders. He'd had to tack another hundred thousand dollars onto his bail bond to get the judge's permission to leave Atlanta, but he thought it would be worth paying the extra premium to see his team play one of the division contenders.

Like most of the other stadiums in the National Football League, Rainbow Stadium in Honolulu had been converted into a giant collection of luxury boxes so that the only outdoor seating was limited to the end zone areas.

The kickoff had been scheduled for 10 o'clock in the morning in order to attract as many stateside viewers as possible.

Sam was looking through his binoculars. His eyes were focused over the south rim of the stadium in the direction of the blue Pacific. It was a beautiful sight, he thought. There were only a few cottony clouds in the azure sky. He could see the wind surfers, the Catamarans, and the Sun Fish, all tacking across the gentle swells that moved inexorably toward the beach. It was the bluest water Sam had ever seen. He happened to look up and see a streak of white in the sky. It looked like a vapor trail from a high flying jet, but this one was arching downward toward the ocean. He watched it until the leading point disappeared into the water. A few seconds later he saw a towering geyser shooting high up in the air. The spray seemed to hang in the air for several seconds. On the surface of the ocean he could see a circular crest of water spreading out in all directions as though someone had dropped a boulder in a pond. As it moved closer to shore, the sailboats began capsizing and people were falling into the water.

As he was watching this Sam could feel the floor of his luxury box shaking. He turned around and looked down at the people in the end zones. They were scrambling over the top of each other frantically trying to get to the aisles.

A quavering voice came over the PA system. "Please stay in your seats and remain calm. I repeat, please stay in your seats and remain calm."

Down on the field he could see that the players had their helmets off and were just standing there with dazed looks on their faces.

The faces of the people with him in the luxury box were as white as sheets. They were all too stunned to say anything. No one had any idea of what could have happened.

"Bring her some water!" Someone near Sam was yelling as he crouched over a middle-aged woman lying on the carpeted floor.

"Jesus H. Christ," whispered Sam.

The game had been cancelled. The PA announcement had come a few minutes after the ground had stopped shaking.

After almost two hours of bumper to bumper traffic with people leaning out of their cars screaming at each other, Sam was finally back at his suite in the Royal Hawaiian. The first thing he did when he walked in his room was turn on the television.

"Hell." The screen was all snow. He picked up his cell phone and called Doug's law office thinking he might still be there.

"Doug, it's Sam. We just had the damndest thing out here—"

"Sam! Are you okay!"

"Yeah, but it scared the livin' shit outa' me and everybody else in my box."

"I bet it did," said Doug.

Sam said, "A guy down in the lobby said something about a missile, but that's all I know.

There's somethin' wrong with my damn TV."

"The networks here are saying that the North Koreans fired a missile that landed about a mile south of Oahu."

"Christ almighty! I saw it Doug! Biggest damn waterspout you ever saw. Wiped out every boat in the area."

"O'Banion's supposed to be making an address in a few minutes." There was a pause, and then Doug said, "When are you flying back?"

"I'm booked on a flight that leaves tomorrow mornin', but I'm sure this could damn well screw that up."

"The Smithers were supposed to leave for Maui tomorrow."

"What do you think this'll mean for your race against Thompson?"

"I don't know. I hadn't really thought about that."

"Well, I'll let you go so you can listen to that fart O'Banion tell us how he's gonna save the world."

"Okay. And Sam. Thanks for calling. It's nice to know you're all right."

"Give my love to Priss."

A few minutes later Doug turned on the television in the corner of his law office.

Paul O'Banion's face came on the screen. He was sitting behind JFK's desk at the Oval Office. There was a look of fierce intensity on his face. You could see his jaw muscles as he began to speak.

"My fellow Americans, today, Sunday, October tenth, twenty ten, the nation of North Korea launched a nuclear missile aimed at our

Hawaiian Islands. By doing so, the North Korean government has committed an act of dastardly cowardice. Only by the grace of God did the missile fall short of its intended target. Had it landed on Honolulu, hundreds of thousands of innocent Americans would have lost their lives. This does not diminish the tragic fact that more than thirty innocent people who were near the missile when it struck are presently unaccounted for and presumed to be dead." He lifted his chin slightly.

"My fellow Americans, this unprovoked act of aggression by the North Korean government will not go unpunished. A few minutes before this broadcast, I spoke on the telephone with the Secretary General of the United Nations..."

Doug slapped his knee. "Here we go again, running to the UN. God damn it, for once let's do something on our own!" "...and I have been assured by the Secretary General that she, on behalf of the world community, will issue the strongest possible statement of condemnation against—"

Doug flicked off the remote and threw it on the couch.

He leaned back in his chair and closed his eyes. How could we have allowed this to happen? he asked himself.

He started thinking back to the 1990's. He remembered that was when the North Koreans had first been suspected of building a secret nuclear weapons plant. They had denied it, of course, saying they were only building a nuclear reactor that would generate electricity for their fledgling industries. President Hinton had bought their story and had given them millions of dollars to help them finish their nuclear reactor. The North Koreans took the money and kept right on working at a location they wouldn't let any outsider inspect. And then they started test-firing missiles that soared over Japan and landed in the north Pacific. And the United States government never did anything about it.

Doug shouted out loud, "Maybe this will finally wake us up!"

Chapter 20

His silver hair was glistening in the noon day sun. It was combed
straight back, the ends just above the top of his starched white collar.
He was standing there on an elevated platform. Fleecy white clouds
drifted lazily in the blue sky above the large crowd of people. They had
gathered there at the Westin Peachtree Plaza to hear him speak. The
silver hair and white linen suit made Nat Thompson look like a tele-
vangelist about to give an impassioned speech for Jesus.

The railing of the wooden platform was draped with a large red,
white, and blue banner. The platform itself was located directly in front
of a grand arched entrance to the seventy two-story steel and glass
cylindrical office building. Eight city officials, including the Mayor,
were seated in folding chairs in a row across the rear of the platform.

There was a crowd of at least five thousand people out on the street.
They were jammed together behind a line of sawhorses and more than
a dozen policemen were strung out in front of the barricades.

The Chairman's beady eyes were scanning the crowd as he stood
there listening to the applause that followed the Mayor's introduction.
It was a very nice turn out, he thought. Mike had done a good job of
making the arrangements.

He reached behind the podium and took a quick sip of water. The tip
of his tongue slithered from side to side across his slit lips. And then at
last Congressman Nat Thompson began to speak.

"Thank you very much for that kind introduction, Mayor
Cogburn." He glanced over his shoulder and said, "And thank you,
Mrs. Cogburn, distinguished members of the Atlanta City Council,

and all of you for comin' hea' today." The loud speakers amplified the nasal sound of his voice.

"Ladies and gentlemen, today is a troublin' time for this great nation or ours. It is a time when we face threats both at home and abroad. Despite all the good things that have been done since I've been fortunate enough to be your representative in Congress, the challenges are still there. And there are those who don't want us to succeed. But ours in a strong country, a prosperous country, thanks to the hard work of our Democratic Majority in Congress and the leadership of President Paul O'Banion." There was loud applause from the street.

"It was the leadership of President O'Banion which provided us with a United Nation's resolution callin' for the reinstatement of an economic embargo on North Korea. It was also the leadership of the Democrat Majority in Congress which raised the minimum wage to ten dollars and hour so that workin' families will have a chance to make a decent wage to support their families."

A loud roar echoed in the canyon of office buildings, followed by spontaneous chanting, "We want Nat! We want Nat! We want Nat!" At the far edge of this sea of humanity, The Chairman could see two old women. They were holding up a cloth banner, the size of a large beach towel, with bold red lettering: KEEP NAT AT BAT FOR US.

Nat was thinking, these people really do love me.

"Ladies and gentlemen, today is a time that requires a steady hand on the tiller to help us navigate through these turbulent wata's now facin' us. Now is not the time to turn things over to someone who has never faced anythin' more challengin' than a simple minded country jury."

More loud applause and shouting.

He held up his big hands until the noise lessened. As he began to speak again, he stood up on his tiptoes. "My friends, I have been proud to serve you during the last six years as the Chairman of the House Appropriations Committee of the United States House of Representatives. Some folks in Washington who know about such things say that my chairmanship is about *the* most powerful and influential position a person can have in the United States Congress. And why is that?"

Someone in the crowd yelled, "Tell us Nat!" This was followed by ripples of good natured laughter.

The Chairman smiled and said, "I will, thank you, sir. It's because the House Appropriations Committee decides how all that money we send to Washington gets spent." He paused, reveling in the certainty that he had them all in the palms of his hands. "And because Nat Thompson is the Chairman of that powerful committee up in Washington, you, and thousands of folks like you here in Atlanta, are the primary beneficiaries." The canyon of office buildings rocked with the sound of their cheering.

He waited for a minute and then swept his right arm through the air. "Nat Thompson always has been and always will be the best friend in Washington this, the greatest city of the South, has ever had." The applause was deafening and he had to wait again. When the cheering subsided he said, "And because of that, you, my friends, will continue to get your fair share. Indeed, I would venture to say *more* than your fair share of what Washington has to offer."

The crowd erupted again in a frenzy of cheers and shouts and waving arms.

And then the chant broke out again, but this time even louder. "We want Nat! We want Nat! We want Nat!"

He held up his hands again as though he wanted them to stop but wishing their cheering could go on forever. The noise finally lessened to the point where he could make himself heard.

"I ask you, ladies and gentlemen," he said in a voice that was now suddenly quieter, but more intense, "do we dare risk throwin' away all the things that the Chairman of the House Appropriations Committee can do for you?"

An ocean of sound, "No!" echoed through the surrounding downtown office buildings.

"Of course you don't." He was up on his tiptoes again. "My friends, you've got far too much common sense for that. And to the best of my God given abilities, so long as I can draw breath, I will continue to be your servant. Thank you and God bless you."

The Chairman stood there and smiled and watched them clapping their hands and heard them cheering and yelling his name. He noticed an old man in the front row. He had on a straw hat with Nat's campaign buttons all over it. The old man was shouting and screaming so wildly that he seemed on the verge of apoplexy.

The city officials and Mrs. Cogburn gathered around Nat and he began shaking their hands. They were all smiling and nodding. A minute or so later Mike came up and whispered something in Nat's ear.

The crowd was heaving toward the platform, pushing against the sawhorses. The police had their arms outstretched trying to hold them back and away from the long black Mercedes limousine that was pulling up to the curb. The Chairman was finished shaking hands and was walking over to his car. The driver held the door open and the Chairman gave the people around him one more quick smile, a satisfied little grin, as he swung his pressed white pants inside.

The shiny black limousine began moving away from the curb and the crowd began parting like the Red Sea parted for Moses, and the Chairman of the House Appropriations Committee rolled out of sight behind the loud rumbling of the six motorcycle police escort.

At the very moment of Nat Thompson's triumphant departure down Peachtree Street, in another part of the city there was a much different kind of police activity underway. It was going on in one of the rooms inside a ten-story limestone building located near the old Fulton County Stadium. It was a rather nondescript building except for the fact that there were iron bars on all the windows.

On the third floor of that building two men were sitting on metal chairs facing each other across a rectangular shaped oak table, slightly wider than a card table. The room was bare of any other furniture.

Across the top half of the wall facing the man with the scar on his left cheek was a mirror, which made the brightly-lit room seem larger than it actually was.

Virgil Wilson sat there with a forlorn expression on his weary looking face. He could see in the mirror that his gray hair was sticking out on each side of his head and that his eyes were bloodshot. He was wearing all white pajamas-like clothing with the words, FULTON COUNTY JAIL, stamped on the back.

He hadn't slept since they'd taken him into custody. The wino in his cell had sung all night long. He'd also peed on the concrete floor and Virgil could still smell the stink. He rubbed his sore eyes.

Virgil rubbed his sore eyes. He was dying for a cigarette.

"Mr. Wilson, now that you've heard me read you your rights under the law, is there anything you want to say?"

The police lieutenant was a barrel chested man in his thirties. He was dressed in a pair of tan slacks, a short sleeved white shirt, and a wide coffee colored tie.

"I ain't saying anything."

"Do you want to call a lawyer?"

He wondered whether he should. He was squinting. The bright lights were hurting his eyes.

"Well?" said the lieutenant impatiently.

Virgil just sat there scratching his belly. His eyes had a vacant look. He had never trusted lawyers. Not since his ex-wife's lawyer had convinced a judge to let her have the house and the car. At the time of their divorce, that was everything in the world that Virgil had owncd.

"Mr. Wilson, I'm going to ask you one last time. Do you want to call a lawyer?" The police lieutenant's voice was loud this time.

Virgil glared at him. "Maybe I do and maybe I don't."

"Mr. Wilson, we've got a tape of you and your partner at the used car lot."

Virgil was looking down at the backs of his hands, trying to think of what to say. How could they have seen it? he wondered. He'd been so careful about waiting until well after midnight to move the motorcycles from the garage of the abandoned filling station to the used car lot. And he was certain that no one had followed him. How the hell could they have known about it?

The police lieutenant was staring at him, still waiting patiently for a response.

Virgil scowled at him and said, "So you saw me moving some motorbikes, so what?"

The policeman leaned closer. "We can prove you stole the motorcycles. Do you want to read this." He reached in a manila envelope and pulled out a sheet of paper.

Virgil watched the lieutenant lay it on the table in front of him. He looked down and started reading.

AFFIDAVIT OF BRIAN P. MATHERN

I, Brian P. Mathern, affiant herein, duly sworn by and before a Notary Public in and for Fulton County, Georgia, do hereby swear to the truthfulness of the following: That I am the current Manager of Inventory for Cycle City Motors, 32455 North Freeway, Atlanta, Georgia, and that in my capacity as Manager of Inventory, it is my responsibility to maintain all records relating to the acquisition of motorcycles purchased for resale by my employer, said Cycle City Motors; That on October 15, 2010, the following described motorcycles purchased were listed on the records as being the property of Cycle City Motors:

Harley Davidson	Model Z 100	ID No. 54399771
Harley Davidson	Model Z 100	ID No. 56009834
Yamaha	Model K 40	ID No. 87993742
Yamaha	Model K 40	ID No. 89492051
Yamaha	Model K 50	ID No. 89537784

Suzuki	Model R 200	ID No. 22069431
Suzuki	Model R 200	ID No. 24348908
Suzuki	Model R 250	ID No. 26358903
BMW	Model X 88	ID No. 90334186
BMW	Model X 88	ID No. 98745388
Honda	Model T 300	ID No. 86994035
Honda	Model T 350	ID No. 87889640
Honda	Model T 350	ID No. 88349801

Further, affiant sayeth not.

Brian P. Mathern
Manager of Inventory
Cycle City Imports

Thus dated this fifteenth day of October, 2010
Debra P. Smith
Notary Public, Fulton County, Georgia

The policeman was pointing at the affidavit. "Each of those ID numbers you see there matches the ID numbers we found on the motorbikes you took to the used car lot."

Virgil's mind was racing. He felt as though he couldn't breathe. He told himself to try to think of something. Maybe this was all they had. He tried to speak calmly. "That don't prove nothin'. I sold those bikes to people who came into the showroom. You take the trouble to look at the invoices, you'll see that. And as far as haulin' 'em over to that used car lot, well, we was just holdin' 'em there so they could be fixed up for delivery later on."

The policeman shook his head and reached into the manila folder again. "Do you want to see these?" He was holding several sheets of paper.

Virgil's face was turning white.

"They're affidavits from each of the people you conned into filling out those pre-application forms."

He knew it was all over. He hung his head down, feeling as though his world had come to an end.

As soon as Charles Danberry received the news of Virgil Wilson's arrest from his source at the Atlanta Police Department, he called Sam. "I've got some great news!" boomed the lawyer's baritone voice. "Virgil Wilson's been arrested for stealing motorcycles."

"Hot damn! I knew that little sumbitch would get his rear in trouble again," said Sam elatedly.

"Well, he certainly has. I'm going to go see Ben Wattenberg first thing tomorrow morning. They don't have a snowball's chance in hell now of using his testimony to win a conviction against you."

"Thank the Lord," said Sam, feeling as though the weight of the world had just been lifted from his shoulders.

He heard his lawyer's voice again, "I still think Virgil Wilson lied about you because somebody paid him."

"Who'd want to do somethin' like that?"

"I don't know, but I'm going to try to find out."

Chapter 21

The news of Virgil Wilson's arrest made the front page of the *Atlanta Monitor*. The boldly printed headline read: **STAR WITNESS IN PROBE OF SAM BRINKMAN ARRESTED ON FRAUD AND THEFT CHARGES.** Doug read every word of the news report. According to the *Monitor*, the U. S. Attorney's office was said to be "reassessing the feasibility of the case against Sam Brinkman in light of recent developments."

Doug had gotten Sam's call the night before the story broke. Priss had just finished taking their frozen dinners out of the microwave when the phone rang. After hearing his friend's excited voice telling him the good news, Doug had shouted, "Sam, that 's the best news I've heard in a long time!" They had all gone out to dinner to celebrate and had polished off two bottles of Dom Perignon.

Doug knew there was a lot to celebrate. He felt certain that Virgil Wilson's arrest would prove that Sam's accuser was a liar and would restore Sam's reputation as an honest man. Doug also realized that it could give his campaign a fresh start. Once the U. S. Attorney's Office dropped their charges, he thought, the cloud of suspicion hovering over his relationship with Sam should disappear. People will understand that Sam is a good and decent man who simply wants to help me change the country for the better, Doug thought. But he also knew there wasn't much time. The election was less than three weeks away.

It was almost 8:30 in the morning and Doug's head was still throbbing from too much champagne the night before. Priss was still in bed. He put the newspaper down on the breakfast room table and took a last sip of coffee. "God," he moaned, rubbing his face. He picked up his jacket and walked out the door.

The traffic was heavy and it was after nine o'clock before he got to the old building with the "Crane for Congress" sign in the cracked display window. He parked out front and walked inside.

"Oh, hi Doug. Where's Priss?"

The woman speaking to him was an attractive black woman in a tailored wool suit with shoulder pads. Jane Morrow was married to an eye surgeon. She had been a Crane volunteer since the first day volunteers started coming to the campaign office.

"She was still in bed when I left," he said walking toward her. "I'm afraid we celebrated a little too much last night." They shook hands. "I guess you heard about Sam."

She nodded. "That was really great news." A telephone rang. She walked over to one of the long folding tables and picked it up. "Crane for Congress, may I help you?"

He mouthed the words: *I'll let you get back to work.*

Another phone near where he was standing started ringing. He reached over and picked it up. "This is Doug Crane, may I help you?"

He heard an elderly sounding woman's voice say, "I really admire what you're doing, young man, and I'd like to make a contribution of twenty dollars to your campaign."

"Thank you very much." He sat down in a metal folding chair and shifted the phone from one ear to the other. "I really appreciate your support."

The door opened and two young women walked in. One was much taller than the other was. They looked at Doug and smiled at the same time.

More phones started ringing. The two young women dropped their purses on a table and went to work answering calls.

By 10 o'clock all of the other volunteers had arrived. There were now nine people in the room, including Doug, all talking and writing as fast as they could. The room was a babble of conversations, ringing phones, and flashing hold buttons.

The door opened and Doug looked up. It was Priss. She was standing there with her mouth open.

Doug shouted from the far side of the room, "Priss, we've raised over five thousand dollars in less than an hour!"

She ran over and picked up a phone.

Sam was standing in the middle of one of his giant furniture show-rooms. He was looking up at the sixty-inch screen of the Sony television set that he had rented for this special occasion. He used the remote to scroll through some channels until he found the station that was carrying Doug's broadcast. His round face lit up with a wide, gap-toothed smile. He raised his big arms in the air and yelled, "All right everybody, come on over hea' and listen to what my friend Doug Crane's got to say! He's runnin' for Congress and he's a damn good man!"

A couple of sales people and a few customers ambled over to the big screen TV.

They looked up and saw a close up of Doug, from the middle of his chest to the top of his head. He looked calm and composed in his dark brown jacket and canary yellow tie. Over his shoulders there were rows of books in the background and Sam knew they were broadcasting from Doug's law office.

The camera panned back. Doug was sitting nonchalantly on the corner of his desk.

"He sure is a good lookin' young man," said a grotesquely fat woman in a tent-like pink cotton dress. She was one of the few paying much attention when Doug started speaking.

Sam reached for the remote and turned up the volume. Doug's voice boomed out across the furniture showroom.

"During the last three months…" Heads all over the store were suddenly turning in the direction of the loud voice. Sam flashed a sheepish little grin and turned the volume down, but only a little. "…it's been my privilege to get to know many of you. You've been kind enough to let me visit with you at your homes, your churches, and your workplaces. I've gotten to know a lot about your concerns, and I hope you've gotten to know something about mine."

A family of five wandered over to join the group in front of the big screen.

"I've found out that a lot of you are working very hard to support your families. Almost every married couple I've met has said they were both working. They told me they have to if they want to get ahead.

"I found that most people in the Tenth District aren't satisfied to just live on what the government gives them. They know they can have a better standard of living if they work hard. But they're struggling because their taxes are too high. And the reason taxes are too high is because Washington is spending too much of their money."

By now more than twenty people were crowded around the Sony. All their faces were looking up at the big screen. Some were nodding their heads as he spoke.

"The politicians and bureaucrats in Washington think they can do a better job of spending our money than we can. But the truth is that you can do a better job of looking after yourselves if Washington would just leave you alone. People are fed up with what's been going on in Washington for the last twenty years."

People were still coming up from around the store.

Doug stood up and put a hand on top of his desk. "It's time for a change so that the federal government doesn't withhold almost half of our paychecks. So that labor unions don't control who we can work for and what we can earn. So that we all pay lower taxes, and not just the wealthy people and the big corporations that can afford to hire tax lawyers and accountants and lobbyists. And it's time for a change so we can finally get rid of the source of all the confusion and all the wasted hours most working people have to spend each year trying to figure out what they owe the federal government. The Internal Revenue Code should be abolished."

"Damn right!" shouted a man holding his wife's hand.

"And we can't keep ignoring the need for a strong national defense. What happened in the Persian Gulf and in Hawaii demonstrates how dangerous such short sightedness can be.

"My opponent will tell you that he's been a champion of the national defense industry and that he's brought billions of dollars in defense projects to the Atlanta area. I can't deny that he has. But ten years ago, he also fought to kill the Republican's bill to begin the implementation of an anti-missile defense system. Why? Because the construction site for the missiles was going to be located in Houston and not Atlanta. And the bill died."

"But if we'd had such a defense system in place, that North Korean missile could have been knocked down long before it barely missed killing hundreds of thousands of people in Honolulu. Because of the Democrats and Nat Thompson, we don't have that kind of protection. Think what might happen if some tyrant in some rogue state decides to target Atlanta? We might not be as lucky as those folks on Oahu were. So ask yourselves, is it really in our best interests to keep a man in office whose sole mission in life is to bring home the bacon."

There were shouts of approval and loud clapping from the large crowd in front of the Sony.

"I'm not going to tell you that Doug Crane can go up there to Washington and single handedly turn things around overnight. It's going to take a lot of hard work by me and a lot of other people in Washington who believe in smaller government and more personal responsibility. And even then it won't be easy. During the last twenty years our sense of self-reliance has become sedated by the drug of federal dependency, and it's going to be very difficult for us to kick the habit." His blue eyes narrowed slightly and his voice became more intense. "But I promise you this. With your support, I will fight like hell to change things."

There was another burst of applause from the showroom floor.

"Our ancestors came here almost a hundred and seventy five years ago, which was a little more than two decades before the War Between the States. They settled in a dusty wasteland at the end of a railroad line and gave that God forsaken place an appropriate name: Terminus. As tough as conditions were, our forefather's fought and worked and prayed, and during the next hundred and fifty years their little community grew from nothing until it became one of the largest and most prosperous cities in the world."

There was total silence now among those listening to his mesmerizing words.

"And then it started to decline. Bars and drugs and porno houses and same sex marriages and murders and all manner of other human mischief took hold of our lives. We lost our values. We lost our way."

There were tears welling up in Sam's eyes.

"Some might say it's too late, that we can't turn back the clock to the way things used to be. That there's no reversing the decline of the American civilization. But I don't believe that. And I pledge to you today that if you elect me to serve as your representative in Congress, I will fight to restore those traditional values that have made this a great country. I may be only one man, but I will be a man with a mission to change things for the better."

"Thank you, and may God give us all the strength to do what's right."

Sam had tears rolling down his big face. And so did many of the people around him. And the tide began to turn in Doug's favor.

Ab Connell was sitting in his large corner office in the Longworth House Office Building, looking out the window at the statute of Freedom on top of the huge dome. Over the years the soot had given the white stone of the Capitol a grayish cast, a look that was in keeping with the Majority Leader's current mood. He had been reading the *Washington Post* story about the dismissal of the case against Sam Brinkman. The news had given him a feeling of anguish and uncertainty.

He looked over at his secretary who was leaning over a file drawer. "See if you can get Nat Thompson on the line."

A minute later he heard a beeping sound and picked up the phone.

"Hey, Nat. How are things down in Atlanta?" He tried to sound cheerful.

"I suppose they could be better." The Chairman's voice was flat and nasal.

"Yeah, the Brinkman dismissal was a crappy break for you."

"Has it made the *Post*?"

"I just finished reading the story, two columns on page two."

There was no response from Nat.

The Majority Leader hesitated, not quite knowing how to ask his next question. "I wanted to see what you think. I mean…is there any possible negative fallout about this Virgil Wilson guy?"

"What's *negative fallout* supposed to mean?" There was a derisive tone in The Chairman's voice.

"Well, I don't know. It's just that this guy seems like a pretty shady character based on what the paper said. I mean, all this stuff about how he conned people into filling out those phony applications."

"Ab, I have no control over how people behave or what they say. Virgil Wilson brought charges against Sam Brinkman for reasons only he knows."

"I understand what you're saying, but the point I'm making is that with a guy like that, you don't know what he might say next. He could say anything, you know, maybe even something crazy like you put him up to doing what he did."

"He could. But people won't believe him. 'Cause he's a fraudulent liar."

"Yeah, I guess you're right." The tone of this affirmation sounded a little tentative.

Ab still had a feeling of uneasiness. He wondered if it was really as simple as Nat made it sound. The nasal voice interrupted his meditation.

"Is there anything else you wanted to talk about?"

"No. I guess not."

Nat hung up without saying good bye.

The Majority Leader looked back out the window again. The rear view of the Capitol across the street looked as gloomy as it had before. He watched as a bus pulled up to the curb belching a cloud of tar-colored smoke.

Ab closed his eyes and leaned back in his chair, praying that what Nat had just told him was true.

Chapter 22

Rhonda Sanchez had flown down to Mexico City to see her father. He had looked so much older to her. The twenty years he had spent in prison had taken a toll on his health. It had hurt her so much when they took him away. She could still feel the pain. She remembered when it had happened.

Her family had lived in a large hacienda on a hill near Mexico City. When she was growing up, she had rarely seen much of her father because he was always traveling. He had been an executive with a large company that had owned businesses all over the world. She had spent most of her time either playing with her friend, Rosa, or going shopping with her mother.

Her mother had been a very beautiful American woman, who had first met her father during one of his business trips to the United States. He had been flying to Miami and she had been an airline stewardess on his flight. She remembered that her mother had told her that he had invited her to dinner at a hotel in Boca Raton, Florida. A few weeks later, they had spent their honeymoon at the same hotel, the Boca Raton Golf and Beach Resort.

The daughter was gazing out the window at a solid bank of clouds that looked like a gigantic white mattress. There was a brief flash of sunlight on the cottony horizon. Her mind suddenly pictured the magnificent four-karat diamond ring her father had given her mother. He had always given her the best of everything…until the day they took him away.

She had been only 10 years old when it happened. After he was convicted, they had taken him from his jail cell in New Orleans and put him in the Atlanta Federal Prison. That was where he had spent the next twenty years of his life.

It had almost killed her mother. She could still remember the sound of her uncontrollable sobbing and the look of anguish and despair on her tear streaked face. It had broken her mother's heart. And it had broken mine, too, she thought.

Her mind shifted to a vision of the way her father had looked during their visit. It was his last year in prison. When she had walked into his little bare room, she remembered how shocked she had been at his appearance. His hair had been as white as his shapeless prison clothes. There had been deep lines on his face that was once so smooth. He had offered her a feeble smile and a trembling hand, and she could not hide the tears in her eyes.

Her mother had told her that they had put her father in jail because of the lies of an evil man who had lived in New Orleans. The man had told the American authorities that her father had been involved in doing bad things with drugs.

It was not until she had been in college that she had learned more. Her mother had said that the man responsible for sending her father to jail was an oilman. He had been doing business with her father and had accused him of being the mastermind of a money-laundering scheme involving drugs. She also had learned that the oilman's name was Boyd Smithers.

For years, the name Boyd Smithers was but a distant memory stored in some dark forgotten place of her consciousness. That is, it had been until this very morning when she was flying back from Mexico City to her apartment in New York.

She was among the highest paid fashion models in New York. She had appeared on the cover of *Vogue* and *Cosmopolitan* and a few weeks earlier had signed an eight-figure endorsement contract with Revlon. Her friends were mostly other highly paid models, male and female, famous photographers, writers, and artists. Not many among her sophisticated and cultured circle of Manhattan friends had much interest in politics. Those who did hated conservatives, especially Southern conservatives whom they viewed as unenlightened redneck, Neaderthal Ku Klux Klanners.

Rhonda was relaxing in her large leather seat reading the *New York Times* when she saw something that caught her eye. It was in an article that included an interview with a young man running for Congress in Georgia. He had seemed so self righteous, she thought, so holier than thou with all his shit about family values and self-responsibility. Then she read the words near the end that sent chills down her spine: "…congressional candidate Doug Crane is the son-in-law of a wealthy former oil man, Boyd Smithers."

She dropped the paper on her lap, her dark brown eyes suddenly on fire. She felt a blinding sense of rage as she said thought, The man who put my father in jail is some rich bastard whose right wing extremist son-in-law is running for Congress.

Rhonda glared down at the paper again. There was a picture of a young candidate's face. He was smiling. The daughter of Enrico Sanchez felt a burning desire for revenge.

They had moved Virgil Wilson down the hall to a new cell. The day before a judge had denied his lawyer's request for a reduction in his bail bond. The con man was waiting for his trial date to be set.

He was sitting there on the edge of his hard bed, scooping a spoonful of Jell-O off of a metal plate. The bed had three coils of springs covered by a thin cotton mattress. The side of the frame closest to the wall was bolted to the concrete and the other side had chains running at a 45-degree angle from the corners to bolts attached higher up on the wall. At the rear of the cell was a toilet with a horseshoe shaped seat that smelled of urine.

As he sat there on his bed with his bare feet on the concrete floor, Virgil could hear the sound of loud rap music. It was coming from the cell next to him. He put his spoon down and placed his hands over his ears and shut his eyes. He had no idea what time it was. The room was windowless.

Virgil was a man in deep despair. He had lost almost all hope. But as bad as things were for the con man, given his current circumstances, there was one small glimmer of light at the end of the dark tunnel. It shone there in the back of his troubled mind and it kept him from losing his sanity. It was the memory of his meeting with Nat Thompson.

When Virgil had gone to see the powerful congressman to sell him information about Sam Brinkman, he had known there might come a day like this when he could use what had happened at that meeting to his advantage. It was his insurance policy.

He remembered his preparations for the meeting. He had been in his room at the Holiday Inn getting ready to go. He had put two strips of white adhesive tape over a small recorder and stuck it to his chest. It wasn't until the congressman's secretary had told him he could go into her boss's office that he had reached inside his shirt and flipped the switch.

As he sat there on his jail cell bed, tracing his two-inch scar with his finger, Virgil Wilson's eyes shone with a devilish light.

She was tired by the time she got back to her apartment. The cab had smelled of stale cigar smoke and the driver had not stopped jabbering from the time they had left the airport. She felt a huge sense of relief when her apartment building on Park Avenue finally came into view.

She leaned over the front seat and handed him a hundred-dollar bill. She climbed out and flashed a dazzling smile at the uniformed doorman who started gathering her suitcases off the sidewalk. She breezed through the revolving doors and rode the elevator up to her floor.

She walked in and turned on the living room lights.

A moment later the doorbell rang and she went to the door.

"Thank you Henry," she said as he set her bags down on the parquet floor.

"Will that be all, Miss Sanchez?"

"Yes," she said, handing him a twenty-dollar bill.

She left the bags on the floor and walked through a large living room. In the center of the room was a grouping of snow white upholstered furniture arrayed in front of a stone fireplace with a black marble hearth. The ceiling had track lights focused on several large impressionistic paintings.

She went into the bathroom and turned on the water. A mosaic of peach colored stones decorated the ledge surrounding a porcelain tub large enough to accommodate a professional basketball player. She took off her gold loop earrings and faced a mirror that extended the length of the counter top. Her long and graceful fingers began undoing the pearl buttons of her cashmere sweater. She took off her light wool skirt and walked into her closet. There were two rows of clothes on each side, one on top of the other, in a space that seemed big enough to park an SUV.

She finished undressing and sat down on the chair in front of the mirror.

Rhonda Sanchez had a classically beautiful face. Her cheekbones were high, like her mother's, though her eyes were more like her father's, evenly spaced and a dark chocolate color. She also had her father's aristocratically straight nose and perfectly contoured jawlines converging on her round chin. Her hair was long and straight, the color of champagne, and it shone like fine silk.

She moved a hand up to her long neck. The mirror reflected an image of flawless, smooth skin, the color of light butterscotch. There was a small mole hidden in the shadow of her left breast.

She stood up and looked at herself, cupping her hands under her breasts. There was a frown on her face. She said to herself, They're too big. She had heard the whispers of the clothing designers that her blouses never hung the way they were supposed to when she walked down the runway. But she also knew that she had the face of Aphrodite and the lines and curves of an otherwise perfectly proportioned body. And so she'd gotten away with having breasts that were larger than those of any other famous fashion model. And despite the petty criticism from the dress designers, she could tell by the look in the eyes of the men in the audience that she was someone very…desirable. She liked it when they couldn't take their eyes off of her. It gave her a feeling of power.

She heard the rhythmic sound of the water filling her Jacuzzi-bath tub. She climbed in and stretched out under the soap bubbles. She closed her eyes and felt the jets of water massaging her. The tension and fatigue from her long flight slowly began to fade.

As she lay there her thoughts returned to the story in the *Times*. Doug Crane. His picture had been shown above the column in the paper. She had to admit that he was very good looking. He reminded her of a New York Jets quarterback she'd once dated. The memory of the quarterback brought a smile to her face. She glanced over at her king-sized bed remembering the night they had spent together.

She finished her bath and climbed out of the tub. After drying off she put on a salmon pink silk robe and sat down in front of the mirror. She looked at her hair. She hated the thought of dying it, but she knew she had to do something to disguise the way she looked. Her face was too well known. Even a redneck Southerner like Doug Crane might have seen one of her lipstick commercials on television.

She sat there staring into the mirror for a long time. Finally she dropped her head and breathed a deep sigh, having made up her mind to do it. Black.

Chapter 23

He felt the tightness in his chest again. And then another sharp pain, always in the same place. He cursed under his breath, trying not to let the people in the audience see what was happening.

Their faces were a blur to him now. He felt like he was going to faint.

He grabbed hold of the side of the podium and with the other hand groped in the hip pocket of his white jacket for his bottle of pills. "…and so my fellow Atlantans…"

His fingers felt the bottle top and he managed to get it off. He tilted the bottle into his hidden palm and felt them spilling out. "…the journey we have traveled together during this campaign…"

There, two of them. He quickly popped them into his mouth, and began chewing with an awkward little grin, then swallowed. "…is about to come to an end."

He reached for a glass of water and took a sip.

"You are the guardians of our rights and privileges" A few seconds later their faces were beginning to come back into focus. "…and you must not let them be taken away by those who seek to destroy what this great country has to offer for those who are unable to help themselves." He was beginning to feel a little better. The pain in his chest didn't sting quite as much.

"I ask you to do your duty on November third. Not for Nat Thompson. Not for the Democratic Party. And not even for this great country, my friends. No, I ask only one thing: I ask that you vote for Nat Thompson for the sake of your families."

A wave of applause poured out of the audience.

Yes, he was definitely feeling better now. He knew he could finish. And he did.

A section of the World Congress Center, the huge convention center across Marietta Street from Centennial Olympic Park, had been partitioned with a giant curtain at one end and a brightly lit stage at the other. The people in the audience applauded for several more minutes. But their enthusiasm seemed somewhat restrained compared to the wild adulation of the street crowd a few days earlier. And almost a third of the folding chairs were empty.

The Chairman wiped his pale forehead with a white handkerchief and made his way off the small stage.

Mike Ruby came running up to him with a look of concern on his face. "Are you all right, sir?"

Nat brushed his arm away. "Of course I am, Mike. I just had a momentary…problem, but I'm fine now."

The rest of his entourage was gathering around him, like worker ants around their Queen, as they all made their way toward The Chairman's dressing room.

He waved them all away except for Mike and they went inside and closed the door. Mike helped Nat take off his jacket, which had dark circles under the armpits.

"Someone bring me a drink," he said, stretching his right arm. "Wild Turkey on the rocks." He rubbed his sunken milky snake eyes and looked in the mirror. Little crack-like lines spread out from the reddish puffiness around his eyes. The silver hair was still exquisitely combed in perfect lines of little furrows running straight back across his scalp.

Mike handed him the glass of bourbon and watched his boss take took a long drink.

"Have you seen this?" Mike said, handing him a newspaper.

Nat looked at it and frowned. "Fuck."

The race had gotten tighter. He was only ahead by five points.

Doug no longer had time for his half-hour workouts at the Q Club. Every waking hour was devoted to a speech, a hand shaking appearance, or a strategy session. Had he tried to squeeze in some time on the Stair Master, he knew there would be too many people asking too many questions. He had attempted to compensate by doing a hundred pushups and two hundred sit-ups in the living room. He would spread a towel on their Oriental rug beside the coffee table and get his heart pumping for thirty minutes every morning while listening to classical music on the stereo. But he had to keep the music low, because at 5 a. m., Priss was still asleep.

She was usually up by 6 a. m. when he was finishing his shower. And she was on this particular morning.

He walked into the breakfast room, adjusting the length of his tie.

She was seated on a tall stool at the kitchen counter. She had on a pale blue velvet robe and was eating a bowl of cereal while reading the morning paper. He walked over and kissed her on the cheek.

"Sam called while you were doing your pushups."

"I wondered who that was calling this early."

"He apologized, but said he wanted to give you the final numbers on your speech last night," she said, referring to his speech at the football stadium at Jesse Jackson High School. "Wait a second, I wrote it down." She got up and walked over to the kitchen counter and looked at a piece of paper beside the telephone. "Here it is. Five thousand six hundred and eighty six."

His face lit up. "Wow! I knew we had a big crowd, but that's fantastic!"

She sat back down at the breakfast table. "Sam said it was the largest crowd they've had since Jesse Jackson High won the District Championship two years ago."

He was pouring a glass of orange juice. He took a sip, then gazed into space. "I think my message may have finally caught on."

She wiped her mouth and said, "What's your schedule today?"

"First up is a television interview on Channel Two at 9 o'clock. Then at 10 I've got an appearance before the Veteran's of Foreign Wars at their meeting hall downtown. Then at noon I'm supposed to give an address at the Cobb County Republicans in Smyrna. Then at 1:30, I've got another television interview, this one on Channel Six, and at—"

"I know about that one," she said. At three he was supposed to be at his downtown headquarters to make phone calls for an hour.

He glanced at his wristwatch again. "I better run." He kissed her on the cheek, and dashed toward the front door.

"What about your cereal!"

"Later." His voice was mixed with the sound of the screen door slamming.

The Fulton County Prison where Virgil Wilson was spending his days and nights provided a room where prisoners could make telephone calls to the outside world. The words printed on the glass door were bureaucratically succinct: PRISONER COMMUNICATIONS.

Prisoners were allowed to make telephone calls once a day between the hours of 7 and 8 o'clock in the evening. The room was a brightly lit and large enough to accommodate ten callers, although it was rare that that many showed up at the same time. The telephones were spread out across on a long counter, each one in front of a metal stool that was bolted to the floor. A small measure of privacy was provided by wooden partitions that divided each space into little topless cubbyholes. A white number was painted on the dark green wall in front of each dialing station, starting from left to right and numbered from 1 to 10.

One of the Fulton County Prison rules was that an armed guard be stationed inside the communications room next to the doorway whenever a prisoner was using the room. Given the dimensions of the room, the optimum location for making a confidential telephone call, one that was least likely to be overheard by the guard, was from space Number 10 since it was almost thirty-five feet away from the guard.

Virgil Wilson had taken careful note of these conditions when planning to make the most important telephone call of his life. For five straight days, at around 6 o'clock in the late afternoon, he had told the guard who brought him his supper that he needed to use the telephone. And to Virgil's surprise, each time he had gotten permission to do so. But despite his good fortune, every time he had gone into the communications room, he had found that things had never been quite right. On the one occasion when he had been lucky enough to find a seat at space No. 10, there had been someone sitting in space Number 9, a fat man with tattoos on his arms who was talking loudly in Spanish to his mother in Tijuana.

But tonight conditions were much better. There was only one other person in the room, an old man mumbling quietly at space No. 3. It would have been better to have a few more distracting voices, but Virgil thought that this might be his last chance. So he decided to make the call.

He felt his heart pounding as he picked up the phone. He stole a glance at the clock on the wall and saw that it was almost 8 o'clock. He pulled a worn piece of paper out of his pocket and punched in the number he had written down. He rubbed his unshaven face with his free hand as he listened to the repetitious ringing sound, wishing with all his might that someone would pick up the damn phone. He finally heard a clicking sound that was followed by a recorded message:

"Thank you for calling Chairman Nat Thompson's office. If you need to speak with someone about a pending piece of legislation, and you are not calling from a rotary phone, punch one followed by the star symbol. If you are calling about an undelivered or misplaced check or another payment matter involving a federal agency, punch two followed by the star symbol. If you are calling to arrange a visit to the capital and would like to schedule an appointment..."

"Son of a fucking bitch," he muttered. His face was turning red.

Finally, after two more choices, he heard, "...if you would like to leave a message with the operator, please press zero and listen for the beep, and then begin speaking, or if you wish you may return to the main menu and listen to a repeat of this message."

He rolled his bloodshot eyes and wondered what he should do. An instant later he realized that since this was the only time he could call, he had to go ahead and do it.

"Shit." He stabbed the zero button.

"Please leave your message after the beep..."

The phone cord was wrapped around his white knuckles. He whispered, "Come on you fuckin' beep."

He finally heard it. "This is Virgil Wilson. I'm in the Fulton County Prison here in Atlanta. You better figure a way to get me out of here. And soon. If you don't, it could be real trouble for you, Congressman Thompson. I've got a tape recording of our meeting and..."

He heard another beeping sound and realized that his recording time had expired. As he hung up he looked over his shoulder and saw that the guard was watching him.

Chapter 24

The President's normally ruddy complexion was darker than usual because of the tan he'd acquired playing golf in the Hawaiian Islands. A pineapple company had paid for all five days of his vacation including his six hundred-dollar a night suite at the hotel on Lanai.

Cole Fruit Company's generosity just happened to coincide with the passage of the Pineapple Security Act of 2008. That bold piece of legislation banned the importation of pineapples from foreign countries. It was during his State of the Union message that the President had passionately beseeched Congress to do something about the public health danger posed by imported and untreated pineapples grown by foreign farmers. The President had called upon Congress to take immediate action to stop what he called "this Trojan horse of bacteria and disease."

At the present moment, the President had equally troublesome concerns. The big Irishman had a scowl on his face as he sat in the Oval Office listening to the Majority Leader.

"Dirk Simpson says Nat's only ahead of the Crane kid by five points," Ab said glumly, referring to the Democratic Party's top pollster of congressional races. "And he sees some further erosion ahead." The bushy eyebrows were knitted in a deep frown.

The President walked over to the corner of the room and reached for his new TearDrop putter. "What the hell is he *doing* down there?"

"He needs help, Mr. President," said Ab weakly, holding up the palms of his hands.

"What do you suggest?" Paul O'Banion was bending over and swinging his putter.

"I think you oughta' go down there. Maybe ride in an open limo through downtown with ole' Nat right there by your side and you both waving to the crowd. Be a great photo op for him…and *you*, Mr. President," he said in an optimistic tone.

The President raked a golf ball in front of his left toe. "Well, I'm not so sure about that. If he's sliding in the polls like Dirk says he is, I may be better off to help somebody else." He stroked a put. "Shit." The ball rolled to the left of the crystal ashtray that was on the carpet about ten feet away from where Paul O'Banion was standing.

"They love you in Atlanta, Mr. President. They really do." A line of yellow teeth appeared below the gray mustache.

"This God damn carpet needs to be replaced."

The Majority Leader's eyes suddenly lit up. "Hey, I've got a great idea! You could fly down next week and spend a morning in Atlanta, and then helicopter on over for a round at Augusta National. It's not that far away, you know."

The President stopped his putter in midstroke and looked over at Ab for several seconds without speaking. Then he frowned and shrugged his big shoulders. "I'm supposed to be in Montreal next week for an economic summit with the G Seven." He straightened up and scratched his head. "Augusta, huh…I guess I could send the Vice President to Montreal." And then his tanned face contorted into a grimace. "No, I just remembered. They've got the greens torn up down there. They're putting in a new type of bent grass."

"But Mr. President, Nat needs—"

Paul O'Banion held up a beefy hand. "You tell him to get his ass over to see Mel Cranford." The President was referring to the President of the Georgia Federation of Federal Employees. "Cranford was up here not too long ago. He told me that there are more than ten thousand federal employees in the Tenth Congressional District of Georgia and they all belong to his organization. If Nat can get Mel's help in turning those people out, he should be okay. But he doesn't have much time, so he better get his butt in gear."

"All right, Mr. President." Ab forced a smile and shook hands, and then turned to leave.

As he walked into the hallway and was being saluted by the Marine standing by the door, the Majority Leader heard the President cursing the carpet again.

Rhonda Sanchez had just finished checking into her suite at the Atlanta Ritz Carlton. She had used her new American Express card, the one with the name Karla Sanders shown in the lower left-hand corner. She'd thought of the name Karla when she'd seen it pinned on a stewardess' jacket. The surname Sanders was something that had come to her out of the blue. She thought it went well with her new first name.

Rhonda was proud of her new look. This Karla Sanders was a stunningly beautiful brunette, even with the short hair. She had decided to shorten the length so that it barely touched the top of her shoulders instead of draping a few inches over them as her blond hair had. There was also a new part that ran straight back on the left side of her head. These hair changes gave her a more business like look, she thought, in keeping with her new persona as a hard working reporter from the *New York Mirror.*

She had specifically requested that the suite include a fully stocked bar and that the bedroom have a king-size bed. The desk clerk had assured her that the suite would be more than satisfactory in every respect. And she was pleased to find that it was. It had a small sitting room furnished with antiques, including a large oak grained armoire with shelves for a flat screen digital television and a fax machine. She had brought along a laptop computer. She opened it and put it on top of a chest of drawers. She smiled, thinking it added a nice touch of journalistic authenticity.

Another piece of technology that she had brought from New York was a tiny camera no bigger than a thimble. A photographer friend had given it to her and showed her how it worked. She was amazed at how easy it was to spy on someone.

She gazed into space and started thinking about Doug Crane. The trace of a smile appeared on her beautiful face. Now that she was in Atlanta, she was ready to meet him.

She picked up the telephone and punched in a number.

A chirpy voice answered. "Doug Crane for Congress."

"This is Karla Sanders," she said smoothly, " I'm a reporter with the *New York Mirror* and I've been sent down here to Atlanta to do a story on Mr. Crane. It's going to be a full ten columns with a lead in on the front page." She paused for a second to let the impact of her words sink in, then said, "Can you tell me how I can reach him?"

She could hear the sound of pages flipping and then, "Well, I can give you his number at his law office. I'm sure his secretary there would be happy to help you set something up."

She smiled. "Thank you. What's their number?" Rhonda reached for a pen in her purse.

After she jotted it down, she hung up and called his law office.

"Mr. Crane's office."

She repeated her cover story and was told by his secretary that his calendar was fully booked for the next three days.

"How about after that?" she asked, holding her breath.

"Well, he could do it Friday evening at around 7 o'clock, if that's not too late for you."

"That'll be just fine." She smiled.

Nat Thompson was lying flat on his stomach with a cotton towel draped across his rear end. The body being massaged had a blubbery albino look. A black man was rubbing oil into the rolls of white flesh gathered near The Chairman's lower back.

A phone rang. The masseuse, whose white T-shirt had black lettering, CAPITOL CLUB, across the front, reached over and picked it up. "It's for you, Mr. Chairman."

"Keep goin' Fred," said Nat without raising his head.

He took the receiver and held it up to his ear and heard the Majority Leader's loud voice.

"Nat, I hope I'm not catching you at a bad time, but I just got back from a little visit with the President—"

"As a matter of fact, you are. What's on your mind, Ab?"

"Well, O'Banion thinks maybe you oughta go over and see Mel Cranford to see if he can get his people—"

The Chairman interrupted the Majority Speaker with an acid reply, "Does he think I'm an absolute moron. Mel Cranford was on the stage with me last night, for Christ's sake. I've been giving him a blow job for the last three days, and the President wants me to see Mel Cranford."

"Well, he'll be glad to know—"

"Is that about it?" Nat said impatiently.

"Well, Dirk Simpson says things have gotten pretty tight down there, and—"

"Fuck Dirk Simpson. He doesn't know what the hell he's talkin' about."

"Nat, I think you're gonna have to go for a debate, I really do. You gotta do something to change the momentum."

"Screw you, Ab."

Chapter 25

Sam Brinkman felt out of place. The clothes he was wearing didn't seem to fit in with what the other people had on. He'd worn an olive green and orange plaid sports jacket with a wide emerald green tie dotted with white smiling faces. His jeans showed a crease from above his knees to the tops of his soft leather boots that had been shined the day before. The other men at the ultra exclusive Magnolia Country Club were wearing ties in muted shades with little printed patterns or ones in brighter colors with angular stripes. There were charcoal pinstripe suits, navy blazers, tweed sport jackets, and tastefully matching wool slacks, all of which were the type of conservatively stylish attire found in a Brooks Brothers catalogue.

The club members stared at the big man with the orange hair and the loud clothes like he was a man from Mars.

Sam pretended not to notice the way they were looking down their noses at him. He found a place near the swimming pool where he could wait by himself until Doug arrived. There were four stools in front of the little bar located just inside the entrance to the Men's Grill. The Grill was where Doug had told him they were going to meet the Chairman of the Cobb County Republican Party. Doug had said he was a Magnolia member.

Sam Brinkman, being a man who had never belonged to a country club and had no interest in joining one, was unaware that the Magnolia Country Club had been forced to move to its present site seven years earlier.

The trouble had started when Magnolia's Board of Directors decided to file a lawsuit against the Fulton County Tax Assessor's Office. At that time, and for almost a hundred years before then, Magnolia's beautiful Tarra-like clubhouse and its two hundred and fifteen acres of oak and pine shaded rolling terrain were situated close to downtown Atlanta. Many of its members lived in the mansions that surrounded the beautiful golf course.

But as grand as the old clubhouse had been for so many years, by the beginning of the twenty first century the Board of Directors realized that it needed to be completely renovated. So they had persuaded the membership to spend a little over two million dollars to make the necessary repairs and improvements. The renovation work had started on schedule and after two years the work had been completed and the Magnolia Country Club was shining like an exquisite jewel. That's when the tax problem had started.

A Fulton County tax assessor had been driving home from work one afternoon and had happened to look down the manicured esplanade. There at the end, at the top of a gentle rise was the magnificent new clubhouse, fronted by a towering row of white Corinthian columns, tall arched windows, and a circular brick driveway bordered with a profusion of colorful flowers.

To the tax assessor's eyes that marvelous clubhouse had seemed so much larger and grander than it had ever been before. He had told himself that when he got back to the office he was going to look at the current property value shown on his books for this Taj Mahal at the end of the esplanade.

And when he did, he had been surprised to find that the Magnolia clubhouse was being valued at only a little over a million dollars. He had known that it was worth a lot more than that. So when the next property tax bill had been mailed a few months later, it showed a revised valuation of three million dollars. The club's property tax bill had tripled.

Magnolia's Board had been furious when they received the notice of their tax increase. This had never happened before. At an emergency meeting of the Board they had decided to file a lawsuit against the county, demanding a reduction of the assessment.

At about this time, the great, great grandson of a slave buried on a Georgia cotton plantation was running for Commissioner of Fulton County. His name was Robert Lincoln and he was a bright young man, a Howard graduate with a law degree from the University of Georgia. He had also served as a Dekalb County criminal prosecutor. Robert Lincoln was an athletic looking young man with an especially fine tuned political antenna.

This ambitious candidate, who had been eager to find an issue that would attract the public's interest, had read about the Magnolia Country Club's lawsuit against Fulton County. He started wondering about the current fair market value of the club's beautiful golf course. And although Robert Lincoln had never been invited anywhere near the Magnolia Country Club, he knew that the club owned about two hundred acres near downtown that had to be worth many millions of dollars.

He had started checking the tax rolls and what he found he couldn't believe. Those two hundred and fifteen acres of prime real estate for years had been valued at a puny four million dollars. Based upon his own well-informed knowledge of current real estate values, Robert Lincoln had known that the land was worth at least two hundred million dollars.

And so Robert Lincoln had held a press conference. He had spoken passionately about the unfairness to those less privileged, those hard working citizens who could only dream of playing golf at a fancy place like the Magnolia Country Club. These more humble ordinary folks, through their own burdensome property tax payments, had been subsidizing a small number of people who were characterized by the candidate at an appearance at the Dexter Avenue Baptist Church as "a bunch of rich, Chardonnay sippin', coupon clippin', good for nothin' white boys."

The black and brown faces that had squeezed into the church made famous by Martin Luther King, Jr. had cheered wildly for their new leader, the man who would restore a sense of tax equity among all of Atlanta's citizens, and a few weeks later, Robert Lincoln had won the County Commissioner's race by a landslide.

And when the next property tax bill had been delivered to the Magnolia Country Club, it showed a total assessed value of a hundred and seventy million dollars. The President of the Board of Directors, upon learning of the news, had suffered a heart attack. Though he had later recovered to the point where he had been able to preside at their next regularly scheduled meeting, a still shaken Board of Directors realized that a day of reckoning was upon them.

And so, a month later, they had accepted an offer from a real estate developer to buy the country club's property for a hundred and fifty million dollars. It was soon thereafter that the Search Committee had located two hundred and fifty acres 45 miles northwest of the club's original location and a new Magnolia Country Club was born.

Now a young man wearing a starched white jacket was polishing a glass behind the bar. A portable television was up on a shelf beside a row of whiskey bottles. It was tuned to an Atlanta station that was broadcasting the news.

Sam glanced at his watch again.

The bartender put down the glass and said. "Can I get you somethin', sir?"

"You got a glass of ice water?"

He gave him one and said, "Hey, you're Sam Brinkman, aren't you?"

Sam nodded. "That's me."

"I've seen you on television lots of times."

"Well, if you ever need any furniture, we've got it…and at the right price." Sam was about to ask the bartender what kind of bed he slept on when he noticed something on the television screen. Big letters had appeared: SPECIAL REPORT, and then the news anchor said, "This news is just in. There's been a report that Virgil Wilson, the man who previously accused Atlanta's furniture king, Sam Brinkman, of cheating on his income taxes—which charges were later dismissed—has been found dead on the floor of his prison cell."

"Turn that up!" yelled Sam, his bulging eyes riveted on the screen.

"Investigators have said that Mr. Wilson's body was found in his cell around 2 o'clock last night hanging from a cord running from his neck to an overhead pipe. Big Two News will keep you fully informed of breaking developments on this story as soon as we have them. In other news…"

At that very moment, Doug Crane walked in the door. He looked over and saw the blank stare on his friend's white face. "What's the matter? You look like you've just seen a ghost."

"Virgil Wilson's dead," Sam mumbled still staring at the screen.

She wondered what she should wear. Rhonda Sanchez reached in her closet and pulled out a black velvet top with sequined sleeves and a plunging neckline. She knew that when she wore it it showed about an inch of her deep cleavage. She shook her head, thinking, I'll save that for later.

Rhonda was looking forward to finally meeting Doug Crane. She had waited for three days to see him and now the time had almost arrived. It was a little after 6:30.

She slipped into a black satin skirt, cut an inch above her knees. She picked out a light gray top with a black satin collar and gold buttons up the front. She put on a pair of low heeled patent leather pumps and walked over in front of the full-length mirror.

I look too fucking good to be a newspaper reporter, she thought, stroking her shiny black hair. The eyeliner and claret colored lipstick were perfect. She knew that her dark eyes would cast a hypnotic spell and that her full lips couldn't be resisted. If he's human he's going to want to kiss me, she told herself.

And then she tilted her head to one side. A flicker of doubt crept into her mind. *I want him to see how beautiful I am*, she thought, *but the dress? Is it still too much? Do I really look like a newspaper reporter?*

She shrugged her shoulders. *What the hell, it'll be nighttime. Maybe he'll think I've got a date afterwards.* A thought struck her and she smiled, thinking, better yet, maybe *he'll* be my date afterwards.

A half-hour later she was sitting in the reception room of Doug Crane's law office.

"He'll see you now, Miss Sanders." His secretary was motioning to her.

Her heart was beating fast.

They walked down a hall past open doors until they arrived at a large corner office. There were rows of law books in shelves behind a cluttered desk. He was talking to someone on the telephone. He looked over his shoulder and swiveled his chair toward her and motioned her to take a seat. Then he mouthed, *I'll be right with you.*

She watched him moving his broad hand through his longish sand colored hair. His skin was tanned. She could tell from the slightly dark shadows around his strong jaw that he hadn't shaved since early in the morning, but he still had a fresh, natural look. His shoulders were broad and powerful, even though hidden by his white, long-sleeved, button down shirt. Her eyes traced the curve of his right biceps and triceps pushing against the upper part of his shirtsleeve.

He finally stopped talking, stood up, and held out his hand. "I'm Doug Crane."

"I'm…Karla Sanders. Thank you for taking time out of your busy schedule to meet with me." She flashed him a smile she knew was dazzling.

He motioned for her to sit down in an armchair in front of his desk. As she did she made sure to hike her satin skirt a couple of inches above her knees.

He was leaning back in his chair with his hands behind his head. "Why does the *New York Mirror* want to talk to a country boy like me."

She liked the way he smiled and his clear blue eyes were really something special, she thought. "Because you're running for Congress."

"There are lots of people running for Congress all over the country."

"Your being too modest, Mr....do you mind if I call you Doug?"

"Not at all."

She crossed her legs and saw him glance down at them. "Doug, why don't you tell me about yourself."

"Miss Sanders—"

She held up her palm and smiled again. "If your Doug, I'm Karla, okay."

He chuckled and fingered the knot of his tie. "All right, Karla. Asking a politician to talk about himself is like asking a used car dealer to tell you about a car. I'm not sure you want to hear it all."

"Try me, Doug," she said coolly flashing him another sparkling smile.

"Well, I grew up about two hundred miles south of here in a little country town called Albany. It's on the banks of the Flint River. Cotton and peanut fields mostly, although there's a little tobacco there too. My Dad's still down there on our farm. He's almost eighty...say shouldn't you be taking notes."

She didn't blink. "I've got a terrific memory. That's the reason they hired me."

"Okay. Where was I?"

"You were talking about your dad."

"Right, well, I graduated from a little school called Albany Academy and then went to the University of Georgia and then..."

She listened to him for about another thirty seconds and then she started wondering what he looked like in the shower. She crossed her long legs again, hoping he would look at them again. But he didn't. He only kept talking.

"You can skip that part," she said, waving her hand and not really having listened to anything he'd been saying. "What our readers are gonna be interested in is more about the man himself. What makes Doug Crane tick? Tell me, what really turns you on?"

She saw the look in his eye. That got him, she thought, smiling and looking straight into his blue eyes. She could see he was adjusting the knot of his tie again. Yes, she thought, he's definitely starting to feel it.

But just as she thought he was warming up to her, he looked off in space and said, "Politics is probably the one thing that really gets my blood going. I feel like I really *can* make a difference about what's going on in this country."

She listened to him blathering on for another minute or so and thought, Is this guy for real?

And then she saw him glance at his wristwatch.

"Gee, I hate to say it Karla, but I've got to be somewhere in ten minutes." He was standing up and holding out his arm to shake her hand.

She reached out her hand and held his for several seconds before letting go. They stood there looking at each other until she finally spoke. "I need seven more columns."

"Well, I'm afraid I've probably bored you long enough for now."

She said, "I'm down here on an expense account. The *Mirror* is very generous, you know. I'd like to buy you a drink at the Ritz Carlton."

He reached over for his jacket. "Thanks, but I've gotta run. Call my secretary in the morning. Maybe we can talk a little more later." He was walking briskly out the door.

She stood there and watched as he walked away, thinking, This has never ever happened to me before.

Chapter 26

Nat Thompson saw the stunning looking brunette walk into the bar at the Ritz Carlton. She was simply the most beautiful woman he had ever seen. And she was alone.

He had been there having a drink with Mel Cranford. The hook nosed man with the gray toupee who was the President of the Georgia Federation of Federal Employees had had one martini and then had left. He had walked right by her as she was walking in.

Nat wondered who she was.

He had never taken much interest in women, except for those rare occasions when he had paid a thousand dollars for a night with someone very special. But he couldn't remember the last time that had happened. He hadn't had the time.

He thought about all the other congressmen he knew that used women whenever they wanted them. It was so easy. The politicians on Capitol Hill made a living by seducing people. The power they had was like an aphrodisiac. But Nat didn't want to spend his time fooling around with women. He was too busy working. But this young woman's face and figure had aroused a feeling in Nat Thompson that he hadn't felt for a long time.

He looked at her again and saw that she was still sitting by herself. He decided to go over and see if he could buy her a drink.

She was stirring her drink absentmindedly when he came up to her.

"Can I buy you a drink?"

"I've already got one," she replied without looking up.

"Well, let me buy you another." He stuck out a big hand. "I'm Congressman Nat Thompson."

She looked up, her dark liquid eyes suddenly alive. "Oh…you're the one who's running against Doug Crane."

His slit lips smiled and he sat down.

She shifted in her seat, crossing her long legs.

He leaned forward and said, "You live here in Atlanta?" He glanced at her chest.

"No, I'm from New York."

"New York, well. You're a long way from home, Miss…"

"Sanders…Karla Sanders."

He held up his empty glass and caught the eye of a waiter and then looked back at her. "And what is it you do in New York, Karla?"

"I'm a reporter for the *New York Mirror.*"

"Is that a fact." He glanced down at her leg that was exposed from just above her knee. He could feel his heart beating. "They send you down hea' to do a story?"

She nodded. "I'm doing a story on Doug Crane."

"Well, we've got a lot better things down hea' that you can write about." He looked at her eyes, those glistening and darkly mysterious gems. He could smell her perfume and he leaned a little closer to her. "Why, you could do a story on Atlanta. This is the most excitin' place in the world," he said, trying to impress her with his worldliness.

She looked at him blankly while stirring her drink.

The Chairman's beady eyes were alive with excitement now. "You can do anythin' hea'." He swept an arm through the air, trying desperately to create the impression that he'd already experienced everything life had to offer.

"What do you know about Doug Crane?" she said.

He shrugged his shoulders. "Oh, I think he's a nice enough young man. But he has no experience. And as well intentioned as he may be, he doesn't know a damn thing about how to really help people."

The piano player started playing a Gershwin tune.

He promptly changed the subject. "Are you staying hea' at the hotel?" he asked nervously.

She nodded, looking in the direction of the piano player. They sat there without speaking for a long time and then she looked over and said. "Does he have any girlfriends?"

"Who?"

"Doug Crane."

He frowned and said. "Hell, I don't know. Wouldn't be all that surprisin' if he did." He changed the subject again. "I'm stayin' hea', too. Always do when I have a late meeting downtown. I've got a suite up on the fourteenth floor." He leaned closer to her. "You ought to see the view. " He waved his hand in the air and said, "The whole city right there in front of you, all lit up like a Christmas tree."

She was still looking in the direction of the piano player. He watched her finger touch a gold loop earring under her soft black hair. He moved his leg a little closer toward hers and felt contact at his knee. She shifted her hips away from him. She was moving her head slightly from side to side as she listened to the medley from *Porgy and Bess*.

He couldn't help looking at the top of her black velvet dress. It was moving ever so slightly against the contours of her magnificent chest.

He suddenly felt a sharp pain in his chest. He grimaced and reached in his coat pocket for his bottle of pills.

She turned and said. "Are you all right?"

"I'm fine," he stammered.

"You don't look fine."

He swallowed the pills and desperately tried to regain his composure.

She sighed and reached for her purse.

He felt panic and despair. She was standing up to leave.

"It was nice to meet you, Congressman Thompson." She was holding out her hand.

"Wait, I haven't bought you that other drink."

She gave him a last dazzling smile and started walking away.

She closed the door and walked through the sitting room into the bedroom.

While she was undressing, she thought about how repulsive Nat Thompson was, an ugly slug of a man in the white suit. She rolled her eyes thinking, Did he really believe he had a chance in the world of sleeping with someone like me? I wouldn't let that ugly pig lick the sole of my shoe.

There had been other men like him who had thought they were too important and too powerful for her to resist—men with villas in Europe, men who owned professional sports teams, and even a United States Senator. It was true that she had slept with some of them. But only if she found them interesting *and* physically desirable. The Georgia congressman didn't come close to meeting either standard. Rhonda Sanchez could have any man in the world she wanted.

And then she thought about Doug Crane. He was different. He had an innocence and boyish exuberance that made the other men she'd been close to seem old and jaded.

She lay down on the king-sized bed and looked up at the blades of the ceiling fan slowly turning in circles.

She wondered what she should do next.

He was nice…maybe too nice. She almost felt sorry for him, knowing that what she was going to do would probably destroy his reputation forever. But it was the only way she could think of to punish his father-in-law for what he did to her father. She glared up at the ceiling as she thought of Boyd Smithers. She sighed and said to herself, It's too bad that the only way to pay him back for what he did is to destroy his son-in-law. She visualized Doug Crane's face again and thought, He has the bluest eyes I've ever seen.

She glanced up at the corner of the ceiling and looked at the dark spot. The camera was still there. She closed her eyes and tried to think of a way to get Doug Crane into her bedroom.

Four floors above Rhonda Sanchez's room, Nat Thompson was sprawled out on his own king-sized bed. His white belly was hanging over his Jockey underwear. On the bedside table was a half-empty bottle of Wild Turkey.

Through the fog of the booze, he was gazing up at the ceiling thinking about Karla Sanders.

I almost had her, he thought. She was beginning to loosen up, I could sense it. And then my fuckin' heart had to turn on me again. If only she'd waited a minute longer, everything would have been okay.

He could see it all so clearly. *She's having that second or third drink, feeling a little tipsy, and putting her arm around my neck and laughing at one of my dirty jokes. Now she's whispering something very sexy in my ear. Now she's sticking her tongue inside my ear. And now she's giving me a look that says, I want you to take me up to your room.*

He could see her laying there beside him now. Her lacy black brassiere straining to contain those massive tits. God, he whispered, reaching for the glass of bourbon again.

He lay back down and felt his heart racing. He took a deep breath and told himself that if he didn't stop thinking about her he was going to give himself a heart attack.

He got up and went into the bathroom and sat down on the commode. He started thinking about what Ab Connell had said to him. He wondered if he should debate the son of a bitch Crane. He knew he had to do something, but he knew damn well that debating an articulate good looking guy who was half his age was very dangerous. If he wasn't careful the whole thing could blow up in his face. But he also realized things were slipping away. He knew he had to do something to turn things around.

He flushed the toilet and walked over in front of the mirror. He stood there unsteadily for a few seconds, then said out loud, "Mr. Chairman, you look like shit."

Priscilla was laying in bed reading when Doug walked in the door.

He came over to her and kissed her lightly on the lips.

"Have you had anything to eat?" she asked. He nodded and walked over to a chair and sat down. As he was taking off his shoes, he looked up at her and said, "Did you hear about Virgil Wilson?"

"No." She put down her book.

"He's dead."

"What? What happened?"

"They found him hanging from a pipe in his cell. I heard about it while I was out at the Magnolia Country Club. Sam was with me. I also got a call from Charles Danberry," he said, walking over to his closet.

"What did he say?"

"Charles said there was no sign of foul play. The investigators are saying he committed suicide."

"What do you think?"

"I don't know," he said, running a hand through his sandy hair. "Charles said he was going to try and get a copy of the autopsy report."

She pulled up the shoulder strap of her silk nightgown. "Sam must've been stunned."

"He was," said Doug as he finished undressing. "I'm gonna take a shower."

He walked into the bathroom and closed the door. He turned on the hot water as high as it would go and got in. The steam and the heat were hitting him on his chest and he was beginning to relax. But then he suddenly thought about the water bill. "Shit," he whispered remembering he hadn't paid any bills in the last two weeks. He finished showering and dried off.

She was reading her book when he walked back in the bedroom.

"Have you been paying the bills? Priss."

She nodded, and he felt a sense of relief.

He pulled the covers up and stared at the ceiling for several seconds, then turned and put his arm around her waist.

"Do you feel like reading?" he asked.

"I'm almost through with this chapter. I'll turn the light out in just a second."

He turned over and put the pillow over his head. As he lay there with his eyes closed, he started thinking about the newspaper reporter from the *New York Mirror*.

Chapter 27

"Ladies and gentlemen, on behalf of the Women's League of Voters, I would like to thank you all for coming here tonight." Al Wilder was attired in a shiny royal blue double-breasted suit. His *faux* black hair was glistening in the spotlight.

The Atlanta History Center Auditorium, located in the wooded environs of Buckhead, was packed to capacity. There was a forest of camera-mounted tripods and a horde of kneeling photographers in the space between the front row of seats and the stage, the floor of which was about four feet above them. There on the stage the three men were standing and facing the audience, each behind a wooden podium that was spaced about six feet away from the other.

Al Wilder was standing in the center of the stage and to his the left was The Chairman, wearing his customary all white, light wool suit with a silk maroon handkerchief showing over the top of his breast pocket. The silver hair was combed straight back, and the tinted talc makeup covered his pale skin so that he looked unusually robust.

On the right side of the moderator was Doug Crane who was wearing a dark pinstriped suit and a white buttoned down shirt with a navy blue tie with angular white stripes. His soft light brown hair was combed to the side and wasn't plastered against his skull like Nat Thompson's was. With his evenly set blue eyes, the strong jaw line, and athletic build, Doug looked more like a men's clothing model or a movie star or a professional quarterback than he did a lawyer or a politician.

Al Wilder was speaking again. "First let me explain the rules for tonight's debate. Each speaker will be allowed a two minute opening statement, after which I will ask the first speaker a question, and after his answer, the second speaker will be allowed to offer a one minute rebuttal."

Nat Thompson was wiping his forehead with a white handkerchief. He had taken the precaution of swallowing two of his heart medicine pills right before coming out on stage. He took a sip of water and tried to concentrate on what the moderator was saying.

"After which I will read a question from the audience."

Doug glanced toward the audience. Priscilla was sitting in the front row next to her parents. He caught a glimpse of her through the bright lights and the trace of a smile flickered on his face. He looked back over at the moderator who was still explaining the rules of the debate.

"There will then be an opportunity for each speaker to give a two minute closing statement."

Al Wilder paused to catch his breath, then turned toward Nat. "Congressman Thompson has won the toss of the coin and has decided to make his opening statement first." He nodded in Nat's direction. "Congressman."

"Thank you Al, and thank you, the members of the Women's League of Voters for sponsorin' this event tonight." He swept his hand in the air and stood up on his tiptoes.

"And I also want to thank all of you in the audience, whether hea' or watching at home, for takin' the time to listen to this debate and consider the differences between my opponent and me on the impo'tant issues facin' us in this election."

He glanced down at his notes and then continued. "It has been my great honor and good fortune to represent the people of the Tenth Congressional District of the State of Georgia for more than thirty years. And durin' that time…"

It was impossible to tell from the audience whether Doug was listening to what he was saying. Doug's head was bowed; he looked like he might be reading his own statement. In fact, he was. He'd rehearsed it with Priss until almost midnight after she had suggested a few changes. He knew how impo'tant his opening statement was going to be. A few moments later his mind shifted to what Nat was saying. "…and because of my service as Chairman of the House Appropriations Committee, one of the most powerful and impo'tant assignments any Congressman can ever hope to have, and an accomplishment I owe to the blessin's of the good Lord, Nat Thompson has been able to act as your servant in deliverin' the things you need. As we march into the next decade…"

Doug glanced at his watch. Nat's time should almost be over, he thought. He took a deep breath and listened to the old windbag mouthing his self-serving platitudes."…the uncertainties facin' us require the steady hand of a man with experience, wisdom, and yes, leadership. And all of these qualities, I humbly submit to you my friends, are those I have acquired during the last thirty years of my service to—"

Al Wilder held up his hand. "Thank you very much Congressman Thompson," he said smiling and touching his black horn rimed glasses.

He turned toward Doug. "Mr. Crane. May we have your opening statement, please?"

Doug cleared his throat and looked toward the camera with the little red light on top.

"Thank you very much, Al, and thank you, the members of the Women's League of Voters for allowing me to be here tonight to discuss the issues of this campaign. The reason I'm running for Congress is that I want to change the way our government works. I want to dramatically reform the monolithic federal bureaucracy we now have so that it gives us more freedom to manage our own lives and lets us keep more of our hard earned money. To achieve that goal I know we're all going to have to change the way we all think about what government should do for us and what we should do for ourselves." His voice sounded calm, deliberate, and sincere.

"I know that may sound like a pretty ambitious objective for someone like me who's never been a politician and who doesn't have the experience in Washington that my opponent has. And maybe, as my opponent has said on so many occasions, I am naive about the way the Washington establishment does business." He put his right hand on the side of the podium and his eyes seemed to take on a more intense look. "But Doug Crane doesn't *want* to do business as usual." His voice was a few decibels louder. "Doug Crane won't play the game of trading favors by dishing out government contracts, special tax breaks, and all sorts of other government goodies just so he can be reelected. No, Doug Cranc is going to go to Washington to change things, and…"

To those in the audience who were watching Nat Thompson, he appeared to be calmly taking notes. His head was bowed and he was writing something on the little writing surface behind the podium. In fact, he was drawing a little stick figure of a man with a sword stuck through its heart. "…one of the first things I'm going to do after I'm elected is to introduce a bill for term limits." He lowered his voice, and then continued. "And I pledge to you tonight, that if you elect me, I will not serve more than four years. Two terms is enough for any congressman."

There was a burst of applause from one side of the audience.

"But while I am there, I'm going to fight to reduce government spending, reduce taxes and get rid of our zillion page tax code that nobody can understand, not even those three hundred dollar an hour tax lawyers. And I'm also—"

Al Wilder was holding up his hand again. "Thank you Mr. Crane. Your time's up."

"Now it's time for me to ask you both some questions. I'll start with a question for Congressman Thompson." The moderator turned and said. "What do you believe is the most important thing you can do for the people of the Tenth District?"

The Chairman's snake like eyes lit up and a little smile formed on his slit lips. "Well, I think the most important thing I can do is to keep right on doin' what I've been doin', using my position as Chairman of the House Appropriation's Committee to make sure that the needs of the good people of the Tenth District are taken care of. Durin' the time I've been privileged to serve in Congress, I'm proud to say that I've literally brought thousands and thousands of jobs to the folks who live in my district. So many in fact that The Tenth District now has the lowest unemployment rate in the entire state of Georgia. We've got more air bases, munitions plants, federal agency offices, primary and secondary public schools, post offices, and libraries than any other district in the state. And I think it's safe to say that if Nat Thompson hadn't been your Congressman, you wouldn't have all those things."

There was a loud burst of applause from one side of the audience.

Al Wilder said, "Thank you, Congressman Thompson. Mr. Crane, you have thirty seconds to respond."

"What Congressman Thompson failed to mention was that most of those jobs he brags about are dead end government jobs. And unlike jobs in the private sector, they have to be paid for out of the taxpayer's pocket. But, ladies and gentlemen, we don't have to rely on the federal government to create employment opportunities for us. We can create an environment where a small business owner can prosper and where jobs can be created without placing a burden on the taxpayer. And the reason unemployment is low is because of the fact that so many people are working for the government. Well, unemployment may be low, but our taxes are going through the roof."

There were sounds of cheering and loud clapping from Doug's supporters.

"All right," said the moderator, "let's move on to a two part question for you, Mr. Crane. What is it in your experience that you think gives you the ability to serve in Congress, and what's your response to those who say they won't vote for you because they don't want to risk losing someone with as much influence as Nat Thompson has, given the fact that he's the current Chairman of the House Appropriations Committee?"

Doug blinked and directed his blue eyes at the camera with the red light. "Well, let me answer the first part of your question by giving you a little information about my background. I grew up working in the cotton fields of my father's small farm in South Georgia. My father was a cotton farmer. We never had much money, but I was lucky enough to get a baseball scholarship to the University of Georgia. After graduating second in my senior class, I went to Duke Law School where I was Editor of the *Law Review*. After I got my law degree, I came home and went to work in the Albany County District Attorney's office. I later served for six years as District Attorney and then my wife Priscilla and I moved here to Atlanta. I'm now a partner with the firm of Baldwin and Bell.

"I'm proud to say I've come a long way from the cotton fields of South Georgia to where I'm standing tonight. But I'm really not much different than thousands of other people here in Atlanta who've worked hard to make something of themselves. Most of you watching tonight have as much intelligence and common sense as I do, and we all know there is something fundamentally wrong with our country. With all due respect to my opponent, I don't think he does, even though he *is* the head of a powerful committee in Washington. And that's why I want to replace him."

There was loud applause and shouting from the Crane side of the audience.

Al Wilder held up his hand again. "The next question if for Congressman Thompson." He looked down again and started reading. "What do you believe is the most important challenge facing the people of the Tenth District?"

"Al, there are do many challenges we face today: hunger, illiteracy, health care—I could go on and on." Nat put his big hands on the podium and raised up on his tiptoes again. "As I stand here listenin' to Mr. Crane running down the good things the government has done and talking about *the private sector," his* rat face took on a look as if he'd just bit into a lemon, "I realize how totally out of touch he is. When he talks about business, what he's really talkin' about are all those big corporations his rich friends control, and what he really wants is for all of us who don't belong to those fancy country clubs that Mr. Crane and his friends belong to, to just roll over and let them do whatever they want. Well, Mr. Crane, let me ask you this: If we don't need the government to help us anymore, whose gonna help that man who's been laid off from his job or that mother at home with her three or four screaming children that don't have enough to eat? And what about the old folks who need health care but can't afford it? Who's gonna look after them?"

There was another burst of applause and shouts of "You tell'em Nat!"

Al Wilder gestured toward Doug indicating it was time for his rebuttal.

Doug looked over at Nat and said, "That stuff's the same old red herring we've heard bleeding heart liberals like you use so many times before. And as they say where I come from, that dog just won't hunt.

"The truth is all your weeping and wailing about how people can't help themselves is nothing but a deception that liberal politicians use to reinforce the chains of government dependency. And as to that father, mother, old person, or anybody else who in fact can't help themselves because of a *real* disability, I've always supported programs specifically designed to help people who are not able to help themselves. There should be a safety net for them. But we shouldn't be redistributing almost three trillion dollars a year of taxpayer money—which is what we're doing now—to provide benefits to people who can work. What was originally intended to be a social safety net for the truly needy has metastasized into a socialistic monster. Politicians like my opponent have used these government handouts to buy votes. But there's no reason why hard working people should have to subsidize people who can support themselves.

"And as far as your demagogic attack on corporations is concerned, when I get to Congress I'm going to fight to end *all* welfare, including corporate welfare. There' s no reason why a corporation should have to be supported by the government in order to make a profit."

Even some of the Thompson people joined in the ripple of applause that came from the audience.

All this time Nat's face was bowed and expressionless. He was doodling with is pencil again behind the podium. Big drops of blood were pouring out of his stick figure's heart.

The questioning and rebuttals continued back and forth for another fifteen minutes until it was finally time for the closing statements.

"Mr.Crane, since you went last on the opening statements, you will be first in giving your closing statement." The moderator nodded in Doug's direction.

The young lawyer smiled and took a deep breath as though he were trying to compose himself. He looked directly into the camera and said, "Thank you again for giving me this opportunity to discuss the important issues of this campaign. My pledge to the voters of the Tenth District is this: If you elect me to serve as your Congressman, I pledge to you that I will go to Washington and do my best to reduce the size of government, to lower your taxes, and to restore a sense of personal freedom and self-responsibility.

"My opponent has told you that since the unemployment rate is low we should all be satisfied with the way things are. But if you think things are fine, take a look around and see what kind of place we live in. The next time you drive down a freeway, look up at the billboards and see what our local culture has become: ads for strip joints, gay bars, pawn shops, bail bond companies, abortion clinics, and there's even one advertising marriages to Russian women. I ask you: Do we want really want to raise our children in this kind of environment."

The auditorium was almost completely silent now.

"And my friends, it's not just Atlanta, it's all over this country. People have allowed their moral standards to decay to the point where today almost any kind of behavior is acceptable. And why is that? It's because of this narcotic-like dependency we have on the federal government to do things we should be doing for ourselves. And just like a dangerously addictive drug, it's destroying the American spirit. We're losing our sense of self-reliance. All we want are our 'rights' and our entitlements. The Nat Thompson's of the world feed upon this type of mentality. They tell us we're all victims of circumstances beyond our control and the government is the only thing that can protect us. So they drag us into the quagmire of dependency. And the sorry state of our modern culture is the result."

His blue eyes were on fire now. "It's time for us to wake up! It's time for us to regain our sense of self-esteem and self-responsibility and be proud that God gave us the ability to fend for ourselves. We can be what our forefather's have been in the past—strong, resourceful, independent, God loving, God fearing Americans." He could feel his heart pounding now. "We can do it, I know we can."

He paused and took a deep breath, knowing he had reached the end. "With your help on November third, I'm going to win this election and work to restore the values of freedom, self-reliance, and personal responsibility for the people of the Tenth District. Thank you very much."

The two hundred or so Crane supporters erupted into a tumult of shouts and wild applause. It took almost two minutes for them to calm down.

Nat was glaring down at his mutilated stick figure. He coughed and then put his big hands on each side of the podium and waited for the noise to subside. A couple of minutes later he was ready to start.

"Thank you, Al. I also want to thank the Women's League of Voters for puttin' on this debate. One of the most precious rights we have is the right to vote. I urge all of you who are watchin' this tonight— whether or not you decide to vote for Nat Thompson—to please go to the polls on November third and exercise your right as a citizen to vote for the man of your choice. Thousands of America's brave sons and daughters have shed their blood for your right to do so."

He took another sip of water and then looked over at Doug.

"My opponent, Doug Crane, is a nice young man. And, my friends, I don't doubt for a second the sincerity of some of the things he's talked about tonight. But Mr. Crane, as well meaning as he might be, has never spent one day, or even one minute, drafting a piece of legislation or arguing on the floor of a state legislature, much less the hallowed well of the United States House of Representatives. Nor has young Doug Crane here ever spent a late night in the House Appropriations meeting room or in the Chairman's chair holding a gavel and fightin' with all his might and soul for the things the good people of the Tenth District need and deserve."

His voice had gotten shriller and his face redder as he spoke. He could feel the heat of all the stage lights. He took out his handkerchief and wiped the side of his glistening face.

"So when you walk into that votin' booth on November third, you think about which one of us really cares the most about you and your family, and which one of us has a proven record of leadership and experience to best serve the needs of you and your family. When you walk into that votin' booth think about which one of us is most like you, which one of us is a person that you'd feel comfortable callin' or writin' or just talkin' with when we meet on the street about some problem you've got that needs attention from someone in Washington.

"If you do all that, my friends, the choice will be clear. Nat Thompson is, and always has been, a servant of the people. I urge you to allow me to continue to be your servant when you go to the polls next November. Thank you and may God bless you."

There was a roar of applause and shouts of approval from the three hundred or so Thompson supporters.

The two candidates walked across the stage toward each other and shook hands amidst an explosion of flashing lights, shouts from reporters, and cheers from people in the audience. Both men were smiling and hoping they had won, but each man had a distinct feeling of uncertainty that he had.

Chapter 28

La Tooth's was one of the Doug and Priscilla's favorite restaurants in Atlanta. It was famous for its inch and a half thick, aged Omaha steaks. The menu was a la carte and very expensive, but tonight was a night to celebrate.

Everybody was with Doug except his campaign manager. Paul's little girl had just had her tonsils out and he had gone home right after the debate.

La Tooth's didn't take reservations and they were all standing just inside the door, at the end of a line end of people trying to get their names on the waiting list.

"Doug Crane!" A tall man with bushy blonde hair came bounding up to him out of nowhere. "Marvelous performance, young man, marvelous performance!"

Doug held out his hand and the stranger began pumping it up and down like the handle of a water well.

"I'm Henri Mathewson. This is my place and I have a table for your party. Right this way."

"No, no," said the young lawyer, frowning. "We can wait our turn." He looked around at the four other people in his group. "That is, if it's all right with you all."

Priss and her parents and Sam all nodded in unison.

The bushy haired man shrugged his shoulders and walked away like a rejected suitor.

A freckle-faced little girl with a pony was holding up a piece of paper. "Can I have your autograph?"

"Sure," said Doug.

"I'm Art Downing, Angela's father." A professorial looking man in a herringbone jacket and bow tie held out his hand. "You did a wonderful job tonight."

"Thank you very much." Doug reached for his pen, then looked at Angela. "Where do you go to school?"

"Ronald Reagan Junior High. I'm in the eighth grade." She was chewing a big wad of gum.

"I've heard they're teaching Japanese at your school. Is that true?

"I took it last year. It was pretty hard." The little girl was twisting her hips as she spoke.

"I'll bet it was. But you never know. One of these days you might be making a trip to Tokyo." Doug handed her the autographed paper. She gave Doug a wide grin that accentuated the dimples in her cheeks.

"Thanks," she said. Her father was beaming.

"Thanks for asking." Doug patted the little girl on the shoulder. She was still smiling and smacking her gum.

Fifteen minutes and about thirty autographs later, the party of five had made it to their table.

They were seated near a fireplace with burning logs under arched gray stones. On the opposite side of the fireplace from their table was a group of four musicians in black tuxedos gathered around an ebony grand piano. They were playing (the other three, a trumpet, clarinet, and bass violin) selections from Broadway musicals. The melodies mixed with the tinkling of glasses and periodic bursts of laughter from around the cozy room.

"May I offer you the wine list, sir?" A tall waiter wearing a dark suit, thin black tie, and starched white shirt was standing next to Boyd.

"Yes, please."

A bottle of California Russian Valley Chardonnay was ordered for everyone but Sam, who wanted a Jim Beam and soda.

Doug looked around the table at the smiling faces. He wondered if they were really as happy as they appeared with his performance during the debate. He could still hear the thundering applause Nat Thompson had gotten at the end of his closing statement. He wondered how the *Monitor* would see it. He knew there would be a front-page analysis of the debate in the morning paper.

The waiter returned with a bottle of wine in a silver ice bucket and Sam's cocktail. He showed Doug the label of the bottle of wine and then opened it.

"That's very good," said Doug, tasting the Chardonnay. The waiter moved over to Priss and filled her glass.

"Thanks for bringing us here," said Doug, looking at his father-in-law seated across the table from him.

"I'll second that," said Sam, hoisting his drink.

"My pleasure." Boyd said smoothly. "It's the least I can do for someone who's about to become a United States Congressman." He was smiling proudly and holding up his glass of wine. "Let's have a toast." They all raised their glasses except Doug. "To my son-in-law, no matter what the future brings may you always have the wind at your back."

"Here, here!" chimed in Susan. Priscilla leaned over and put her arm around her mother.

The Furniture King said loudly, "And let's send Nat Thompson back home for good so he can find out what it means to work for a livin'!"

The waiter handed them each a menu and they all ordered aged Omaha steaks of various cuts and sizes.

Priscilla was looking at the centerpiece, multi-colored cut flowers in a crystal vase.

"Aren't those beautiful," she said. Her mother smiled and nodded in agreement.

Boyd looked up at his-son-in-law. "I don't see how the differences between you and Nat Thompson could have been spelled out any more clearly than they were tonight. It looks to me like the choice is real simple: Do we stay stuck in the past, or do we pick ourselves up and move into the future." His lined but handsome face had a look of intensity. "You're the future, Doug, there shouldn't be any question about that."

The candidate took a sip of his wine and smiled at his father-in-law. "How's your back feeling?" he asked.

"Oh, it's okay. I've cut back on my riding some and that's helped."

Doug looked at Boyd again and winked, "We need to get Sam down there and see if he can handle 'Mean Red'."

Sam shot back, "Hey, you watch out. I'll get you behind the wheel of one of my eighteen wheelers and we'll see if the big city lawyer can handle some real ridin'."

Doug laughed and turned back to Boyd. "My Dad told me he drove over to your place the other day and paid you a visit."

"He did. He told me about a new fertilizer I'm gonna try next Spring. Said he'd had good luck with it."

Sam was watching one of the musicians strumming the bass violin. The Furniture King was tapping his fork on the table with a big gap toothed smile on his face.

The waiter returned with a large platter of fried crab claws. He leaned over and set it on the middle of the table.

"Oh, those look good," said Susan.

Sam reached over with one hand and picked up the platter and held it in front of Susan.

"Have some. You too, Priss."

Priscilla said, "I remember the night Doug and I got married, we had a big platter of crab claws just like this."

The music continued to play while they all enjoyed the crab claws, the wine, and later, the sizzling steaks.

It wasn't until they were eating their desserts that Doug noticed her. She was standing near the bar at the far side of the room and she was looking directly at him. It was the reporter from the *New York Mirror*.

Nat had reserved a private dining room at the Westin Peachtree Plaza Hotel. He was there with his Director of Community Relations, Linda Farnsworth, along with a half dozen other staff members, his campaign manager, and Abner Connell, who had flown down from New York to see the debate.

There was a dense cloud of gray cigar smoke hovering above the long table. The Chairman was seated at one end. On his right side was Ab, and across from him was Linda Farnsworth, a mousy looking young woman with narrow set eyes and dull brown hair.

Ab said, "You kicked his ass, Nat, you really did." He was stirring his Chivas on the rocks.

The Chairman was holding up his glass to a pretty young cocktail waitress who was wearing a sleeveless white silk blouse and a very short red ruffled skirt. "Bring me another one, would you honey."

Mike was looking at his wristwatch. "We should get a pretty good reading in about seven hours."

Ab glanced down at Linda Farnsworth's wide black rubber watchband, thinking that it looked like something his grandson might wear.

"It went better than I thought it would," said Nat, his slit lips curving into tentative little smile.

"I'm *telling* you, Nat, you kicked his ass."

The waitress returned with a fresh Wild Turkey. Nat's smile widened. He looked over at Ab and winked and they both watched her as she walked away.

At the other end of the table Mike was pouring himself a glass of wine.

Nat said, "There's something I've been meanin' to mention to you, Ab." "What's that."

"Linda here gave me the idea the other day. She said we ought to start havin' some of our committee hearings down here in Atlanta. Give the home folks a better sense of what we do up in Washington."

Ab looked at Nat as if his friend had suddenly gone stark raving mad. "What in the hell are you talking about. Can you imagine what people would think if they could see what your sausage factory is really like, how it's about as pretty as a hog with lipstick. Come on Nat, you'd be crucified."

Nat held up his hand. "Hang on a second. We'd do some things in a different way than we do in Washington. We'd keep the real horse tradin' private, the same as always. What I'm talkin' about, and what Linda has suggested, is after we've done all the hammerin' out on the budget up in Washington, we get some of the members down hea'— I'm not sayin' they'd all have to come, but enough of them to make it look like a real session. We polish it up some, maybe even have a little dress rehearsal, and then present it for the folks to see. It would be a real educational experience."

"Gee, Nat, I don't know. That sounds to me like you're putting on some sorta theatrical production. It might look kinda phony."

"You 'aint listenin'! I said we were gonna do it right. There's no way the folks around here are gonna know we're not doin' some serious government business." The Chairman's face was getting red.

Linda touched him on the wrist. "Sir, remember your blood pressure."

"Look, it's just that nothing like that's ever been tried before." Ab continued. "Every regularly scheduled committee meeting has always been held in Washington under the House rules of procedure. Sure people have town meetings all the time, but hearings to decide on the annual budget, even if they are just…*recreations*—that's gonna be a tough one."

The Chairman took a deep breath and then plowed ahead. "Linda's idea is that we get a little funding for a new buildin' here in Atlanta where we assemble the committee members, put it somewhere on Peachtree Street near downtown where we could have maximum visibility. I think the Speaker will go for it, if you sell it the right way."

The waitress had come back and was standing by their table.

Ab waved a hairy hand. "Miss, bring me another Chivas on the rocks."

"You tell the Speaker this little demonstration project can be done entirely in keepin' with the House rules."

Ab was watching the waitress walking back toward the bar.

The morning after the debate *The Atlanta Monitor* ran the following headline: THOMPSON AND CRANE DUKE IT OUT TO DRAW. The paper's assessment was based upon telephone calls made to a thousand randomly selected people in the Tenth District. The results were that fifty one percent had favored Doug Crane and forty nine percent had favored Nat Thompson, a statistical dead heat. Neither candidate had been able to deliver the knockout punch he'd hope for.

With less than a week to go, the race for the Tenth Congressional seat was still too close to call.

Chapter 29

Rhonda Sanchez had caught a cab back to the Ritz Carlton from LaTooth's. When she had walked into her bedroom she had glanced at the digital radio on her bedside table and saw that it was a little after 11 p. m. She had taken off her low-heeled shoes and the jacket to her navy blue suit, and was now lying on her king-sized bed with her eyes closed. She heard the distant sound of a car horn from somewhere down below.

Her mind played back the events of the last few hours.

After the debate had ended and most of the people in the audience had left, she had waited in a far corner of the auditorium, in the shadows of the balcony. She could see the cluster of people around him, the smiling faces and nodding heads, all of them standing in front of the stage. They were patting him on the shoulder and on the back and he was smiling and saying words she couldn't hear. He really did have a wonderful smile, she thought.

They finally started moving up the aisle, still talking and laughing and smiling and acting as though they thought Doug had won the debate. She watched them walk past her and, as they did, she heard someone mention the name of the restaurant where they were going to have dinner. As they were walking through the double doors leading out into the lobby, she'd started moving toward the aisle.

When she came out into the lobby, she could see them pushing through a glass revolving door at the front of the Omni. The very pretty woman with the long black hair must be his wife, she had thought. Rhonda remembered the name Priscilla from the *Times* article. She saw the white haired man walking beside her and felt a sudden chill go down her spine. He had to be Doug Crane's father-in-law, Boyd Smithers, the man who destroyed the Sanchez family.

Rhonda's adrenaline was pumping and her mind was racing. It was as though some uncontrollable force that had taken hold of her had compelled her to follow them. But it wasn't just her hatred of Boyd Smithers that drove her to pursue them. There was something about Doug Crane, some indescribably powerful sexual impetus that pulled her toward him. This muscular country young man with his penetrating blue eyes was unlike anyone she had ever met.

He had spoken so passionately during the debate about all that shit she didn't care about. What a waste, she thought. She had wanted to reach out and touch him, and tell him to save his passion…for her.

She had followed them outside and saw them climb into two of the cabs waiting at the curb. As they pulled away she waved to the next one in line and walked over and got in the back seat. She told the driver to take her to the restaurant she had heard them talking about.

A few minutes later she was downtown, pulling up to the curb on Luckie Street. She could see the green awning and the name "LeTooth's" in ornately drawn white lettering over the entrance to the restaurant.

When she got inside, there were still a half dozen people between where she was standing and the candidate's group that was still waiting for a table. She watched as he signed the autograph for the little girl. When the waiter finally took them to their table, she made her way into the smoky bar next to the dining room and ordered a drink.

She remembered the expression on his face when he had looked over at her and seen her standing there. It had taken her a long time to catch his eye. But when she finally did, he had given her an unmistakably lingering look, and she had known that he was feeling the same sexual electricity she was.

She heard voices in the hall and her mind returned to the present.

She blinked and rolled over to one side. Her beautiful face became more pensive as she lay there listening to the low hum of the ceiling fan. Her mind began searching for a way for her and Doug Crane to come together.

An idea came to her in a flash and her eyes opened wide. She jumped out of bed and started pacing the floor. She was smiling and suddenly bursting with energy. She raised a fist high in the air. "Yes," she yelled.

Doug was about to leave his office. He was scheduled to give a speech at noon before the Fulton County Realtor's Association. It was raining and he was reaching in his closet for his umbrella when he heard his secretary's voice come over the intercom.

"Mr. Crane."

"Yes, Jane."

"It's Mr. Danberry on line one."

He walked over to his credenza and punched the button on his speakerphone. "Hello, Charles. How are you?"

"Fine, listen Doug, it's about Virgil Wilson. Do you remember my saying that I wanted to take a look at his autopsy report."

"Yes, I remember."

"Well, I just spoke with the coroner's office this morning and they're telling me they have no record of an autopsy ever having been requested."

"What! How can that be?" Doug knew that whenever there were suspicious circumstances surrounding a homicide, the law required that an autopsy be conducted.

"Something else very unusual," the defense lawyer said gravely.

"What?"

"They cremated his body."

"Why would they do that?" Doug said frowning.

"It's supposedly a new policy at the Coroner's Office that was instituted because of overcrowding at the prison cemetery."

"Didn't somebody try to claim the body?"

"They won't tell me."

"Charles, something very strange is going on here."

"I know." There was a pause, and then, "I've got a trial starting tomorrow, but as soon as it's over I'm going to go see the County Commissioner about this."

"Well, good luck. And let me know what you find out."

"I will."

Shortly after Doug left the office for his meeting with the realtors, Jane received a telephone call from a young woman who said she was Nat Thompson's personal secretary. She said that the Congressman was staying at the Ritz Carlton and that he wanted to meet privately with Doug.

Doug's secretary finished taking the message. She had written it down on her message pad in big letters: THOMPSON WANTS TO MEET WITH YOU! THE RITZ CARLTON ROOM 1006 AT 8PM.

There had been an accident on the freeway and it had taken him a long time to get back to his law offices at Balding and Bell from his last political event of the day, a speech at a Ramada Inn to the Atlanta Junior Chamber of Commerce. It was almost 7 when he walked in and saw the stack of messages on his desk. He glanced over at them and froze. The one from Nat Thompson's secretary was on the top of the pile.

His blue eyes were opened wide as he stood there staring at the words on the pink slip. "What in the world is this all about?" he mumbled.

His secretary was walking in the door and saw his shocked expression. "I tried to call you, but—"

"That's okay. There's still time." He gazed out the window at the autumn drizzle wondering why Nat Thompson would want to talk with him.

An hour later he was knocking on the door of room number 1006 at the Ritz Carlton.

He heard a feminine voice from within. "Come in."

He glanced at the piece of paper in his hand to be sure he had the right room number, then opened the door and walked in. He looked around at the elegantly furnished sitting room. There was no one there.

"Nat, are you here?" he said loudly.

He heard a woman's voice again. "In here."

It was coming from the bedroom. The door was halfway open. He could see the corner of a four-posted bed next to an antique chest of drawers.

He walked over to the doorway and looked in.

She was laying there on top of a silk sheet, wearing nothing but black lace panties, which narrowed to the width of a string at her round hips, and a low cut black brassiere which concealed only the lower half of her magnificent breasts. Her skin was as flawless and smooth as a baby's and was a light tan color except for a narrow band of white at her hips.

Her shiny black hair cascaded over the pillow and she was twirling a strand of it in her fingers and motioning with her other hand for him to come closer. "I want you," she whispered.

She was the most incredible thing he had ever seen. His heart was pounding. He started moving toward her bed as if drawn by some powerful and irresistible force. She was holding out her arms to him. At that moment he heard a sound from the elevator out in the hall. Something suddenly clicked in his brain.

He shut his eyes and stood there for a few seconds. She reached for his hand and he felt the warmth of her touch. And then he blinked a few times as though waking from a bad dream. He pulled his hand away from her and turned around and started to leave.

"Wait. Don't go."

He forced himself to keep walking, but he kept hearing the sound of her words and seeing her...lying there.

When he got on the elevator, his heart was still pounding.

Chapter 30

The shadows cast by the huge white tent began to lengthen across the asphalt parking lot as the large crowd of blue-collar federal employees milled around like farmers at a tobacco auction.

There was the smell of barbecue chickens and sausage links and a circle of blue-gray smoke spiraled into the air from above the black iron cooker that was so big it looked like a small locomotive.

Mel Cranford was standing there in front of the barbecue pit with an arm draped over Nat's shoulder. The Chairman was holding a drumstick and chewing, and the corners of his slit lips were glistening with grease.

"Ya'll come on over here and say hello to Congressman Nat Thompson!" The union boss was waving to a group of people standing by the beer keg.

Nat had taken his tie off and had put it in his pocket. His shirt collar was open, but he still had on his wide lapeled white coat. He tossed his drumstick into a barrel and wiped his hands off with a paper towel.

An elderly black man strolled over to say hello. You could see the edges of his kinky white hair showing under his flat, short billed cap that snapped in front. Nat's face broke into a broad grin and he stuck out a big hand. The federal employee smiled, revealing a gold front tooth, and accepted the handshake with a little bow of his head.

Nat said warmly, "How are you, sir. I sure do thank you for comin' out here today. What's your name?"

"Charles Washington," the man replied quietly.

Mel Cranford chimed in. "Charles here has been delivering the mail for over forty years."

He gave the old man a playful jab and said, "Isn't it about time for you to hang up that mail bag, and start doin' a little fishin'."

"I'm plannin' to…next February."

Mel said, "Well, you be sure and go vote for Nat here on November third. That's a week from next Tuesday. Can you remember that?"

The old man nodded sleepily.

Nat put his hand on the mailman's shoulder. "And Charles, you be sure and tell your wife…," The Chairman frowned and said, "You married?" The black man nodded. "Well, you tell her and any of your kin' folk to be sure and vote for me, you hea'. If this fella Doug Crane gets elected he's gonna take away all the things I've done for you all. You wouldn't want to lose your Social Security and your Medicare, would you?"

"No sa'."

"Well then, you get out there in your neighborhood and tell all the folks they need to go vote for Nat Thompson." The Chairman gave the mailman a parting pat on the shoulder.

Mel said, "Go get some of those chicken wings, Charles." Then the union leader started waving to a group of people by the beer keg. "Hey Bob! Come on over here and say hello to Congressman Nat Thompson."

A fat man with a toothpick in his mouth turned and looked in their direction. He started ambling toward them. He was wearing blue jeans and a baseball hat with the words "Atlanta Vultures" written across the front. The fat man named Bob came up and stuck out his hand, spilling his beer as he did.

Mel turned to Nat. "Meet Bob Dolty. Bob works part time at Local 432."

Nat worked his slit lips into another big smile. "Pleased to meet you, sir." He was holding another drumstick and didn't try to shake hands. "What do you do when you're not workin' down at the union hall?"

"I got a five hour shift at the Department of Human Resources." The man with the toothpick in his mouth stuck a finger between his swollen belly and a wide leather belt which had the name BOB across the back in what appeared to be branded lettering.

"Well, you tell your friends to be sure and vote for me next Thursday. If Doug Crane gets elected, there's no tellin' what's gonna happen to folks like you."

The fat man was scratching his armpit. "You're damn right I will, Nat. We got a stack of your brochures and I'm gonna be handin' 'em out to everybody in my neighborhood."

Nat's beady eyes were shining like pearls.

Two hours later, Nat Thompson was back at the Ritz Carlton, sitting on a sofa with his shoes off and rubbing his sore feet.

Mike was with him. "You've got to be at the American Legion meeting in thirty minutes,

Mr. Chairman. Here's your speech." The campaign manager handed him some sheets of paper.

"Fuck."

Mike closed his briefcase and took off his wire-framed glasses. "I think it'll go over well. It really drives home the point about how important you've been to our national defense."

"Bring me a drink, would ya'." Nat closed his eyes and took a deep breath. He was still thinking about the barbecue with the Georgia Federation of Federal Employees. "Thanks," he said taking the glass from Mike. "I really owe Mel Cranford. He worked his butt off for me today. All afternoon he's callin' his people over to come say hello to me. He knows them all by their first names, you know." He sipped his drink. "A real pro, that's what Mel Cranford is." He offered a wry smile. "Maybe he's the one should be runnin' for Congress."

He savored the bourbon again, and started thinking about his next event. "These American Legion guys oughta' be kissin' my ass. After all, I'm the one who talked O'Banion into sending the Seventh Fleet over to North Korea to shut down Pyongyang." He put his glass down on the coffee table and started rubbing his feet again. "I only wish that son of a bitch Wilder had asked more questions about national defense durin' the debate."

Mike nodded his head and said, "Yes, that was a little unfortunate for us, but I do think you drove home the point that you're the one with the power to protect our vested interests, including our national security interests."

There was a knock at the door.

Mike said, "I asked room service to bring you something to eat before we go."

The young man walked across the room and opened the door. A waiter in a crisp white jacket rolled a cart covered with a white table-cloth into the room.

After Mike tipped him, The Chairman walked over and lifted the ornately designed silver cover and peered down at the plate. There on the bone China plate was a grilled strip steak, mashed potatoes topped with a puddle of gravy, and what looked like spinach in a cheese sauce.

Nat sighed. "Hell, I ate so much chicken and sausage this afternoon, I think I'll pass on that. You can have it if you want." He started walking toward the bathroom. "I'm gonna take a shower."

"Okay, but we need to hurry, Mr. Chairman. We've got to leave in twenty minutes."

"Fuck."

"Ladies and gentlemen, the Captain tells me that you are now free to adjust your seat backs and tray tables and move about the cabin as you please. We hope you will enjoy your flight to New York and we thank you again for flying Delta."

Rhonda Sanchez had the window seat in the third row of the first class section.

She reached down and felt her purse under her seat, thinking again about the tiny surveillance camera inside it. She sighed and gazed out the window. She was hoping that her photographer friend could do something with what she had. Even though Doug Crane hadn't actually gotten into bed with her, the camera had captured him walking toward her and taking her hand. There was also the unmistakable expression on his face. She could still see it, that look in his blue eyes that had told her how much he wanted her.

She shut her eyes and the beautiful fashion model face grimaced. If only he hadn't turned away. She breathed an audible sigh, then told herself, that it didn't matter anymore. She'd done what she set out to do. It didn't matter that they didn't make love.

But she knew that was a lie.

A gray haired man across the aisle looked over at her and smiled. He was an aristocratic looking gentleman and he reminded her of her father. She remembered her last visit with him a few weeks ago in Mexico City. He looked so old, she thought. She had always found it strange that he had never said anything about the circumstances surrounding his being sent to prison. But she remembered that he had mentioned the name of a young woman who used to work for him at that time. He had told her that Veronica Montez had been very intelligent and very beautiful, and that she reminded him of Rhonda. But he also had said that she had failed him during a very stressful period of his career. He hadn't elaborated and Rhonda had wondered what had actually happened between them so many years ago.

"Ladies and gentlemen, the Captain says we should be beginning our approach to LaGuardia in approximately twenty minutes."

She closed her eyes and tried to rest as she listened to the droning sound of the jet engines.

The morning after Rhonda returned to New York she took the film from her little surveillance camera to her photographer friend to have it developed. She told him that the film should be carefully edited to show as little of her face as possible, not trusting the dyed black hair to be enough to keep her from being recognized. And when she got back to her apartment she started thinking about how she would pass the tape on to the media. Perhaps, just put it in an unmarked envelope addressed to the *New York Mirror*, she thought, smiling at the irony.

Later that evening the television in her living room was turned on and she was listening from the kitchen where she was fixing herself something to eat. The program being broadcast was a rerun of *Unsolved Mysteries* and the host of the show was talking about how a viewer had solved the mysterious disappearance of a loved one by looking up her name in the white pages of the New York City telephone directory.

It suddenly occurred to Rhonda that she might try to look up the name and telephone number of Veronica Montez. She leaned across the kitchen counter and reached for the telephone book. She flipped through the pages and found that there were five women with the name Veronica Montez shown at various addresses within the New York boroughs. One of them had a Manhattan address. Rhonda looked at her phone number, knowing that the odds of this being the same woman who used to work for her father were one in a million. After a moment of hesistation she decided to take a chance and punched in the number. It rang several times and Rhonda was about to hang up when she heard a woman's voice.

"Hello."

"This is Rhonda Sanchez. I was trying to reach a woman named Veronica Montez who used to work for my father many years ago. His name is Enrico Sanchez."

There was dead silence at the other end of the line.

"Hello, Ms. Montez, are you there?"

"Yes...I am." Her voice sounded flustered.

"Well, did you know my father?"

"Yes," she said quietly.

"You did! I can't believe it!" Rhonda took a deep breath and then said, "Could we possibly get together for a cup of coffee?"

There was another pause at the other end of the line, and then, "I guess so, but—"

"There's a little coffee shop on West 34th which I think is pretty close to where you live.

How would six o'clock tomorrow be?"

"Okay, but it's been so long ago."

"Good. I'll look forward to meeting you."

"All right."

Rhonda hung up and looked over at the television set. The host of *Unsolved Mysteries* was talking about a new mystery now, but the fashion model's mind was still concentrated on the one involving her father and the woman named Veronica Montez.

Rhonda had arrived at the coffee shop fifteen minutes early in order to get a table. The room was crowded, but she had managed to find an empty one near the rear of the room. It was only big enough for two chairs and was covered with a red and white checked tablecloth bearing a few brown stains and two empty coffee mugs.

A waiter came by to take her order.

She looked up. "I'm expecting someone. We'll order in a few minutes."

He nodded and went over to another table. A few minutes later Rhonda glanced at her watch again and saw that it was six o'clock.

About ten minutes later Rhonda saw a very attractive looking woman who looked like she was in her forties standing in the doorway and looking around the room. Rhonda stood up and waved her arm and the woman started walking toward her. As she approached, Rhonda could see that she was in fact a very beautiful woman, with high cheek bones, full lips, and creamy skin the color of light coffee. Her clothes were tastefully conservative, a knee-length cranberry colored suit revealed her shapely legs and full bosom. Her glossy black hair, that showed only a few strands of white, was tied at the back of her perfectly shaped head with a white silk scarf.

Rhonda held out her hand and said, "You must be Veronica Montez."

The stranger smiled and said, "I'm sorry I'm late."

Rhonda looked at her again and wondered if she might be a fashion model herself.

"One of my law firm's clients had an emergency."

"You're a lawyer?"

"Yes, I'm with O'Malley and Friedrichs."

The waiter reappeared and they both ordered coffee.

"What do you do here in New York, Ms. Sanchez?"

"I do some modeling, mostly fashion magazine layouts and shows for designers."

Veronica Montez's eyes widened. "Wait a minute. You're the Revlon girl. I've seen you on television and in magazines. It's nice to meet a celebrity," she said smiling.

"Well, I appreciate your taking the time to meet with *me*. I know that it's been a long time ago since you saw my father. I don't know if you're aware of it, but he got into some trouble and…spent several years in prison."

Veronica nodded without changing her expression.

Rhonda continued. "He told me that you used to work for him, but he's never really talked about what happened to him in New Orleans. Several years ago my mother told me that the reason he went to prison was because of the lies of a man named Boyd Smithers. She said he falsely accused my father of being involved with smuggling drugs."

The lady lawyer's expression became somber. She frowned as she said, "I'm not sure you're going to want to dredge up old memories, Rhonda."

"But I want to know what happened."

"Even if it causes you a lot of pain?"

"What do you mean?"

"Rhonda, I don't think reliving the past is always the best thing to do. Sometimes it's better to leave things alone."

"Please, I *have* to know."

Veronica shifted uneasily in her chair, crossing her legs. "All right, but I hope you're strong enough to handle what I have to say." She breathed an audible sigh and then continued, "When I was in my late twenties, your father sent me to work for a small oil company in New Orleans that was owned by Boyd Smithers and his partner, a man named Jim Ferriday. Your father's company had acquired a controlling interest in S & F Oil Company, and I was to be in charge of managing its finances. But your father wasn't really interested in trying to make money by investing in the oil business." She hesitated and looked down at her hands. The she said quietly, "His purpose was to use the oil company as a means of laundering drug money. You see, your father and I were both working for a Colombian drug cartel."

"What! That's a lie! He couldn't have!"

Veronica reached across the table and put her hand on Rhonda's forearm. "I'm afraid it's the truth."

Rhonda sat there stunned and tears started to stream down her beautiful fashion model face.

Two days after her meeting with Veronica Montez, a thick manila envelope was delivered to Rhonda's apartment. She opened it and found a note from her photographer friend.

Rhonda,

    Hope you like the way it turned out.

    The guy sure as hell looks like he was hot for you. Good luck, gorgeous.

                         Roy

Rhonda put the note back inside the envelope and walked into the kitchen. She walked over and opened the lid of the garbage can and dropped it in.

Chapter 31

Doug had gone straight home after leaving the Ritz Carlton. By the time he got there it was almost 9 o'clock. When he walked through the front door, he didn't hear a sound. "Priss?"

He walked through the living room and into the kitchen. He looked over and saw a yellow sticky note on the front of the refrigerator. Her handwriting said, "Gone to supper with Mom and Dad. See you later. S."

He went into the study and opened his briefcase. He picked up the remote control and aimed it at the stereo on his bookshelf. The clear plastic top lit up and the disc tray swirled into position, followed by the crisp piano chords of Chopin's Polonaise.

He tried to look over some of the position papers that he and Paul had been working on, but his mind kept drifting to the scene of Karla Sanders' bedroom at the Ritz Carlton. "Hell," he whispered. He couldn't get the vision out of his head. He could still see her lying there and motioning to him and then whispering…

He sighed and stuffed the stack of papers back in his briefcase. He got up and walked into the bedroom. She'd left the overhead light on. He took off his clothes and put on a sweatshirt and gym shorts and laced up his running shoes. Maybe some exercise will help clear my mind, he thought.

He walked outside and when he got to the sidewalk he started jogging in place. There was no one in sight. The streetlights illuminated the two-lane asphalt road in front of their house. To his left it rose up a hill and curved around to the east toward an elementary school. In back of the school was an oval shaped dirt track, a lap of which was about a half mile. Doug had been able to use the track at night because of its proximity to the street lights.

It took him less than five minutes to jog over to it. He picked up his speed once he got to the oval track. The reddish soil was lined with white powder and bore evidence of a herd of footprints. He ran around the track listening to his feet pounding the dirt and an occasional barking dog. And ever so slowly the image of Karla Sanders' incredible body lying there in her king-size bed slowly began to recede.

When he got back home, Priss still hadn't returned. He took a long hot shower. As he was drying off, he heard her come into the bedroom.

He started thinking about what he was going to tell her about what had happened at the Ritz Carlton. "Just tell her the truth," he whispered to himself, "You didn't do anything wrong." But then, as he stood here looking at himself in the foggy mirror, a feeling of uncertainty swept over him. Maybe I shouldn't say anything, he thought.

Why should I tell her what happened and make her wonder how I could have allowed myself to get into that kind of situation? But then, not telling her would mean I have something to be ashamed of, and I don't...do I? He squeezed his eyes shut and thought, No, I don't. I was a just the innocent victim of some kind of a setup. She'll understand. But what if she doesn't?

All of these conflicting thoughts were cascading through his mind as he walked back into the bedroom. He still hadn't made up his mind what to tell her.

She looked up and saw him tying his bathrobe. Priss said, "Hi sweetheart." She was folding clothes and stacking them on the foot of the bed.

He walked over and kissed her on the cheek. "How are your folks?" he said.

"They're fine. They were sorry you couldn't join us for dinner tonight."

He took hold of her hands and looked at her for a long time.

She said, "Is something wrong?"

He was still trying to find the right words to explain what happened at the hotel. He took a deep breath. "Something very…unusual happened tonight, Priss."

"What?"

"A few days ago, Jane got a call from someone who said they wanted to do an interview. The person who called said she was from the *New York Mirror*."

Her eyebrows arched upward, "The *Mirror,* gee, that sounds great. But you never said anything about that."

"I was going to. Anyway, she came up to my office and we talked for a while and before we got very far into it, I had to leave to go to a meeting. I told her that she could call me later to schedule a time to finish the interview."

She was standing there with a quizzical expression on her face.

"And then, this afternoon, Jane got a call from Nat Thompson's office. The message was that he wanted to meet with me at the Ritz Carlton."

"What?"

"That's what the message said." He took another deep breath. "So this evening I went over to his hotel. I went up to his room and knocked on the door. A woman's voice told me to come in and I did. It was a large suite with a sitting room, but no one was there. And then I heard the woman's voice again. It was coming from the bedroom and I walked over to the doorway and looked in."

He paused and then began to speak in a quieter tone. "It was the reporter from the *New York Mirror.* She was lying in bed wearing just her underwear."

Priss clenched her fists and squinted. "That, sick desperate old man. How could he do something like that!"

Doug shook his head. "I thought she was whom she said she was until…" His blue eyes were looking into space.

"Do you think you should call the police?"

"She's probably checked out of the hotel by now. And even if she hasn't, it would be my word against hers."

"God, he'll do *anything* to win this election, won't he," she said angrily.

He nodded, feeling a great sense of relief now that he had told her and that she understood that Nat Thompson had tried to set him up. Of course it had been a trap. That was the only logical explanation. Karla Sanders was probably just a high priced prostitute hired by Thompson who also happened to be one hell of an actress.

A few hours after they had turned the light off and gone to bed, Priscilla woke up. The covers were twisted around her legs and she reached down to untangle herself. She put her head back down on the pillow and closed her eyes, but she couldn't go back to sleep. She was lying there with her eyes wide open staring up at the dark ceiling and listening to Doug's heavy breathing.

She felt a burning desire to tear Nat Thompson's eyes out. She kept thinking, How could someone be so low that they would use some she-devil temptress to try and seduce my husband?

She thought about how much pleasure it would give her to see her husband defeat that despicable old man next Tuesday. How good it would feel to watch his ugly, weasel face on television making a teary-eyed concession speech to all his imbecilic supporters. She could see him now, desperately trying to put a spin on his landslide defeat by the thousands and thousands of people who had known that her husband was so superior to Nat Thompson in every way.

She glanced over at the red glowing numbers on her digital clock. It was almost 3 a.m. She reached down and pulled the covers over her shoulders again and told herself not to move. She tried counting to a hundred. But the pale, weasel face still wouldn't go away. She kept tossing and turning. She realized that if she didn't stop moving around she was going to wake up Doug. She pulled back the covers and slipped out of bed and then groped in the darkness for her book on the bedside table until she felt it.

She walked into the den and turned on the light switch. She lay down on the couch and started reading.

After ten minutes she hadn't finished the first page. An idea came to her. She got up off the coach and walked over to her desk. She turned on the computer and logged onto the Internet. She typed in the website address for the Library of Congress and began searching for information about Nat Thompson's past.

At 5 a. m. she heard the alarm in the bedroom go off. It was the Sunday morning before the election.

She could hear Doug making coffee in the kitchen. But her mind was too absorbed in what she was reading on her computer screen to pay much attention.

Sometime later he came into he den. He was wearing a brown cord suit and striped tie and was holding his briefcase.

He smiled and said, "You're really turning into a computer geek, you know."

"Oh, I'm finding out all sorts of interesting things about Nat Thompson."

"Well, see if you can get a print out on his criminal record at the Atlanta Federal Prison. I could use it." He walked over and kissed her on the cheek. "I'm gonna go see what torture Paul's got planned for me today."

"Okay." She turned around and reached for her mouse again.

"Oh, and Priss."

She looked up again. "What?"

"Thanks for everything. I mean, during the pressure all these weeks of the campaign, there were times when I realize I've been sort of a horse's ass, but you've always hung in there for me, and, well I…I love you."

She gave him a warm smile reached up for his hand.

When he got to his office, Doug saw a copy of the *Atlanta Monitor* lying on his desk. He put down his briefcase and started browsing through it.

Reading a newspaper was an old habit of Doug's, one he'd found hard to break, even at a time when so many people, including Priss, preferred to sit at their computer screens with their mouses in hand and scroll through all the news information sources now available on the Internet. But to Doug, there was something especially satisfying about the tactile feeling of reading the news the old fashioned way.

Before his campaign had started, Doug would've read every word of every important news story, including the editorials written by conservatives like George Will and William Saffire. He had usually ignored the mushy moderates like David Broder. And although he rarely had agreed with the liberal writers on anything they had to say, he frequently read the opinions of Anthony Lewis and Al Hunt. When he had, it would usually make his blood boil and he'd hammer away on his word processor and fax a long rebuttal to the editor.

Before he announced his decision to run against Nat Thompson, only a few of his letters to the editor had ever been published. Now almost anything he wrote found its way into some local publication. In fact, Doug thought that one of the most satisfying things about his campaign was the knowledge that whether or not he won the race, at least he was finally getting a chance to make his opinions on national public policy known to the public.

But he still didn't have the time he'd like to have to read the paper. He turned a page and found the editorial section. The headline of the left-hand column shocked him.

REASON SAYS STAY WITH NAT THOMPSON

He had felt as though someone had hit him in the stomach with a sledgehammer. A few seconds later, the shock wore off and he got mad. "God damn it! How could they do this!" He was so angry he was only able to concentrate on the first couple of lines.

Although our hearts might tell us to vote for Doug Crane, the charismatic young conservative Republican who has conducted a thoughtful, issue oriented campaign in his battle to unseat veteran Congressman Nat Thompson, our minds tell us to stay with a proven leader. There is simply too much at stake for the people of the Tenth Congressional District to forfeit the power and influence of their longtime representative, the current Chairman of the House Appropriations Committee. Congressman Thompson's record demonstrates that...

His fury boiled over. He jumped up and started ripping the paper to shreds. It was as though all the tension and anxiety that had built up inside him during the last few months had suddenly exploded in one huge outpouring of anger. He kicked his trashcan across the floor and then slumped back down into his leather recliner.

A moment later his office door slowly opened. An Hispanic looking man holding a vacuum cleaner cord was peering into the room. He said hesitantly, "Is something wrong, sir?"

Doug looked up at him and raised his hand apologetically. "No, sorry I disturbed you."

The door closed and Doug leaned back and stared at the ceiling and whispered, "Get a grip on yourself." He looked back down on his desk. He saw the legal size sheet Paul had prepared describing the day's itin-erary. His eyes scanned it. He shook his head and then began to laugh.

What a cruel irony, he thought. Item number one was a breakfast meeting at 8 a.m.with the Atlanta News Writers' Association.

Chapter 32

By the time Doug got back home after his breakfast meeting with the news writers and appearances at four churches in his district, it was the middle of Sunday afternoon. When he walked into the den, he was surprised to see that Priss was still sitting in front of the computer.

"Are you *still* at it?"

She was staring at the screen.

"Come over here and look at this," she said without moving her head.

He walked over to her. She said, "After you left, I logged onto the Web sites of about a half dozen newspapers. I looked for everything I could find during the last five years relating to Nat Thompson's money raising activities. Then I pulled up everything they had relating to all the bills he introduced in Congress during that same five-year time period." She turned toward him and said, "I found eight direct relationships between the financial contributions he received and the pieces of legislation he sponsored."

Doug shrugged his shoulders. "Sweetheart, you've got to understand, they all do that. That's the way the game is played in Washington."

"Maybe so, but take a look at this one," she said pointing to the screen. He leaned closer to the computer monitor and she started explaining what was shown. Pointing to a line she said, "Do you see that? Over a three-year period prior to July of 2008, a man named Luke Dorning contributed almost fifty thousand dollars to two of Nat Thompson's congressional races. According to a *Monitor* article I found, this guy Dorning was a real estate developer who owned about fifteen thousand acres of land about a hundred miles south of Atlanta."

She moved her finger down the screen. "Those are the dates that the news accounts of Dorning's contributions to Thompson's campaigns were published.

"Now, if you look right there, you'll see that on July 30, 2008, Nat Thompson introduced a bill in Congress called the Air Defense Consolidation Act, which provided for the acquisition of a new takeoff and landing site for the Air Force's new B-3 Bombers. And according to this story in the *Washington Post*," she said, moving her finger down the screen again, "Thompson's sales pitch was that by building the runways at a central location in the southeast, we could close some older air bases in the same region which would lower the Pentagon's operating expenses."

Doug had pulled up a chair. His eyes were riveted on the computer screen.

She looked over at him and smiled. "Now here's where it *really* starts to get interesting." She took the mouse and scrolled down the screen, then stopped. "Look at that."

His eyes focused on where she was pointing.

"You see right there. That's the *Monitor* story in the business section they ran on November 3, 2008. This was a report noting that Luke Dorning had sold those fifteen thousand acres located a hundred miles south of Atlanta. He sold it to the Pentagon for eighty-two million dollars pursuant to the funding authority contained in the Air Defense Consolidation Act." She rocked back in her chair and said loudly, "That's Nat Thompson's bill! Doug. It was payback time!"

"Hang on a second. How do you know the eighty-two million wasn't a reasonable price based on what this Dorning guy paid for it?"

She smiled and said, "Because I did a little research to see if the *Monitor* might have published something in the business section on his original purchase price for the property…and they did." She was pointing to the screen again.

"Look at that. Do you see what it says? 'On September 10, 2006, Dorning Properties, Inc. purchased 15,026 acres of land located in the southern part of Macon County for $ 8.6 million.'

"That's less than six hundred dollars an acre, Doug. At that price it had to be scrubland with no more than a few volunteer pines. I bet it was just cow pasture. Dorning and Nat Thompson ripped off the taxpayers for almost seventy-five million dollars." Her voice had risen a few decibels.

Doug was sitting there shaking his head.

"And you want to know what other little goodie I found?" She scrolled down the screen and stopped. "Look at that." She pointed her index finger at the screen.

"That's a story from the *Miami Tribune* dated February 10, 2009." She started reading: "'Congressman Nat Thompson entertained guests at his elegant new home in West Palm Beach. The guests included his friend, multimillionaire developer Luke Dorning of Dorning Properties, Inc.'"

She leaned back. "You want to bet that sometime shortly before he closed on that West Palm Beach mansion of his, there wasn't a deposit slip and a check with Luke Dorning's signature on it going right into Mr.Chairman's bank account?"

Doug sat there staring at the screen, his eyes as big as saucers. It was several seconds before he said anything. He finally said softly. "I've always known Nat Thompson traded favors to win votes, but this..." He stood up and walked over to the window.

"What are you going to do?" she asked.

He was running his hand through his hair, looking out the window. "I don't know. I need to talk to Sam and Paul."

"I'll print out everything if you'd like."

"Thanks."

She highlighted the portions of her research shown on the monitor that she wanted copied and then clicked the cursor on the print icon.

They sat there listening to the repetitious high-pitched whining sound as four pages emerged onto the gray tray.

Doug looked at her rubbing her lower back and realized how tired she must be. "Why don't you go lie down and take a nap. You must be exhausted."

She handed him the pages. "Yeah, I think I will."

They stood there facing each other. "Thanks for all your help, Priss." He kissed her softly on the lips.

"All in the line of duty." She smiled and walked into the bedroom and closed the door.

He walked over to his desk and picked up the telephone. He was in luck. In a matter of minutes he was able to get the operator to set up a conference call with both Sam and Paul.

Doug told them what Priss had found, referring to the specifics of Nat Thompson's self-dealings that were shown on the printed pages.

When he finished, he heard Sam's thundering voice, "God damn, Doug, we gotta get this stuff out now! Let's call the *Monitor* and tell them what we've got."

Doug said, "What do you think, Paul?"

Doug's campaign manager, in his usual cautiously circumscribed manner, gave a carefully considered response. "I think we need to weigh all the ramifications of this. If we take these things to the *Monitor*, they may very well assign one of their investigative reporters to look deeper. And they might end up running a front-page story. It's certainly sensational enough to sell a lot of papers. But we've got to remember that the *Monitor* just gave Thompson a ringing endorsement in their lead editorial. They're on record with all that garbage about what a proven leader he is and how much he's done for Atlanta over the years. So they may want to beg off, especially this close to the election."

"Well, hell," said Sam, "Doug could just say screw you and hold his own press conference."

"That's an option, all right," said Paul. "But we'd need to be very careful that everything we said is fully verifiable, and I'm not so sure we can do that without more information. The fact that he bought a mansion in West Palm Beach right after Dorning's land was purchased smells bad, but it's also only circumstantial evidence. We'd need to get hold of either his or Dorning's bank records to prove there was a kickback, but I don't think we've got enough time to do it. And Doug, you could also have a perception problem by coming out with all this stuff right before the election. People might see it as an act of desperation."

Sam boomed, "To hell with perception, we're in a dogfight. We gotta go out with our guns blazin', show that bastard that—"

"I don't know, Sam. I think maybe Paul's right. It could look like a desperation play on my part."

Sam was still steaming. "Do you doubt for one second, that if old Thompson could bring the hammer down on you with a story like this, he wouldn't do it."

"I'm not Nat Thompson, Sam."

And so, at the close of the last weekend before the election, the race between Nat Thompson and Doug Crane was still too close to call. It was one of less than a dozen such races going on around the country, the results of which could determine whether the Republicans or the Democrats controlled the United States House of Representatives for the next two years.

Under these circumstances, it was not surprising that the national media turned its bright spotlight on the Thompson-Crane race in Georgia.

It was just before sunrise on Monday morning and the only sound in the living room of the Crane residence was Doug Crane's heavy breathing. He was just about to finish the last of his one hundred pushups. He suddenly heard a loud rumbling sound coming from outside.

He got up off the Oriental rug and went over to the bay window and looked through the wooden louvers. He couldn't believe his eyes. It was parking right in front of their little house. He could see the broken branches falling off the trees. The cab of the Mac truck was connected to a long flat bed in the center on which was a silver satellite dish, about ten feet in diameter.

"What the…"

Priss came running into the living room tying her bathrobe. "What in the world is that noise?" she said frowning.

He offered her a wry smile and then waved a hand toward the window. "Take a look."

She went over to the window and looked outside. And then the doorbell rang.

Doug said, "I think this means it's showtime."

Chapter 33

Unlike his younger opponent who had decided not to hold a press conference, on Monday morning, less than twenty-four hours before the polling places were to scheduled to open, Nat Thompson summoned the press to hear what his campaign manager described as "a very important" announcement. The site chosen for this occasion was the entrance to the Nathaniel Thompson Veterans' Administration Hospital, an imposing, newly constructed three-story red brick building with beds available for over five hundred patients. A majestic six-column portico fronted the building, at the center of which were eight-foot tall double doors painted a milky white color and topped by a half moon of glass inlaid with radial spokes of wood.

The Chairman was standing in front of this grand entrance and his pale face was beaming. Behind him and fanning out to each side were more than a dozen very old people, many with blankets draped over their bony shoulders. All of these geriatric stage props were sitting stoically in their sparkling chrome wheelchairs. Each one had a nurse in a starched white uniform standing behind each wheelchair. While they were waiting there you could see that every now and then one of these nurses would lean over to adjust a hearing aid or wipe away some drool.

Down at the foot of the concrete steps which led to the hospital's grand entrance was a grassy area, about ten feet wide, between at least fifty rows of folding metal chairs that fanned out on each side. About a dozen television cameramen had set up their equipment near the front of this grassy aisle. The press representatives had staked out seats in the front row. At the rear of this expansive lawn could be seen the

Greyhound charter buses parked in the lot behind a row of oleanders. The buses had delivered sixty eight members of the Atlanta chapter of the Veteran's of Foreign Wars, a large group of Mel Cranford's federal employees, a busload of Teamsters, and thirty-two members of the Atlanta Electrical Union. By the time they had all taken their seats there was not an empty folding chair. On this beautiful fall morning they were all eagerly waiting for the little man in the white suit, their perennial benefactor from Washington, to step up to the podium and make his important announcement.

Nat was smiling and patting the hands of each of the old folks and pretending to be interested in whatever it was a few of them were muttering. Most of them looked like they had no earthly idea of where they were. When he had shaken the last trembling hand along the row of wheelchairs, he turned and walked over to the podium. A burst of applause rang out from across the lawn.

He looked down his long narrow nose, his beady eyes scanning the large crowd, and suddenly his slit lips broke into an even broader smile and his chest expanded with his feeling of self-appreciation. And then he raised a big hand and the crowd grew quiet. It was as though some chubby Roman emperor was about to address his legions before sending them off to fight the Visigoths.

"Thank you very much ladies and gentlemen for bein' hea' today. It always give me such a wonderful feelin' whenever I come to this hospital which provides such wonderful care and treatment for folks like those you see seated behind me. It is a great honor for me to have my name attached to such a marvelous facility." He smiled and glanced up at his name etched in stone above the portico.

"Today, it gives me great pleasure to announce to you that upon my reelection to Congress I intend to introduce the Long Term Health Care Act of 2010. This act will provide, for the fist time eva', a new one thousand dollar federal grant to each and every family that has someone sufferin' from a stroke, Alzheimer's disease, or any other kind of serious physical disability which make it impossible for 'em to look out for themselves."

There were cheers and loud applause, and he paused and savored their lively demonstration of praise for his compassion.

"And, my friends, I'm not talkin' about just the people who're in institutions like this one. If they're at home, and my bill is passed, they're gonna be gettin' a check for one thousand dollars, just like the folks you see behind me."

This elicited an even louder burst of applause and cheers, which came before he could finish his sentence.

"Now I'm sure my opponent, Mr. Crane, would tell you we can't afford to take care of our old people, that we've got other priorities that are more important." From all across the lawn came a loud, "Boooooo!"

He held up his hands, then stood up on his tiptoes and raised his nasal sounding voice as much as he could. "But I tell you, we can't afford *not* to because there are no higher priorities than helpin' the people who need help!"

There was thunderous applause echoing off the grand portico.

"And so my friends, when you go home tonight and you see Grandma or Grandpa sittin' there in their bathrobes, lookin' off into space with that blank look in their eyes, maybe thinkin' about how they rocked you in their arms when you were little or how they took you to the doctor to get your booster shots, I want you to think about what that extra thousand dollars could mean for them and for you. I want you to think about how nice it would be to have a nurse come in one or two days a week, and how nice it would be for you to spend some time doin' the things *you* like to do, instead of pushin' that wheelchair down to the park so you can watch Grandpa or Grandma feed the pigeons.

"Nat Thompson knows what it feels like to have to be responsible for someone who can't take care of themselves. Many years ago my grandmother had a stroke and couldn't do anything but stutter a bunch of gibberish until the day she died. Poor ole' Granny was that way for ten long years. And whenever I'd come home from Washington, I'd go see her out at my dad's farm. I used to read to her from her favorite book, *Gone with the Wind*. So I know what it's like to look after somebody like that. I know how hard it can be on families to have somebody like Granny livin' with 'em."

Many in the crowd down below were nodding and sniffling as he spoke.

"I'm sure if a rich boy like Doug Crane had a problem with his grandmother, he'd just ship her off to some fancy nursing home, 'cause he and his in laws have got more money than they know what to do with." He was sneering now. "A one thousand dollar grant for long term health care doesn't mean much to rich folks like them. But it sure does to you and me."

There were shouts and yells and some people were jumping out of their seats. He was waiting for the noise to die down so he could be heard. It finally subsided.

He looked off in the distance to add to the dramatic effect of what he was about to say next, and then rose up on his tiptoes again. "Well, I'll tell you something, Mr. Crane. There's thousands of other folks in the Tenth District besides those of us here today that can't afford to ship their grandparents off to nursing homes that cost more each month than what most of us pay on our home mortgages." He turned to the side and swept his arm behind him. "And a lot of poor old folks like these hea' would be out on the street if it weren't for places like the Nathaniel Thompson Veterans' Administration Hospital."

There was another wave of ear splitting applause and shouting.

"Thank God we've *got* places like this! He dropped his voice a few decibels. "I can't tell you how proud it makes me to see my name carved in stone above the hallowed entrance to this great hospital where so many wonderful old people have been taken care of over the years.

"My friends, public health care hospitals like this are a lot like the Bald Eagle. They're a precious national treasure and a symbol of our national spirit of compassion. And like the Bald Eagle, they are an endangered species because of cruel and heartless penny pinchin' Republican budget cutters like Doug Crane."

More shouts and yells poured across the lawn and he held up his big hands to quiet them so he could finish.

His nasal voice filled with as much intensity as he could muster. "I promise you on my mother's grave that as long as Nat Thompson draws a breath, he'll fight for the good health of your loved ones!" His fist pounded the podium.

The crowed was cheering wildly, everybody was now on their feet.

He held up his palms. "The Doug Crane's of this world will not prevail so long as you, the good people of the Tenth District, don't let it happen. And I know in my heart that you won't. You're gonna go to work spreading the message of this campaign, and you're gonna tell your wife, your husband, your boyfriend, your girlfriend, your aunt, your uncle, your grandfather, your grandmother, your nephews, your nieces, your cousins, your boss, your friends, and anybody else you can think of to go to the polls tomorrow and vote for Nat Thompson!"

They were chanting, "Nat! Nat! Nat!"

He had to shout to be heard. "Tomorrow mornin', the fate of our loved ones will be in your hands. I ask that you vote to protect them by returning me to Washington so I can do what's right for them and for you. God bless you and God bless America!"

There was thunderous applause that could be heard for blocks away and it lasted for several minutes. It wasn't until the noise finally began to die down that a reporter on the front row shouted a question: "Congressman Thompson, how do you intend to pay for the thousand dollar federal grant!"

The little man in the white suit was walking off the portico, smiling and waving and ignoring the reporter's question.

Not far from the Nathaniel Thompson Veteran's Administration Hospital was Booker T. Washington Community College, a rather shabby construction in comparison to the majestic new hospital building that bore The Chairman's name. And it was in the musty auditorium of that run down community college, which auditorium also doubled as the school cafeteria, that Doug Crane was talking to a group of about a hundred students.

A few of the cracks that spread across the dirty windowpanes of the east side of the auditorium could be traced to round holes which were in fact bullet holes. The top sashes had been opened this particular morning on the day before Election Day. It was a pleasantly cool fall morning and because it was so nice outside, there was no need for either air conditioning or heating. This was fortunate since those systems rarely operated the way they were supposed to at Booker T. Washington Community College.

The students were all seated on folding wooden chairs. Most of the faces in the audience were either black or brown, and, as the school's president finished his short introduction, they all seemed to have a look on their faces that said, this was going to be really boring.

Doug was standing in front of the cafeteria serving area where there was a line of plastic hoods over galvanized metal food containers. He could see the boredom and skepticism on their young faces. He had taken off his jacket and his sleeves were rolled up to his elbows.

"Thank you, President Barton. And thank you all for inviting me here today."

He paused as he looked around the room and then said. "I want to tell you about a man who sold me a suit the other day. His name is Horace Jefferson. He's a very friendly man. Horace told me grew up in Harlem. He was the youngest of ten children and when he was little, he said he was always the last one who got to use the bathroom."

This provoked a little laughter from the few who were listening.

"Horace had to go to work when he was ten years old to help support his family. He used to gather up the discarded pages of old newspapers that he'd find scattered in a ditch behind the public housing project where he lived. And then he'd sell them to a paper recycling company for two cents a pound. After he did this for about six months, he'd collected enough money to buy his first pair of leather shoes."

More of the students were looking at Doug.

"He told me that when he had put that pair of new shoes on for the first time and had smelled that new leather and seen what a fine shine they had, he decided then and there that he was always going to have nice things." He paused, then said, "And I'm here to tell you that today Horace Jefferson has those nice things.

"That boy from Harlem who saved all that old newspaper so he could buy a pair of leather shoes is now the number one men's clothing salesman in the United States of America. After he sold me that suit I was telling you about, he showed me his award. It was a big mahogany plaque with a bronze plate that was inscribed: *To Horace Jefferson, National Salesman of the Year, 2009*. And above that was a laminated color photograph of Horace shaking hands with the President of the United States."

The students were all on the edge of their seats now.

"Horace wouldn't tell me how much money he makes a year, but he did say he sold over two million dollars worth of men's clothes last year. And I did happen to notice his gold Rolex watch and the diamond stickpin he had in his silk tie, so I'd guess he's doing okay."

This produced wide smiles and even a few high fives.

Doug walked up to the first row of folding chairs. Sitting there were two Chinese, one Japanese, two Mexicans, three Blacks, and two Anglos. Doug looked slowly down the row into the eyes of each of these young people, all the while thinking, they are our future.

"The point of this story is that if you work hard enough you can do the same thing that Horace Jefferson did."

Their faces suddenly broke into wide smiles and the young people in the musty auditorium-cafeteria started clapping their hands.

Chapter 34

The dawn of election day was chilly and gray. A layer of altostratus clouds blanketed the sky. Just above the eastern horizon was a glimmer of reddish and golden light.

On this potentially historic day in the life of the young lawyer from Albany, Georgia, Doug Crane started the day as he usually did, by doing his pushups and sit ups and running six miles at the elementary school's dirt track. He was nearing the end of his run. But unlike all the other days when he was a solitary runner circling the dirt track in the solitude of the tall pines, on this morning he was accompanied by a small army of reporters.

In the beginning, when Doug had first arrived at the track and was shaking hands with them, all of the attention had made him feel like a famous celebrity. He had been surprised at how many of the press people had flown in from out of state. Some of them were wearing elastic knee braces, others had sweatbands around their foreheads. He had thought the experience of a morning jog with the press would be fun. But after the first lap, he had begun to feel like a reclusive Hollywood star being trailed by the paparazzi. They had all been peppering him with a cacophony of questions: "Has Nat Thompson run a dirty campaign? Will you get any black support? Do you think you can win? What are you going to do if you beat him?"

During the last twenty-four hours of the campaign, Doug had been on the verge of losing his voice, so it hadn't been easy to make his voice heard. He was relieved when, after about three laps, many of them had started falling behind. By the last lap they were all walking.

He waved at them and smiled and jogged back home. Some of them were bending over with their hands on their knees.

After he got home he showered and put on the new suit he'd bought from the Brooks Brothers store near his law office. It was a charcoal pinstriped suit, a light weight wool, which he matched with a white button down Sea Island cotton shirt and a canary yellow tie with a pattern of claret colored lines that were horizontally wavy.

Priss had left earlier to put up some yard signs and hand out brochures at Robert E. Lee High School, which was where Doug would be casting his vote.

He finished dressing and got in his Volvo. As soon as he pulled out of the driveway he could hear the sounds of their engines starting up. The news vans were parked on both sides of the street in front of his house, except for the large space directly in front that was occupied by the Mac truck and the flatbed trailer carrying the satellite dish.

As he headed down the street toward Robert E. Lee High, he glanced in the rear view mirror and saw the vans following him. He was leading a caravan and feeling a little like the Pied Piper as they made there way down the winding road past the pines and the houses with their well tended lawns. He saw a man dressed in a bathrobe picking up his newspaper. He straightened up and stood there, staring at the procession of vehicles bearing the names of local television stations.

Doug glanced in the rearview mirror again. At that very moment the front wheel of the van immediately behind him struck a deep pothole and a silver hub cab came flying off. A few seconds later Doug could see that the van was maintaining its pace as if nothing had happened.

He saw the school building come into view. It was a rather old looking four-story, dark red brick building. On each side of front door were four somewhat pretentious looking Ionic columns with flaking white paint. On the west side of the main building were four large gray aluminum structures, set side by side. They were each the type one might see divided in half bearing WIDE LOAD signs and bracketed with motorcycle escorts as they traveled down highways. They were being used as temporary classrooms for the overcrowded school.

Doug parked his car at the curb of a circular driveway surrounding a grassy area and a tall flagpole with a large flapping American flag. A sign bearing a pointing arrow was stuck in the grass. He followed the direction indicated which was toward a nearby concrete walkway. He could hear the sounds of the cameramen unloading their equipment.

He got to the end of the walkway, pushed a bar on the double doors, and walked down a hallway with a glossy linoleum floor until he saw a door with a sign that said: "Voting Inside."

He went in. Three women, one young and pretty and the other two looking like they were in their seventies or eighties, looked up at him in unison and grinned and waved and called him by his first name. Many of the twenty or so people standing in line reacted in the same friendly way.

There were ten voting booths lined up on the far side of the room with curtains that hung from an overhead rod. When closed, one could only see a person's legs from about mid-calf down.

Doug was shaking hands with a friend when he suddenly heard the door open. He turned and saw the boisterous gang from the television stations sweeping into the room. They began setting up their equipment like an invading army making camp for the night.

Doug frowned and held up his hands trying to calm the commotion. "Come on fellas. These folks are trying to make some important decisions here." A few of the news people had little self-conscious grins on their faces as they continued setting up tripods and connecting wires.

Doug was standing at the back of a line of about ten people that extended to a table with a cardboard sign taped to it reading "A to K".

"You don't have to wait in line." A bluish white haired woman wearing glasses as thick as bottle tops was motioning for him come up to her table.

He hesitated for a second and then thought about all the things he had to do today. With a little grin and his palms facing up, he looked at the people in front of him and said, "If you folks don't mind…?" Heads nodded and faces smiled and they patted him on the back and he went up and signed the registration form, then picked up his voting card. The kindly old woman led him to an empty booth.

"Hold it Doug!" boomed a cameraman's voice. The tripods with cameras and bright lights were moved into position forming in a tight semicircle in front of the candidate's booth.

Doug turned around and looked at all the people watching, suddenly feeling very self conscious and a little embarrassed by all of the attention.

"Okay, you can go in now," said a man holding a boom over his head.

After he got inside, Doug closed the curtain and opened the booklet on the platform in front of him. He started flipping through it and saw a long list of candidates grouped in elections for various national, state, and local offices. There was also some lengthy wording shown on the last two pages about two local bond elections. He flipped back to the first page and saw that the Tenth District Congressional race was listed about two thirds of the way down.

He gazed down at his name, "Douglas R. Crane, Republican," and was suddenly filled with a deep sense of pride. He took a deep breath and stuck the pin into the tiny hole next to his name, hoping and praying that enough other people would be doing the same thing during the next several hours. He finished voting and pushed the curtain open and looked out into the bright lights.

His blue eyes sparkled as he extended his arm high in the air with his thumb raised. All of the people standing in line, about thirty or so, were looking at him and smiling and clapping their hands.

As he walked out the door, Doug felt like he was living in a dream and floating on a cloud.

At that precise moment Nat Thompson was feeling more like someone had driven an ax through his skull. He was leaning toward his bathroom mirror, with his big hands pressed flat on the marble counter top. The Chairman was looking at the strands of silver hair matted in the drops of perspiration dotting his pale, lined forehead.

"Mike! Call down to room service and tell them to send up a bottle of Excedrin!"

"Right," came the campaign manager's voice from the sitting room.

"And make it extra strength!" Nat rubbed his fingertips against his temples, trying to ease the throbbing pain. "God," he whispered. He tied the sash of his cashmere robe around his large waist and walked into the sitting room.

He slumped down onto the couch and tried to make himself comfortable. His head was resting on a tufted satin pillow and the heels of his bare feet were propped up on the armrest of the velvet-upholstered sofa. He put his forearm over his eyes and said weakly, "So, let me have it."

"Well, the car will be here at 8:45. You vote at 9. At 10 you'll do an hour on the Al Wilder Show. We need to be there at 9:30."

"Damn it, Mike, you know I hate that radio call-in bullshit."

"I know you do, but that's a very valuable time slot and we need to take advantage of it."

Nat rolled his eyes. "Okay, okay. What else?"

"At 11:45, you've got an interview at Big 2 News. Then at twelve-thirty you're back here for lunch with the Mayor and the City Council members."

"I hope that turd Williamson isn't comin'," said Nat referring to the only Republican member.

"He wasn't invited."

"Good."

"After lunch, you're at your downtown headquarters from 2 to 3. I've got three stations sending crews over for a photo op for the five o'clock news. Then, from 3:30 to 4:30 you're at the Westin Peachtree Plaza for a tea with the Democratic Women of Atlanta."

"Christ, Mike. Can't you do any better than that." He was massaging his temples again. "Where's that fucking Excedrin. Call room service and tell them—"

There was a knocking sound at the door.

Mike got up and went to answer it.

"It's about time." He heard the door open and Mike saying, "Thanks."

The campaign manager came back in and handed Nat the bottle of pills then went to get a glass of water.

Nat summoned up the strength to pull himself up from his prone position. "What time is it?" he asked.

"It's almost 8 o'clock." Mike handed him a glass of water and Nat swallowed three of the white pills.

"What's the weather like?"

"Cloudy, a high of about sixty expected, with a twenty percent chance of rain," said Mike.

Nat said, "No reason there shouldn't be a good turnout."

"If it's twenty-five percent or better of the registered voters we should be fine," said Mike with an air of confidence.

Nat closed his eyes. "Give me the rest of it."

"Okay." Mike was scanning his notes again, "At 5 you're back at your downtown headquarters making calls for an hour."

"When do I get to pee?"

Mike's methodical tone continued. "From 6 to 7 you're hosting a cocktail party back at Westin Peachtree Plaza for the Greater Atlanta Teachers' Union. We've got the ballroom on the first floor. Then you're up here watching the returns until your victory speech at CNN Center."

"Jesus." Nat breathed the words wearily as he thought about what lay ahead.

Mike glanced at his watch. "You've got to get dressed, Mr. Chairman."

Nat heaved an audible sigh and shuffled off toward the bathroom.

Chapter 35

It was 7 o'clock in the evening and the digital television in the corner of the Crane's living room was tuned in to the local news. The screen they were looking at was up on the shelf of a cherry armoire that was the size of a small closet.

"You're just in time," said Priss to Doug as he walked in the front door. Paul was right behind him carrying a heavy briefcase.

She was sitting on their sofa that was upholstered in a fabric decorated with colorful exotic birds. She was sitting between her mother and father. Boyd was leaning over the coffee table reaching for a cheesy dip that Priscilla had made. The rectangular shaped coffee table was made of a cinnamon colored yew wood and had an ornate floral design bordering its edges. Susan was doing needle point work on a pillow resting on her lap.

Doug had his jacket draped over his arm and with his other hand he reached up and loosened his tie. Priss' first thought was, *He looks dead tired.*

Sam came walking in from the kitchen holding a can of beer.

"There's the man!" His big face lit up. "We're gonna do it Doug! I can feel it!" He was raising his big arm and clenching his fist.

Boyd looked up at Paul and said in an anxious tone, "Have you done any exit polling?"

Paul was chewing a cracker with a pensive expression. He swallowed then said, "Just a raw numbers count. We haven't had the time to question people. It looks like we've had a good turn out in our precincts, but so has Thompson. In fact, this could be the biggest turnout in the Tenth District we've seen in the last twenty years."

"Turn that up!" yelled Priss. She was pointing to the television screen.

"…And we now have some very early returns in the race between long time incumbent Nat Thompson and his Republican challenger, Doug Crane. With only five percent of the precincts reporting, we show that Thompson has 7,689 of the votes cast, to Crane's 7,422, obviously too close to call at this very early stage. In the race for Attorney General…"

"Damn, that's a close sun of a gun," said Sam, wiping the yellow dip off his chin.

There was a rumbling noise from outside. Priss got up and walked over to the window and peeked through the shutters.

"They're back." She stretched out the word "back" and gave Doug a look rolling her eyes.

The doorbell rang and Doug went to the door.

"Big 2 News, Mr. Crane." A man with the build of a lumberjack wearing a baseball cap was standing there grinning. He was carrying a folded aluminum tripod across his broad shoulder.

Doug could see the others, carrying more equipment, walking up the driveway.

He looked at the man with the baseball cap. "You fellas are welcome to come in, but I'm afraid we haven't got a lot of extra space here in the living room."

The lumberjack sized newsman stepped inside and looked around the room. "I think we can manage." He began unfolding the tripod.

They somehow were able to squeeze everything between Priss' sideboard and the door to the kitchen, a space not much bigger than the parking space for a compact car.

"Help yourselves to a Coke," said Priss, speaking to the four television technicians. "There's an ice chest on the floor in the kitchen."

Doug was sitting in the wing back chair next to the sofa. He was in the process of untying his shoelaces.

The telephone started ringing.

"Could somebody get that," said Doug. As hectic as things had been since he got home, he knew that it was only the beginning of a very long night.

The Chairman was sitting on the velvet sofa, gazing at the ice floating in his glass of bourbon. The short crystal glass showed about an inch of Wild Turkey and was resting on his thigh. His legs were crossed at the ankles and his shoes were off. The Chairman was thinking about how good a shower would feel.

His suite at the Ritz Carlton was a beehive of buzzing people. Mike and Jane were there along with four other members of The Chairman's staff from Washington. Then there was the Mayor and his staff of six, mostly young people, and Mel Cranford and some union officers whose numbers Nat hadn't counted. All of them were chattering away about the heavy turnout and what a good sign that was for Nat's reelection chances and what a big win this was going to be and how Nat's victory was going to guarantee that the Democrats retained control of Congress. A few bored television people were sitting on the floor with their backs against the wall, waiting for permission to turn on their cameras.

Mixed with the hubbub of fragmented conversations was the sound of a voice coming from the television set. The mahogany encased screen was lit up, casting a flickering glow across the sofa where The Chairman was recuperating from his long day of handshaking and talking and smiling and being Nat Thompson, the servant of the people.

"Quiet everybody!" yelled Mike, holding his hands up. His dark eyes were trained on the television. "...and the latest results in the Thompson-Crane race, with fifteen percent of the precincts reporting, show that it's still a virtual toss up with Nat Thompson having 45,989 votes, and his challenger, Doug Crane, with 44,678. It could be a while before *that* one's decided. In other races..."

There were shouts and clapping from around the crowded room.

When the noise subsided you could hear the sound of someone knocking on the door.

Mike went over and opened it. "What's this?" he said.

"Compliments of the Mayor, sir." The bellboy was wheeling in a cart carrying a large silver ice bucket filled with bottles of champagne.

Doug was standing next to the coffee table beside a well-dressed young woman who was holding a microphone in front of his face. They were facing the television camera and waiting for the signal that they were on. And then a red light above the lens came on and someone standing behind it pointed a finger at her.

"I'm here with Doug Crane at his home near downtown where he and his family and a few of his closest advisors are all anxiously watching as the returns come in for the race in the Tenth District." She turned to him and said. "Mr. Crane can you tell us your reaction so far, and what do you make of the fact that you've continued to trail your opponent since the polls closed two hours ago?"

"Well, Molly, I think my message of conservatism and personal responsibility has gotten through to a lot of folks and I'm very gratified by the kind of turnout we've seen today."

"But what about the fact that you're still behind? Mr.Crane."

"We are behind, that's true, but we're only about two thousand votes down and we've still got almost half the precincts unaccounted for, so we've got a long way to go before we'll know how it's going to turn out."

"All right, thank you Doug Crane, now back to you in the studio, Frank."

They turned the floodlights off and Doug smiled and shook the reporter's hand. He turned around and smiled at Priss and leaned over the coffee table.

"Can I get you something?" he asked.

"No I'm fine." She brushed away a lock of his sandy hair that had fallen over his forehead and gave him a warm look. "How are you holding up?"

"Okay, I guess," he said with an uncertain little smile.

"When this is all over," she said in a whisper. "Why don't we go over to the Cloister. Just the two of us."

The telephone was ringing again.

"Sounds like a great idea." He kissed her on the cheek.

"Doug!" Paul was calling from the other side of the noisy room. "It's for you."

He walked over to the phone and looked at his campaign manager. "Who is it?"

"Somebody from New York."

"Who could that be?" said Doug, frowning and taking the phone.

"She says her name is Rhonda Sanchez."

He took the phone. "Hello."

"Doug…I'm sorry."

"Who is this?" said Doug, still frowning.

"I didn't know the truth…I thought your father-in-law…" Her voice broke and he could hear her sobbing.

There was a sudden eruption of yelling and shouting. Doug looked over and saw Sam jump out of his chair with his arms raised. "Yes!" Boyd and Priss were hugging. Paul came over and slapped him on the shoulder. "Hey Doug, you've got the lead!"

Doug still had the phone up to his ear as he watched the jubilation in his living room.

"Listen, Miss…Sanchez, things are a little crazy around here right now. Maybe you could call some other time."

"But…"

He hung up and ran over to Priss who was standing with her arms raised high.

"We're in the lead!" she yelled.

He put his arms around her and picked her up off the floor.

At 1 AM the lights were still on at the Oval Office. The President had a worried look on his ruddy face. He was wearing his black silk robe with its embroidered gold presidential seal on the pocket and leaning back in his big leather recliner. Across his JFK desk was the Majority Leader, bleary eyed and unshaven, in a suit that looked like it needed to be pressed. Ab Connell had been summoned for this late night meeting at the White House to brief the President on the latest results of the congressional elections.

"As of this moment, Mr. President, we're dead even."

"How the hell could that be?" The veins in Paul O'Banion's neck were standing out like chords. He stood up and started pacing the floor.

Ab held out his hands with his fingers spread. "We lost two races I thought were in the bag. Tom Dickinson went down in Kentucky and Mat Adams lost a sqeaker in New Jersey."

"Mother fucking son of a bitch! How?" The president looked like all his blood had gone to his head.

Nat slumped further down in his chair. "We can still pull it out, but it's going to be up to Nat Thompson to win his race in Georgia."

The president got out of his chair and started pacing back and forth. "What's the latest you've got on that?" O'Banion asked anxiously. He looked at Ab and put his index finger between his teeth.

"It's been going back and forth the last couple of hours. Right now Nat's in the lead, but only by a few hundred votes. About ten percent of the precincts are still out."

"Christ almighty, Ab. Why's it taking them so fucking long to count the ballots."

Ab was nervously stroking his mustache. "They had the biggest turnout they've ever had, over a hundred and fifty thousand. So it's taking a lot longer than usual."

The President was tightening the sash of his robe. He heaved a sigh and said, "Well hell, I'm going to bed. But call me just as soon as you hear something."

"Yes sir, Mr. President."

"Priss, can you make another pot of coffee?" said Sam.

"Sure. We could probably all use some." She yawned as she got up from the sofa and walked into the kitchen.

It was almost 2 AM. The television crews had packed up their gear and left around midnight. Priss had just gotten back from taking her mother to the hotel, but everyone else was still sitting there in the Crane's living room, watching and waiting.

Paul suddenly shouted, "This could be it!"

Priss ran back into the living room.

Their eyes were all riveted to the television screen. "…and, after a very long night, we finally have one hundred percent of the precincts reporting in the race for Congress in the Tenth Congressional District, and…oh my, this has really been a cliff hanger, but it looks like there will be a new congressional representative for the Tenth District. Doug Crane has…"

Priss didn't hear the rest of it. They were yelling and hugging and jumping up and down. Sam was shouting, "Break out the champagne! Break out the champagne!" Boyd and Paul had their arms hooked together and were dancing in a circle.

Priss looked over at Doug. He was standing there staring at the screen, as though he couldn't believe what had just been announced.

She walked over to him and put her arms around his neck. "I love you," she said quietly.

He looked at her and smiled. There were tears welling up in his blue eyes.

Epilogue

Having been relegated to his new position of Minority Leader and mindful of the hefty pension that had accrued during his long service in the House, Ab Connell, on the day after Christmas, had announced his resignation from Congress. He had left Washington and joined one of New York's largest law firms and became a marquee name lobbyist. The rumpled looking bushy mustached politician had faded from the public's consciousness until, several months after his resignation, it had been reported on the tenth page of the *New York Times* that the former Majority Leader was engaged to a woman named Monique Langston. The most notable piece of information about the future Mrs. Abner Connell had been the revelation that twelve years earlier Monique Langston was *Playboy's* Playmate of the Year.

After his defeat for what would have been his fifteenth consecutive term in Congress, Nat Thompson had retired to his ocean-side mansion in West Palm Beach. Since leaving Washington he hadn't done much entertaining. His former financial supporters, people like Luke Dorning no longer visited him or even called for a piece of advice. Nevertheless, during the months following his defeat, Nat had received hundreds of cards and letters, mostly from old people in Georgia who still looked upon him as their patron saint. But as flattering as these letters were, without the excitement and challenges of Washington, the Chairman's once dominating spirit had ebbed. He had in fact become a lonely old man.

It was while he was in the process of writing his memoirs, two days before his seventy-sixth birthday, that he suffered a massive heart attack that killed him. The news of his death had appeared on the front page of the *Atlanta Monitor*. The next day his body had been flown back to Atlanta where his flag draped coffin had been placed in the rotunda of the state capitol on Martin Luther King, Jr. Drive. Thousands of mourners had lined up to pay their respects on a sunny fall day, a day that was just short of three years since Nat Thompson's one and only political defeat. They had buried The Chairman at the family cemetery on his parents' farm near Macon. An inscription on his tombstone read simply: *Nat Thompson, A Servant of the People*.

Doug Crane had served for two terms in the House of Representatives. During that short time he had become the most popular conservative leader in the Republican Party since Ronald Reagan. The handsome young man from Georgia had been a passionate and persuasive speaker. But his manner of communicating hadn't been pedantic or abrasively confrontational in the way that was so common among many of his congressional peers. Doug Crane had a sunny disposition and also a charmingly intelligent method of expressing his ideas and beliefs.

The young Georgia lawyer had been able to use this rare combination of charm and intellect during hundreds of hours of House floor debates and committee hearings. And as promised during his campaign, he had introduced bills to radically reform the federal government. And although not all of his proposals were adopted, substantial changes were made. The Internal Revenue Code was simplified, though not as much as Doug had advocated. His bill to introduce strict term limits had passed in the House, but had failed by two votes in the Senate. Doug had also introduced a bill to allow people in the Social Security system to make their own investment decisions about the money withheld from their paychecks. This reform had been bitterly opposed by the Democrats and the leadership of the powerful AARP, but a compromise was ultimately reached to allow a small percentage of Social Security withholdings to be privately invested.

His revolutionary ideas and charismatic personality had attracted the attention of the national media. The country boy from Georgia had become a star on the television talk shows. He had appeared on the *Larry King Show* a half a dozen times. He had also been a frequent Sunday morning guest on *Meet the Press, This Week,* and *Fox News Sunday.*

Near the end of his second term, Doug had flown to Atlanta for a meeting with his closest advisors, Sam Brinkman, Boyd Smithers, and Paul Davidson. They had all urged him to run for President of the United States. Doug told them that he would have to talk it over with Priss. He had explained that she was expecting a baby.

When he got home he walked over to the living room sofa and sat down next to her. He told her about his meeting. "Well, what do you think, Priss?"

She could see the look in his eyes. She smiled and nodded her head.